PAY-OFF TIME

Remo was ready to claim his reward. Chuin already had picked up a pile of local currency from the High Moo. Now it was Remo's turn to collect—on the gorgeous Low Moo's promise of "poom," whatever *that* was.

He didn't dare guess. Low Moo lay waiting for him like a great tawny cat, her unblinking eyes like black jewels.

Remo didn't dare question her, but he could tell that there was something in the air, something sexual but somehow more. Whatever the Low Moo had in mind, it was going to be very different, Remo decided. He closed his eyes.

He was going to let her surprise him. . . .

REALM

The Destroyer

#77

COIN OF THE REALM

Created By

WARREN MURPHY & RICHARD SAPIR

A SIGNET BOOK
NEW AMERICAN LIBRARY
PUBLISHED BY
PENGUIN BOOKS CANADA LIMITED

Dedicated to the memory of late, great Roy Orbison (1936–88), who died seven weeks after this novel was completed. His untimely passing transformed this Destroyer into a memorial to his legendary career, instead of the tribute it was intended to be.

PUBLISHER'S NOTE

This book is a work of fiction. Names, characters, places, and incidents either are the product of the author's imagination or are used fictitiously, and any resemblance to actual persons, living or dead, events, or locales is entirely coincidental.

NAL BOOKS ARE AVAILABLE AT QUANTITY DISCOUNTS
WHEN USED TO PROMOTE PRODUCTS OR SERVICES.
FOR INFORMATION PLEASE WRITE TO PREMIUM MARKETING DIVISION,
NEW AMERICAN LIBRARY, 1633 BROADWAY,
NEW YORK, NEW YORK 10019.

First Printing, July, 1989

2 3 4 5 6 7 8 9

SIGNET TRADEMARK REG. U.S. PAT OFF AND FOREIGN COUNTRIES
REGISTERED TRADEMARK — MARCA REGISTRADA
HECHO EN WINNIPEG, CANADA

SIGNET, SIGNET CLASSIC, MENTOR, ONYX, PLUME, MERIDIAN and NAL BOOKS are published in Canada by Penguin Books Canada Limited, 2801 John Street, Markham, Ontario, L3R 1B4
PRINTED IN CANADA
COVER PRINTED IN U.S.A.

Prologue

The Master of Sinanju reined in his shaggy-footed pony on the beach of what would one day be called Shanghai. The sun shining off the sea which the barbarian Chinese called the Sea of Sudden Typhoons hurt the eyes. He turned to his night tigers.

"Dismount," he called.

Weary and hunger-wasted, the young night tigers of Sinanju climbed off their steeds. One, Sako, sat dazedly on his horse blanket. His eyes were squinched shut in pain. His face, dry in spite of the brutal heat, was the color of soiled ivory.

"Help him," Master Mangko said, holding his scabbard as he dismounted.

Two night tigers assisted Sako from his horse blanket. They laid him on the trackless white beach. The sound of the tide was a *lap-lap-lap* that would not change with the centuries to come.

The Master of Sinanju knelt beside his faithful warrior. He felt the man's ribs. Sako winced in pain at every gentle touch, but he uttered no curse or word of protest.

At last the Master of Sinanju spoke quietly.

"I can offer you no hope, my faithful night tiger. No hope, but one boon. You have only to ask."

"Do it," whispered Sako, and he shut his eyes on the last sight of his life—the Master Mangko, tall and lean, his hair like a cap of dark horsehair over his penetratingly clear eyes.

The Master of Sinanju, kneeling, rested one hand on Sako's fevered brow and the other on his throat. He spoke soothing words until he felt Sako no longer shrink from the touch of death. Sako would not know which hand would strike the blow. Such was Master Mangko's mercy.

The blow came swiftly. The Master of Sinanju lifted a

hand and it hammered in Sako's forehead like an old egg. Sako shuddered and lay still.

They buried him in the sand, close to the sea, so that the Chinese bandits who had wounded him would not get the body. Then they set about to build boats of bamboo and rattan.

They toiled all through the night, with the Master of Sinanju pausing often to cast his gaze inland. The bandits would not be far behind, although they too had suffered casualties.

Night came and the sun on the water no longer burned their eyes. When the young red sun rose, three bamboo boats sat leaning on sands that were as white as crushed pearls.

The Master of Sinanju inspected the rattan lashings of each until he was satisfied with their seaworthiness.

Only then did he give his night tigers a short bow to signify that they had done a creditable job, and the order to push off. The ponies were stripped of their blankets and provisions and given their freedom.

The bandits appeared atop the near hills. They sat on their horses like sullen Buddhas.

"Quickly," urged the Master of Sinanju.

The first boats pushed off.

"With me," Master Mangko ordered. Two night tigers sprang to his side. They understood that they must give the others time to make open water.

The Chinese bandits came off the hills like thunder, the hooves of their horses pounding and splitting on the rocks. Master Mankgo shook his head. The Chinese never learned to treat their horses properly.

There were four bandits. They charged like a breaking wave.

The Master of Sinanju stood resolute in his blue tunic and trousers, a black-clad night tiger on either side of him.

"Remember," he intoned, "if we die, our village dies. We do not fight for our lives only, but for the lives of our fathers and mothers, our sons and our daughters and their offspring for generations to come. The lives of thousands yet unborn depend upon our skills this day."

The night tigers clenched their iron daggers in their hands. Master Mangko drew a long sword from a scabbard. They stepped away from each other to give themselves room to fight.

The bandits howled in ferocity as they bore down on their victims, certain that their great swords were better than the crude blades of the Koreans, and that their war cries had paralyzed the interlopers.

Closer came the horses. And when they were almost upon the three unmoving Koreans, the great swords of the Chinese swept back for the kill.

The Master of Sinanju let out a cry of defiance and he rolled between two converging horsemen. His sword snapped bones to the right of him and bones to the left of him. Shrill whinnying preceded the sounds of the horsemen crashing into the surf.

The Master of Sinanju leapt to his feet. He saw that his night tigers had also snapped the forelegs of their foemen's steeds.

The Chinese were carried into the waves by their terrified, stumbling mounts. They floundered in the water. One was pushed under by the maimed hooves of his mount. He did not return to the surface.

The Master of Sinanju strode into the water. His blade flashed left and his blade flashed right. Chinese heads leapt into the sky like ugly moons.

As a last gesture, the Master of Sinanju dispatched the horses so that they would not suffer. He felt bad about the horses. It was not their fault that they belonged to stupid Chinese bandits.

"You did well," Master Mangko told his night tigers, and together they pushed off in the third boat and joined the others.

Days passed. The water was calm. They fished with string and silver hooks. They ate cold balls of rice boiled the night before.

It was many days' journey later when the sky darkened. They pulled down the gaily colored sails of cotton, fearing a storm. But no storm smudged the sky. The boats were lashed together for safety.

The Master of Sinanju grew pensive of visage. All signs pointed to a storm. Further on they sailed into the darkening sky of clouds. Talk grew less frequent. The night tigers were quiet.

When he felt it safe, the Master of Sinanju ordered the sails raised. But there was little wind to fill them. The universe seemed terribly still. After a time, their hooks brought up no more fish and the night tigers began to mutter of fearsome things.

"Where is the storm these clouds promise?" one asked. "And why do our lines fail us? Are there no fish in this entire sea?"

And the Master of Sinanju was silent for a long time. At length he spoke.

"We have entered the storm," he announced.

The night tigers looked puzzled.

"You do not see this storm because it is not a storm in the sky," Master Mangko went on coldly, "but one of the deepest ocean. This storm is not above us. It is below us."

At that, the night tigers demanded answers, but the Master of Sinanju only gave them his enigmatic back.

And still they sailed on.

On the twelfth day, the ocean changed color. First it was a milky brown, as if the very sea bottom had been stirred by a great hand. And as they sailed onward, ever fearful, the sea color became green. Not the green of certain pools, but the green of sickness, of poison.

They sailed past a floating body but did not disturb it. There was no sign of land for miles in all directions.

Later, other bodies appeared. Men. Women. Some children. As they watched the swells, a body here and a body there floated to the surface, bloated and white. No sharks disturbed these bodies.

"What does this mean?" asked the night tigers.

And for that the Master of Sinanju had no answer either.

When they were twenty days out and still no sign of land, the Master of Sinanju looked up into the night sky. He read the multitudinous stars and consulted a scroll. After a long silence he announced in a sad voice, "We must turn back."

The night tigers were shocked.

"Back? What of our destination? Our hardships to get this far? How can you order us to give up? Our village depends upon the coin of this emperor."

"The coin sent as a guarantee will have to do," intoned the Master of Sinanju, his voice full of doom. "The stars over my head tell me that we have passed the emperor's realm."

"How? It is so big."

"We have passed it because it is no more," answered the Master of Sinanju. "Now, quickly, bring your vessels about before Sinanju is no more as well."

And the Master Mangko, third in the history of the House of Sinanju, settled at the tiller of his boat. Hard times lay ahead for his village. But a more terrible fate had befallen those who had summoned him.

The greatest client state in the history of Sinanju had been swept from the sea's frigid face. The Master of Sinanju would have wept, but he knew he would need all his tears for his own people. . . .

1

The sound of the morning newspaper hitting the flagstone walk awoke Shane Billiken.

His close-set black eyes snapped open instantly. Sunlight streamed in through the glass doors of his bedroom. The pounding of the surf was close. He reached for the nightstand, knocking over a copy of *The Compleat Shirley MacLaine*, and pulled a pair of oversize sunglasses to his eyes.

"It's here," he said hoarsely, sleep clogging his throat.

"Mummuph?" The sleepy girlish voice barely penetrated the silk covers.

"I said it's here," Shane Billiken repeated. He elbowed the sleeping figure.

"Owww!" Bedsheets were clawed off an angry blond head. "Did you have to hit me?"

"The paper. I heard it arrive."

"I'll bet you did. Every morning you hear it. Through twelve rooms and ten doors, you hear it."

"My senses are attuned to the physical universe," Shane Billiken said. "I hear the tread of ants and the whisper of a spider slipping down its web. Now, be a good girl, Glinda, and go fetch."

Glinda shook her blond hair into place. She eased over to the side of the bed. She had the body of a teenager, tanned and fit and unblemished.

"You know it's probably not going to be in there," she said.

"I made a positive affirmation last night. My stars are exceptional. Today will be the start of my new career."

"I want to know what's wrong with the old. You make enough."

"Don't whine. It's negative. You know negativity affects my biorhythms. And don't forget I found you pushing drinks. If you don't like it, I can find another Princess Shastra."

"Not after the Donahue show. We're famous now."

"Just get the paper, okay?"

Glinda pulled on a purple nightgown. She rummaged through a nightstand drawer.

"What are you waiting for?" Shane demanded.

"I gotta find my crystal pouch. You know what my horoscope said. You cast it yourself. 'Don't go anywhere without your crystal.'"

"I meant trips. Not walking to the damned front door."

"You said anywhere. Getting the paper is anywhere. Ah, here it is."

Glinda tied a green Nepalese pouch around her neck with a rawhide thong. She fingered open the drawstring mouth to make sure the crystal was safely inside.

"Come on, come on. I can feel my positive energies fading."

"The ink isn't going to vanish because you can't hold on to your biorhythms, you know."

"Just get it."

Glinda passed out of the room, her gown trailing like a cape. She hadn't bothered to close the front.

She returned a moment later, the pouch nestled between full breasts that bore the unmistakable rigidity of silicone implants.

"Here," she said, tossing a folded newspaper onto Shane Billiken's hairy exposed chest. Glinda folded her hands over her breasts, feeling their hardness, and tapped a bare foot while Shane Billiken rummaged for the obituary section.

His fleshy face was a mask as he read.

"O'Brien . . . Oliver . . . Olney . . . Ott. Damn! It's not here."

"Try page one. After all, he is famous."

"Good thought." Shane Billiken tore the scattered newsprint apart until he found page one. It wasn't on page one. Nor on page two. The entertainment section was no different.

"See?" Glinda said.

"Quiet, I am making a positive affirmation. Okay, the obit wasn't published today. That means he's going to die today. It'll be in tonight's paper. Tomorrow morning at the latest. I can feel it in my bones, Glinda."

"Sure, sure, Shane."

"Hey, how many times have I told you—"

" 'It's magic, and you don't fuck with magic.' I know, I know. I'll meditate on it in the shower, okay?"

"Take off the pouch first."

"No chance. I don't want to fall and crack my neck."

"It'll shrink in the shower."

"I'll take the crystal out and hold it between my legs. Do me a favor, Shane? Put some Kitaro on the CD player."

As the sound of showering penetrated the bedroom, Shane Billiken rolled out of bed. He walked over to his bedroom mirror, examining his square face in the mirror. With a jade comb he straightened his bangs.

"Lookin' good," he murmured. Then he noticed a slight hollow effect when he moved his head from side to side. He would have to eat more ice cream or something. He mustn't lose that face. No one would ever accept him as his idol if the resemblance slipped.

As he walked into his private dressing room, he started to hum an old rock song.

"Only the lonely, dum dum dum dum dee dee dah," he sang.

In his dressing room, he flipped on the CD, grimaced as synthesizer music droned from ceiling speakers, and lifted the Pyrex cover of a cheese container. He broke off a handful of Brie and started nibbling on it. Pieces fell at his feet.

The shower sounds cut off and Glinda's voice penetrated the walls.

"You know, sometimes I think you don't love me."

"I love you," he said, putting on white linen pants. He selected a golden silk shirt, not bothering to button the top three turquoise buttons after he drew it on. He selected a mood charm in the shape of the astrological sign of Taurus and dropped it over his neck. When the charm touched his bare chest, the bull turned blue.

Shane Billiken smiled. Blue was a good augury.

"You didn't say it as if you meant it," Glinda complained.

"I'm a fully Evolved Being. I don't have to sound like I meant it. I exist in a state of perpetual sincerity."

"Say it again."

"I love you." Under his breath he added, "You nimnoid."

"Sometimes I think you just love me for my body."

"No," said Shane Billiken. And this time he really sounded sincere. "I love you for the money you make for me," he whispered.

"Or because I'm the psychic conduit through which Princess Shastra, High Priestess of Atlantis, has chosen to speak."

"You're very special," Shane Billiken said, taking a hit of rhubarb wine from a green glass jug.

"You know, I was reading that Shirley MacLaine book last night, and it got me thinking."

"With what?" Shane Billiken asked his image in the mirror as he primped his hair.

"I mean, what if I'm channeling so good because, like, I really am the reincarnation of an Atlantean girl? I don't mean a priestess or princess, but I could have been a lady-in-waiting or something. Or maybe an Atlantean atomic scientist. Oh, yuk!"

"What?"

"I just found this really gnarly pimple on my tush."

Shane Billiken rolled his eyes behind his impenetrable sunglasses. He would have preferred mirror shades, but Roy never wore mirror shades. Maybe he should send the guy an anonymous note suggesting that wearing mirror shades would be a boost for his image.

"*Yeeowch!*"

"What now?" Shane sighed.

"I squeezed the pimple and got blood. It's, like, all over my legs. What do I do?"

"Think coagulation," said Shane Billiken, opening the sliding glass doors and stepping onto the redwood sundeck. He closed the doors on that sissy mood music. That was the one drawback to this business, he thought. The music sucked.

The sunlight danced on the Pacific. Shane Billiken eased into a deck chair. He flipped through his appointment book. At two o'clock Mrs. Paris was due in for her monthly Aura Replenishment. Better make sure the ultraviolet lamps were working. At three the McBain twins were due to be Rolfed. Shane smiled. Rolfing them wasn't exactly what he had in mind. Maybe he could send Glinda off on an errand before they arrived. Then that yuppie stockbroker, what's-his-name, was coming in to talk about opening a major-city chain of biocrystal generating stations.

Not bad, thought Shane Billiken. By five o'clock he would have pocketed over seven thousand dollars, and that still left his evening free. He took another hit of rhubarb wine.

It was a long way from telling fortunes out of a house trailer at carnivals and psychic fairs all over the country, thought Shane Billiken. And really, he wasn't doing much different. Instead of servicing all comers, he saw only a select clientele of wealthy patrons. They paid fifty times for the same line of patter Shane had been dispensing in his curtained-off trailer cubicle. But they weren't just paying for the patter now, they were paying for bragging rights as one of the select clients of the exclusive Shane Billiken, world-renowned Doctor of Positivity, author of *The Elbow of Enlightment*, *Soul Commuting*, *Crystals and Your Cat*, and his current best-seller, *The Hidden Healing Powers of Cheese*.

It was a sweet deal, lately getting sweeter with the channeling bit he was doing with Glinda.

The wind coming off the Pacific sent the Tibetan prayer wheels positioned at each corner of the redwood sundeck to spinning, and Shane Billiken adjusted his shades. He settled back to enjoy the rays.

He was almost into an Alpha state when the sliding glass door grated open.

"Hey, who's that?" Glinda demanded, toweling her hair.

"What?"

"There. In the ocean. Someone in a boat."

Shane Billiken sat up and looked across the water.

Out in the surf, bobbing in buoy, was a tiny boat. A ragged sail fluttered from a twisted crosspiece.

"What kind of a boat is that?" Glinda wondered aloud.

"Looks homemade. Probably some idiot teenager's." Shane Billiken rolled to his feet and leaned on the rail. "Hey, you!" he called. "This is a private beach. Better not try to land or I'll have to call the cops."

The boat drifted toward shore.

"I think that's a girl in it," Glinda said.

"Didn't you hear me? Private beach. It's posted." Shane Billiken pointed at the signs.

The boat kept coming.

"You'd better stay here," he told Glinda.

"Be careful," she called after him.

Shane Billiken pounded down to the slapping waves. The heat cooked the bare soles of his feet, but he shrugged it off. He had learned to walk over hot coals back in the late seventies when the psychic thing looked to crash and he was considering a lateral career slide into a straight carnival act.

"I said turn back, whoever you are."

The boat was very close now. It was not made of fiberglass, which it would have been had it been some pampered Southern California teenager's boat. Nor was it wood. The hull was dark and ratty like dry vines. They appeared to have been braided. The sail was a faded gold rag. There were holes in it. The boat had taken a terrible pounding, as if it had made an ocean crossing, which Shane Billiken realized was impossible. It was too small. Obviously unseaworthy.

As it drifted in closer, Shane Billiken saw water sloshing at the bottom of the boat. It was not much from being awash. The sole occupant was huddled on a shelf in front of the tiller.

It was then that Shane Billiken got a clear look at her.

It was a girl, perhaps twenty-one or twenty-two. She wore a faded kirtlelike garment that had been discolored by salt and sun. Her hair was all over her face. It was long and black and lustrous, in spite of the flecks of dried salt that clung here and there.

"Speak English?" Shane suddenly asked. It was her face that made him ask the question. At first he thought she was Asian. There was something about her skin—a golden brown like poured honey. But her eyes were not slanted. They weren't round like Caucasian eyes either. They were exotic, and as black as hot little balls of tar.

"I said, do you speak English? Speakee English?"

The girl didn't answer. She was too busy at the tiller. It was obvious that she was trying to beach the boat before it swamped. Shane Billiken plunged out into the surf.

"Whoa," he said as he grabbed the shattered bow. It

felt like a basket in his hands. Reeds, he thought. This is a reed boat.

"Lemme help," he said. The girl shrank from his voice. She looked at him in a curious mixture of fear and wonderment.

"Help," he repeated. "Me help you." He pointed to himself and then at the girl. He worked his way along the hull. The girl retreated to the other side. The water was up to Billiken's waist.

"What's wrong with you? I want to help. *Comprende*? No, that's Spanish. Damn. I don't know any Hawaiian or Polynesian or whatever it is you speak."

Shane took hold of the braided rail and started pushing the craft toward shore. A wave came up and sloshed his neck. The next one tossed brackish seawater into his mouth.

"Hell's bells!" he snarled. "I'm not getting anyplace." He shook his head and swore again. The sunglasses fell from his face and disappeared into the water.

"Now see what you made me do? Those were my trademark."

Despite the violence of his voice, the girl's expression changed. The fear evaporated. The wonderment remained, but she seemed no longer afraid.

For the first time, she spoke.

"Alla dinna Dolla-Dree," she said musically.

"Same to you," said Shane Billiken, spitting salt from his mouth. He was trying to feel for his shades with his toes. He found them when a wave knocked the boat against his chest, and it was all he could do to hold on to the boat. His feet dug into the silty sea bottom. He felt plastic break under one foot.

Swearing, he started to push the boat for shore. Gradually he got it moving. The girl took hold of the tiller, steadying it so that the craft didn't drag.

The water was down around Shane Billiken's knees when the keel grated the sand. He shoved the boat from behind and got the prow onto dry beach.

"Okay, come on. Out of there," Shane ordered, offering his hand.

The girl stood up and shook her skirt. Salt water had stiffened it. Shane noticed that the cloth was of a very coarse weave, and when he reached out to help her onto the beach, his forearms brushed it. It felt like sandpaper. But along the edges of the hem and collar and shortened sleeves was decorative stitching. He touched them instinctively. It was like touching metal wire.

"Silver," he breathed.

"*Berra yi Moo. Hakka Banda Sinanchu. Sinanchu, danna?*"

"Babe, I haven't a clue what you're saying, but my name's Shane. Me, Shane. Get it?"

"*Sinanchu, danna?*"

"Is that your name, Sinanchu?" Shane asked.

The girl grabbed his arm eagerly and spewed out a torrent of words: "*Se, Sinanchu. Ho cinda ca Sinanchu. Kapu Moo an Dolla-Dree.*"

"Whoa, slow down. I don't savvy. What's this?"

The girl was digging under her skirt. Shane Billiken noticed that she had great legs. Better than Glinda's. Come to think of it, her face was prettier than Glinda's. He stared up at the sundeck. Glinda waved back at him. Yes, definitely better than Glinda. And all her parts were probably organic, too. No plastic augmentation.

The girl dug something from under her skirt. It was a leather pouch. It was hung from a string. The pouch rattled when she shook it. She opened it and dug out a handful of fat silvery coins. They resembled old-fashioned silver dollars.

She offered some to Shane.

"*Bama hree Sinanchu*?" she asked.

"Yeah, right," muttered Shane Billiken. He examined the coins. They were crude. He could see the marks of hammering. Probably handmade. On one side there was the profile of a man who wore a crown. On the other was a fish. Maybe a shark. The fish side was ringed with incised lettering. Shane didn't recognize the script.

"*Sinanchu, danna?*"

"*No comprendo,*" said Shane Billiken. He shook his head. "No savvy. No. No."

The excited expression fled from the girl's face. She snatched back the coins and replaced them inside the pouch. The pouch then disappeared under her skirt. Shane Billiken watched every move, marveling at her slim honey-gold legs.

"Wait," he said when she started back for the boat. "Wait here."

"*Rapa dui kuru da Sinanchu,*" she said.

"Right, Sinanchu. Wait here, Sinanchu. Okay? Wait."

He pantomimed for her to stay, then ran up to the redwood sundeck and joined Glinda.

"Glinda," he said. "Baby." He was puffing with exertion.

"Who is she, Shane?"

"This is going to be hard on me, baby."

"What? What is?" Her face screwed up like a baby whose lollipop had been snatched away.

"We're adults. Both of us."

"Yeah?" Glinda bit her knuckles.

"But better than that, we're both Realized Beings. We've been through Yoga together. We've Rolfed together. We've chanted mantras until the sun came up."

"We've been on Donahue together," Glinda retorted. "Don't forget that. You wouldn't have gotten on Donahue without me."

"Baby, don't make this any worse than it is. Remember before, when we were talking about reincarnation?"

"Yeah. But what does that have to do with *her*?"

"Everything. Just listen to me. Okay? Remember when I told you all about Soul Mates?"

"You said we were Soul Mates."

"We are, we are, baby. That's what has made our time together so special. That's why we'll always have these precious memories, no matter what."

"I knew it. You're dumping me. Dumping me for that . . . that ragamuffin who just happened to wash up on your beach. Our beach. The beach you bought with the money we made."

"Baby. Glinda. Please. I'm trying to explain Soul Mates."

Glinda folded her arms. "Go ahead."

"That girl down there, do you know who she is?"

"No. And I don't want to."

"She's Princess Sinanchu. My eternal Soul Mate. She's really from the lost continent of Atlantis, too. But she never died, because she's immortal. She's been at sea for thousands of years, searching, seeking. And do you know what she's been seeking all this time?"

"A free lunch?"

"No, she's been seeking me. Because in a previous existence, we were married."

"You told me that we were married in a former life. How many wives in former lives have you had, anyway?"

"That was a different past life. That was during the French Revolution. But Princess Sinanchu and I ruled Atlantis together. Don't you see how much higher that is, karma-wise?"

"No, I don't, and how do you know this stuff, anyway?"

"It's kismet. You got to trust me."

"I did trust you, you temporal two-timer!"

"Baby, just get a grip on yourself. Go inside and do some Yoga breathing exercises like I taught you."

"Then what?"

"You can pack."

"*Pack!*"

"You can take your time. Just be gone by noon. Okay? Don't make this hard on yourself."

"What about our past life together? Doesn't that mean anything?"

"I forgot to tell you that we got divorced in that life. I didn't want to mention it before because, sentimental me, I thought we could work it out in this one. But now that Princess Sinanchu has found me, I know that it was never meant to be. But take comfort in the true knowledge that we've improved each other's journey through life in these few months together."

"You mean I've improved yours, you . . . you bastard!"

Glinda turned on her heel and stalked through the open door. She slammed it after her, cracking the glass.

"And, Glinda, baby, on your way out, could you cancel today's appointments?"

2

His name was Remo, and he was collecting heads.

It was not as difficult as it sounded. True, the heads that he was collecting were firmly attached to the necks of their owners, and the necks held to muscular torsos by strong tendon and nerves. And the nerves were in turn connected to nervous hands and itchy trigger fingers that rested on the firing levers of a collection of vicious weapons ranging from stubby Uzi machine guns to rocket-propelled grenade launchers. But for Remo Williams, slipping around the perimeter of the self-sufficient solar-powered log cabin deep in the Wisconsin woods, harvesting heads was as easy as picking blackberries, but not nearly as much fun.

For one thing, you could eat blackberries. Remo had no such intentions today.

Remo carried two of the heads by their hair. His fingers felt greasy from an assortment of hair oils. The oils were clogging his pores and their petroleum poisons were leaching into his system. He switched hands and wiped the free one on his black chinos. He had to hold the heads off to one side so the dripping blood didn't spatter on his shoes.

Blackberries didn't drip blood either. That was another downside.

One of the upsides was that people didn't have thorns. But they did have weapons.

Remo saw another guard, a shotgun sagging in the crook of one arm, pause by a thicket to light a cigar. He had virile black hair that gleamed like an oil slick and Remo's cruel face got a disgusted look on it. At this rate, he'd soon have both hands full. It was an unpleasant thought.

Crouching, Remo set his trophies on the ground. He noticed that one eye of one of them had popped open. He shut it.

Then he waited while the cigar smoker drifted in his direction.

It was a clear cloudless day. Yet the guard did not see Remo, even though Remo crouched three inches in front of him. He did not see Remo because Remo was trained not to be seen. And the guard was only trained to watch the skies for helicopters.

When he was hired to protect the life of the man in the log cabin, the guard was told that he would be assigned to the middle ring. The outer ring, he was informed, was posted to take care of ground threats. No vehicle or ground force could get past the outer ring, he was assured. But the outer ring might not neutralize a helicopter on the first try. That was his job. He asked about the inner ring, and was told never to step beyond his defense perimeter without checking with The Man by radio.

So he smoked and watched the skies, less concerned about helicopters than getting skin cancer from standing out in the open like this six days a week.

Like many people, he worried about the wrong things. While his eyes were on the broiling sun, he did not hear Remo Williams rise up from the thicket like a ghost from its grave. Nor did he sense the open hand that swept out for his skull.

He felt the other hand on his opposite side only because Remo wanted him to. Remo needed to steady the man's torso—otherwise there would be a mess. He wanted the head intact, not exploded.

"Wha—?" the man started to say. Actually, he barely got the W out. He reacted to the unexpected touch on his right, and with his attention properly diverted, the other hand slapped his head clean off his neck.

Pop!

Remo backpedaled with the head in his hands, knowing that exposed necks usually spurted like fountains. This one was no exception. The body collapsed and fed the flowers with its most precious fluid.

It was that easy. And now Remo had three heads.

Number four was a short guy. He carried two Uzis, one in each fist, like he expected to use them at any second. The short ones were like that, Remo thought. In all his years in the game of violence, as a Marine, as a cop, and now as an assassin, there was one constant. Short guys were always trigger-happy. There should be a height requirement for gun ownership. Anyone under five-foot-seven could not own a pistol or rifle. They were psychologically unfit.

For that reason, Remo took an extra precaution with the short one. He sneaked up behind him and yanked his arms back. They broke at the shoulder. As the Uzis fell onto the grass, Remo slapped this way and that and the head bounced into his arms.

Four heads now. Upstairs said there would be six guards in all. Six would be a good, convincing number. At least he hoped that Pedro Ramirez, AKA The Man, and the owner of the log cabin, would be convinced after he eliminated all six guards. It would be nice, although not mandatory, if Remo didn't also have to eliminate Pedro Ramirez.

Pedro Ramirez was convinced something was wrong. He sat in the den of his cabin, the sun roof showering him in golden sunshine, thinking that this was better than Miami. But anything was better than Miami, where rivals would whack you while you sunned yourself on your own frigging porch. Whatever the problem, it was fixable.

He grabbed the mike of the portable radio set. The guards were under orders to check in at three-minute intervals in rotation. That way Pedro knew within three minutes, tops, if he had a security problem. Usually sooner, because the perimeter was staked with concealed video cameras. They fed the banks of screens that were duplicated on every inner wall of the cabin. That way, no matter which wall Pedro Ramirez faced, he had his eye on things.

"Santander, come in," he barked into the microphone. He was as brown as an old shoe. Not unusual. Most people who grew up in Peru were richly colored. Most people who grew up in Peru grew up dirt poor and were buried in Peru. Pedro Ramirez might have been buried in Peru, except for the magic coca leaf. It had made him rich. And its derivative, crack, had made him powerful.

He was so powerful that although the authorities of virtually every American and European nation had issued warrants for his arrest, and business rivals had contracts on his brown skin, he was still able to set up housekeeping in the heart of the nation that most wanted him.

"Santander! Bandrillo! Paco! *Sangre de Cristo*, someone answer."

Pedro shot a glance at the video screen. There was no sign of trouble, no unusual movement. Was that good or not? He decided not. At least one of his guards should have strolled on camera by now.

"Pablo! Zenjora!" he yelled. "*Madre de Dios!*"

Over the radio he heard a peculiar sound.

"*Pop!*"

His brown forehead wrinkled. He could not place the sound. It was not a gunshot. It did not possess that popping firecracker quality that denies its deadliness. This was not an explosive sound. It was more . . . meaty.

Remo Williams picked up the sixth and final head. He had to kneel to do it, and catch a loop of hair with his pinky. The other fingers of both hands were occupied with other loops of hair.

It was awkward, carrying three heads in each hand so that they did not bleed all over him, but for what Remo wanted to do, it would be worth it. Especially with the cigarette lighter he had taken off the body of the late cigar-smoking guard.

Remo ghosted past a video camera concealed in the hollow of a dead oak. Even if Upstairs had not briefed him about the camera's location, Remo would have spotted it. It was so obvious. The entire thirty-acre area surrounding the solar-powered log cabin was immaculately groomed. A dead oak tree in the middle meant that it had a purpose other than being a former tree.

Remo stopped at the edge of what Upstairs had, in the briefing, called the inner ring. Remo dropped to one knee and pulled a water-soluble folded map from a back pocket. It showed the location of every buried antipersonnel mine in the inner ring.

The trouble was, Upstairs had forgotten to draw compass points on the map.

"Damn Smith!" Remo muttered, turning the map every which way. He tried to align the map with the dead oak tree. When he thought he had it, he tucked the map into his back pocket and gathered up the six heads. The hair-tonic smell was getting to him.

Remo strode for the place where the nearest mine should be, knowing that he would be exposed to the video camera once he stepped into the expanse of greensward where the mines lay buried.

What the hell? he thought. If they don't see me coming, they sure are going to hear me coming.

Several minutes after the last pop emanated from the radio set, Pedro Ramirez was sweating. Something was truly wrong. The one good thing, he thought, was that he handled his own security problems himself. An underling, faced with the absence of hard intelligence, might hesitate over disturbing his superior. Whatever the problem was, Pedro Ramirez had a head start on it.

Working the controls that governed the pan-and-scan function of the video cameras, Pedro set them for wider coverage.

The camera showed nothing at first. Not even the guards. It was as if they had vanished. Then Pedro realized a flaw in the system. The cameras pointed straight out. They were not set to scan the sky or the ground. The ground was where his six guards must be. There was nothing in the sky, because the roof-mounted parabolic mikes hadn't picked up helicopter blades and the sun roof was wide enough to reveal parachutists or hot-air balloons.

Pedro Ramirez has everything covered. But still he sweated. He had lots of enemies.

The oak-tree camera caught a momentary glimpse of something. He adjusted the controls, sending the camera in reverse. When it framed the man in black T-shirt and pants, he froze the gear.

Pedro leaned closer to the color monitor. The intruder was as lean as a two-by-four. He had deep-set dark eyes and high cheekbones. He was walking through the mine field so quietly that Pedro thought the mike system was broken, except that it clearly picked up the sound of a squirrel-dropping hitting a leaf. Pedro relaxed a little when he realized the man was alone. What kind of fool would send one man to kill him? He shrugged. Probably the same kind of fool who would go.

Grinning a little, Pedro Ramirez watched the man. He was walking around the mine field in a twisting path. The idiot. Better to run through in a straight line, if one hoped to avoid the mines.

They were beautiful mines, too. They had been deployed during the Vietnam war specifically to decimate small units. The unique design actually did no physical damage to the man stepping on the mine. It was those who surrounded him who were riddled with shrapnel. Usually the man on the mine was so psychologically devastated that he had to be removed from combat. Tactically, that meant no survivors.

Pedro watched as the man tramped through the grass. What were those things he carried? Pedro wondered, noticing what looked like bags. Perhaps filled with hand grenades, he thought. Well, he would not worry about hand grenades until the man got through the mine field, which of course he would not. After all, if an army couldn't penetrate that field, what could one man do? Especially one who kept stopping to test the ground with his feet. A stupid amateur.

Remo stomped again. He hit the area where, according to the map, a mine should be. Nothing happened.

"It's always something!" he said, annoyed. He tried moving to the left. He stomped the grass. Nothing. He moved to the right, and felt, under his gum-soled shoes, the light depression that was the result of rain tamping down the loose earth that had been redeposited over the buried mine. He pressed firmly. He was rewarded with the warning click that would have frozen his blood back in his Vietnam days. Today he grinned.

The explosion sent dirt, rocks, and fire spraying outward.

"There," Remo said, lifting one bundle of human heads and talking to them politely. "That wasn't so bad, was it?"

The heads didn't reply. But Remo noticed that the eye of one deceased guard had popped open again. His hands were full and he couldn't shut it. Remo pressed on, searching out more mines.

* * *

Pedro Ramirez jumped in his cushioned chair. He was learning that antipersonnel mines designed to destroy and demoralize small units were not equal to every task. The idiot was going out of his way to set off every mine in the field. As soon as he stepped on one, he went on to another. The explosions didn't seem to faze him at all—and it was a miracle that the concussion didn't trigger one of the grenades in those bags.

The realization of those potential weapons made Pedro Ramirez think that it would not be long until the man was knocking at his front door.

It was time to go to the defense of last resort. Not even a man who walked with impunity through a mine field could overcome Big Bonsalmo, who stood gleaming by the fieldstone fireplace.

Remo came up on the side of the log cabin, which generated its own electricity, was supplied by a private well, possessed no telephone lines, and technically did not exist. Except that there it stood.

Remo set the heads down on the grass and dug out the cigarette lighter. Lifting up one head, he applied the lighter's flame to the thick oily hair. It caught instantly. Remo let it burn a little, and then flung it toward a window.

The smoked glass shattered on impact.

Remo set two more of the heads on fire and ran around to the back. He tossed one head in an upper window and the other in a lower window. The other heads, blazing like torches, shattered strategic windows on the other side. Remo saved the sixth head for last. He carefully closed its stubborn baleful eyes and, setting it alight, gave it an overhand toss to the roof.

Pedro Ramirez did not fear the smoke. His eyes were shielded and he breathed pure oxygen through a breathing aparatus. He did not fear the grenades that he knew had smashed the windows, although it was taking an awfully long time for them to detonate. The fire bothered him not at all, although it was rapidly spreading. He started for the front door. When he moved, he clanked.

But when the sun roof broke into glittering shards, his

heart quailed. The glass bounced harmlessly off and about him. But the thing that landed at his feet was another matter.

It was Santander. His hair was a ball of flame and as it ate into the darkening flesh of his face, one eye twitched open.

Remo watched until the smoke billowed out of every window and chink in the cabin and then walked up to the door, happy to have free hands once again.

He knocked politely. And waited.

Metallic sounds greeted his ears and he wondered for a moment if Upstairs had slipped up. There had been no mention of a midget tank in the briefing.

The door suddenly slapped open and Remo looked up. Remo was tall—about six feet high—but the thing that greeted him was taller by a solid two feet.

It was silvery-gray and plated like an armadillo. It stood on thick legs that ended in clubby feet. The arms hung crooked, like those of an overmuscled gorilla. The head was a box with round glass eyes and a black rubber appendage like an elephant's trunk. The breathing sounds it made resembled those of a hospital respiration machine.

"Do your worst!" the thing said hollowly.

"I beg your pardon?" Remo said politely.

"I said do your worst. I'm not afraid of you!"

"Let's take this from the top, shall we?" Remo said. "I'm here to see Pedro Ramirez, millionaire playboy and chief distributor of crack in the western hemisphere. Could you tell him I'm here, Tobor? Or do robots relay messages?"

"Idiot. I'm Pedro Ramirez."

"You?"

"You're here to kill me, no?"

"Actually, I come bearing options," Remo started to say.

"But I can't be killed," said Pedro Ramirez, smashing a mittenlike gauntlet against his thickly plated chest. It made a bell sound. "Not as long as I'm wearing this. It's titanium plate. Stronger than steel. Over it is bullet-proof Kelvar with a Teflon base. Bullets bounce off. Grenades are nothing to me. I'm impervious to poison gas, fire . . . you got it, I spit upon it."

"Actually, I was hoping you'd just surrender to the authorities. The government wants to make an example of you."

"You'll never take Pedro Ramirez alive."

"I'll go with option B if I have to," Remo said, shrugging.

"Just try," boomed Pedro Ramirez. "Go ahead, see if anything works. Why don't you try shooting?"

"Shooting?" Remo asked vaguely.

"Yeah, don't tell me the little cockroach forgot his gun."

"Actually," Remo said, patting his pockets, "I'm not sure if I thought to bring a gun. I was really hoping you'd just surrender, especially after I went to all that trouble with your guards. You did notice that."

"Yeah. So what?"

"I thought it would convince you of the error of resistance," Remo said, continuing to pat his pockets. "Guess not," he added weakly.

Out of his back pocket Remo pulled a folded slip of paper. He glanced at it and tossed it away.

"What was that?" Ramirez asked.

"Nothing much. Just the layout of your mine field."

"How did you get hold of that?"

"Satellite surveillance," Remo said. "My superior monitored the entire construction of this place."

"Oh," said Pedro Ramirez, who knew the U.S. government wanted him, but didn't know they wanted him quite that badly.

"I can't seem to find it," Remo was saying.

"Too bad," said Pedro Ramirez. "Why don't you just go away?"

"Ah," Remo said suddenly. "Here it is." Out of his right pants pocket he brought out his fist. He held it in front of him as if about to throw a punch. His arm was bent at the elbow.

"That's your fist," Ramirez pointed out.

"Keep your scales on," Remo said. "I haven't cocked it yet." Remo pulled back the thumb of his fist. He made a little click of a sound with his tongue, and his index finger popped out like a gun barrel.

"There," Remo said with a satisfied smile. "Now—last chance. Put your hands up."

Pedro Ramirez did not put his hands up. He spread his arms. "Go ahead, cockroach. Shoot! Shoot!" he howled.

Remo shrugged. He dropped his thumb like a falling hammer and said, "Bang!"

Pedro Ramirez guffawed inside his protective square helmet. His eyes closed with laughter. He didn't see the index finger, pointing at him, move for the center of his chest. He wouldn't have seen it move even if his eyes had been open. For the finger was coming for him at supersonic speed.

The coroner's official verdict was that Pedro Ramirez died of hydrostatic shock. Because Pedro Ramirez was at the top of the FBI's Most Wanted list, he was forced to explain hydrostatic shock to a flock of reporters at the FBI news conference..

"Hydrostatic shock, gentlemen," the coroner said carefully, "is a phenomenon wherein the human body is subjected to a noninvasive impact so great that it results in a chain reaction of internal stress which quite literally disrupts the body cells. This man's mitochondria were destroyed. The result was instantaneous death. We see such a phenomenon when the wearer of a bullet-proof vest is struck by a bullet of sufficiently large caliber—a .357 Magnum round for example—where even though there is no penetration of the protective garment, the impact is as lethal as if penetration was achieved."

One reporter wanted to know what kind of bullet-proof vest Pedro Ramirez wore.

The coroner replied that it was not a vest, but an armored body suit.

Another reporter asked the question that the coroner feared.

"What caliber was the murder weapon?"

"That I am unable to answer at this time," he admitted. "No shell fragments were found at the scene, but the size of the dent in the suit's chest is consistent with a .38 slug."

The coroner was relieved that the logical follow-up question—how could a mere .38 slug cause hydrostatic shock?—was drowned out by a journalist asking him to speculate on which of Pedro Ramirez's many enemies had finally gotten to the drug kingpin.

When the news conference finally ended, the coroner went back to his lab and sat down to put the finishing touches on the official death report. He decided to simply state the details as they existed, and not try to explain how a .38 slug had wrought such havoc—especially when no corresponding slug could be found and the impact point bore a strange indentation.

The coroner lifted the plate to the light. It was bent. And the impact point was unmistakable. Also unmistakable were the tiny rills at the impact site. He couldn't get over how much like the ridges of a man's fingerprints they were. There was even a little slice of a line above the ridges that corresponded to the edge of a fingernail.

But what kind of fingernail could score a Kelvar-Teflon-titanium sandwich?

No kind, he decided. His final report would simply not mention those imponderable details. Some lines of inquiry were better off not pursued.

3

Remo slammed the door behind him and announced, "I'm home."

A peculiar odor greeted his sensitive nostrils.

"You are just in time," a squeaky voice called from the kitchen. Remo followed the odor. It smelled vaguely familiar. It was a food odor, that much was certain, but for the twenty years that he had been a disciple of the art of Sinanju, he had learned to shut out what used to be tantalizing smells. His olfactory organs now only responded to the Sinanju version of the five basic food groups—rice, fish, duck, nuts, and berries.

"Sit," said Chiun over his shoulder as he hunched over the gas stove. The Master of Sinanju, who was barely as tall as the stove, stood on a footstool. He wore a thin white kimono with shortened sleeves appropriate for cooking with fire.

The table was set for two. Remo sat.

"What's cooking?" he asked, sniffing the hauntingly-familiar aroma.

"A celebration dinner."

"Great. But what is it?"

"A surprise," squeaked Chiun. "Close your eyes."

Remo did as he was told. He even folded his hands. He waited. He sensed rather than heard Chiun's sandaled feet slither in his direction. Something hot was poured into the great celadon bowl that dominated the center of the table.

Remo sniffed harder. He felt his stomach juices stir as they had not in many years.

The opposite chair scraped back and the Master of Sinanju spoke up.

"You may open your eyes, my son."

Remo did. The wise eyes of the Master of Sinanju looked at him with crinkled amusement. Merriment lay in their hazel depths. They dominated a face that was the color of aged ivory, making the myriad of wrinkles look somehow akin to youth and not age. Twin puffs of wispy white hair decorated the hollows over his small ears. A fragile beard was stirred by the steam coming from the great bowl. Such was the countenance of Chiun, latest Master of Sinanju, heir to the longest and most celebrated line of assassins in history, and Remo's trainer and adopted father.

"This is a great day for us," he said softly.

"Amen," said Remo. "But what's this? Duck soup?"

"No duck today. Nor fish. And rice we will do without. For this is a day of celebration. I have waited long for this golden hour."

"Great. But what is it? It smells great."

"Patience," intoned Chiun, raising a long-nailed finger. The nail was pointed and slightly curved. "Perfection is fleeting. Do not hurry the moment."

"Tell my mouth. I'm practically drooling. What is this stuff?"

"Egg-lemon soup," whispered Chiun. His voice was reverent.

"Egg-lemon?" Remo said, staring at the steaming bowl.

"Reserved for full Masters only. Oh, this is a glorious day."

"Egg-lemon soup." Remo looked into the steam as if the skies were parting to reveal their innermost secrets for his eyes alone.

"Savor this moment, Remo."

"I'm savoring. I'm savoring," Remo said. It had been over twenty years since he had come to Sinanju, the sun source of the martial arts. Twenty years since he had learned the skills that made its practitioners the most feared warriors in history. Twenty years since he had eaten his last steak. Twenty years since sugar, coffee, processed foods, and alcohol were forbidden to him. Twenty years since his body had been made one with the universe, until his diet had shrunk to rice, duck, and fish, with the occasional organically grown vegetable thrown in for vitamin content. And twenty years since his tongue had touched an unfamiliar food.

"Ah," said Chiun. "I see it in your eyes."

"Steam?"

"No, a twinkle. Egg-lemon soup always brings a twinkle to the eye."

Remo did not reply. He only stared. A new food. A new taste sensation. He had to keep swallowing because his mouth juices were erupting like a liquid volcano. His hands reached for a spoon, but something inside him made him hesitate. A new food. Maybe after this there would be no more new foods. Chiun was right. This was a moment to savor.

"Have you nothing to say?" Chiun inquired at length.

"I'm speechless," Remo said sincerely. "Really, Chiun, this is wonderful. Egg-lemon soup."

"From an ancient Korean recipe."

"This is great. How very thoughtful, Little Father. And only last week you were harping on me to let my fingernails grow long like yours."

"Speak not of trivial quarrels on this auspicious morning," Chiun said magnanimously.

"Sorry," Remo said sheepishly. His eyes were not on Chiun, but on the bowl. It still steamed. But he could see the broth now. It was yellowish-white. And in it tiny dark specks floated. The sight filled his eyes to brimming as the aroma filled his nostrils. Remo felt almost as if he were going to cry with the sheer joy of discovery.

"Egg-lemon soup," he said under his breath. And it was a prayer.

"I will let you pour," Chiun said suddenly, clapping his hands.

"Gladly," Remo said, bolting from his seat. He scooped up the large bowl and ladled out the heated broth, filling first Chiun's bowl and then his own. He replaced the bowl and sat again. He stared into his own bowl. His hands, holding the ladle and a spoon, almost trembled.

"You may go first."

Remo hesitated. Then, dropping the ladle, he dug in. He brought the first hot spoonful to his mouth. He hesitated again. Chiun's eyes were eager as they watched him, his wise old face beaming with pride. This was a sacred moment.

Remo blew on the spoon to cool the broth. He took his first spoonful. It seared his tongue like acid.

"Hooo!" he said, swallowing.

"Good?"

"Strong."

"It has been a long time since your tongue has tasted such nectar. I recommend small sips."

"Okay," said Remo. The second spoonful was pungent. It slid down his throat with all the fire of a shot of good Kentucky bourbon. The third taste was merely sharp. Remo found himself able to take larger doses. He drank up the bowl greedily, not even noticing that Chiun had not even tasted his own.

"More?" asked Chiun.

Remo nodded.

"I am glad you like it," Chiun remarked as he refilled Remo's bowl. Only then did he sample his own bowl. He sipped from the spoon lightly, showing none of the strong reaction that had come with Remo's first flavorful sips.

Remo was on his third bowl when a thought occurred to him.

"This is really excellent, Little Father, but if you were able to eat this stuff all these years, why didn't you?"

"Egg-lemon soup is reserved for full Masters, which I have been for all the years that you have known me, but which you have achieved only recently."

"So, why'd you abstain?"

"Could the father eat so well and let his only child go without?"

"All these years," Remo said, looking up from the nearly empty bowl. "All these years you sacrificed. For me."

"A father's duty," said Chiun, who was not really Remo's father, but in many ways was more, much more than that.

"I am honored by your sacrifice," Remo said quietly. "And only yesterday you were telling me that it was time for me to grow a beard like your own. And I told you to go stuff it."

"A harsh memory, but on this night we transcend such petty arguments," Chiun said loftily. "More?"

"Yes," said Remo, holding out his bowl.

After consuming every last drop, Remo spoke up.

"I feel ashamed, Little Father," he said quietly.

"On such a night?" Chiun squeaked. He brushed Remo's

admission aside as if it were inconsequential. "It is of no moment."

"But I should explain."

"It is nothing."

"But I'd really like to," Remo repeated. "I cut you off, about the beard and the fingernails, because we've had these discussions many times before. But I don't want you to think I don't honor you. I do. It's just that this is America. Customs are different. I could grow a beard, but it's just not me. As for my fingernails, as I've explained to you before, in America only women go about with their fingernails long."

"And Masters of Sinanju," added Chiun.

"Yes, and Masters of Sinanju. But you're Korean. You can get away with it. But the work we do for Smith and America requires that I sometimes go undercover. I can't have long fingernails. I'd stick out. It would defeat the whole purpose. You can understand that?"

And the Master of Sinanju surprised Remo by saying a simple, "Yes, I understand perfectly."

Remo's concerned expression relaxed. He nodded when Chiun held up a steaming ladle. Remo's bowl came up again. This was the fifth bowl, but the soup was so light that Remo felt as if he could drink it all night.

As he dug in again under Chiun's approving gaze, Remo thought of another question.

"One other thing puzzles me, Little Father."

"Yes?"

"I thought we couldn't eat eggs."

"We cannot. But egg-lemon soup is different."

"Oh. I seem to remember you telling me that even the white of the egg was poison to us. The yolk would turn our dead bones to powder."

"And so it would. But this is egg-lemon soup."

"It's lemony, all right. But I don't seem to taste much egg."

"It is there. The lemon simply masks its taste."

"And these crunchy things," said Remo, looking at the dark specks floating in his spoon. "What are they? Almond slices?"

"No," said Chiun quickly.

"Seeds, then? They're very hard."

"No."

"Then what?"

"They are the precious egg bits."

Remo blinked. He looked at his spoon.

"I don't get it. Eggs aren't hard and crunchy." He looked closer. He noticed that the specks were shaped like tiny shards of glass. Some were white. Others a dark brown. He jiggled his spoon and noticed that some of the brown ones were white on the opposite side. What did that remind him of? Remo wondered.

"How do you get an egg to be this hard?" he asked.

"It is simple," Chiun replied. "You take the raw egg, and you break it over a bowl. Then you place the shell in another bowl."

"Yeah," said Remo. He was hanging on every word.

"And there you are," said Chiun, beaming.

"Did I miss a step here?" Remo asked.

"You wish to know the recipe?"

"If that will explain the egg part, yeah."

Chiun shrugged. "It is simple. In a pot you have the lemon broth simmering."

"Right. Lemon broth."

"Then you take the bowl with the eggshells and the bowl with the inedible eggs' hearts."

"That means the whites and yolks. Yeah. Go on."

"Then," said Chiun rapidly, "you pour the first bowl down the sink and the second bowl into the broth, first taking care to crush the eggs into small edible pieces."

"The shells!" Remo roared. "I'm eating eggshell soup!"

"Egg-lemon soup," Chiun corrected, his face stung. "And a moment ago you were raving about it."

"Raving. I'm hysterical!" Remo snapped. "Why didn't you tell me these were shells? I wouldn't have eaten them!"

"But they are good for you. Did you not enjoy your first five bowls?"

Remo's face calmed down. "Well, yeah, actually I did. But now that these are eggshells, it's a different story."

"That is the recipe. Had I used the hearts of the eggs, you would have been dead after your first bowl."

"Yeah, but—"

"I do not understand, Remo. If it was delicious when

you did not know its ingredients, why is it not still delicious after you know these things?"

"It *is* delicious," Remo said defensively, and Chiun's face softened.

"Then eat," Chiun implored. "There is plenty."

"You're still on your first bowl," Remo observed.

"At my age, it is better to eat in moderation. But you are young yet. Come, fill your stomach. This is a happy day."

"Okay with you if I skip the shells?"

"But they are the best part. And you would not spoil this auspicious day by not eating what I have slaved over all day?"

"I won't chew them, then."

"If that is your wish," Chiun said sadly.

"Okay, I'll chew," said Remo. "See?" His teeth went *crunch-crunch* against the bits of eggshell.

Chiun beamed. He looked like a wrinkled little angel.

When the meal was over and Remo had cleared the table, he asked:

"So what do we do now?"

"It is time for Copra Inisfree. We will watch her show."

"Okay," said Remo, but only to be polite. He had no interest in the talk-show hostess whom Chiun found so fascinating.

But when the Master of Sinanju settled on his reed mat before the living-room television, the picture that greeted his eyes sent his happy face into shocked dismay.

"What is this?" he demanded querulously. "Where is Copra the Clown?"

Remo looked. "Guess she's been replaced. This guy is the new hot thing."

On the screen was the name "Horton Droney III" inside a graphic designed to resemble a shouting mouth. The image dissolved into a shot of a cheering studio audience. Then a casually dressed man jogged down the studio aisle, giving high fives to enthusiastic greeters. In the background, Remo noticed that security guards were dragging other audience members away. One took a switchblade away from a black man. Others shouted epithets to the man who, once on the stage, appeared not to notice that not all the commotion was in his favor. He shot the audience a huge smile. His teeth were so big and white the smile made his face seem suddenly dirty.

"Tonight's guests—and I use the term loosely—are a quack and a fraud," said Horton Droney III in a too-loud voice. "The quack's here to plug his book, *The Hidden Healing Powers of Cheese*." A hardcover book flew into Horton Droney's hands. He pretended to flip through the pages. "And a piece of Swiss it is too." He threw the book over his shoulder. It knocked over a standing spotlight. The crowd cheered wildly.

Chiun turned to Remo. "Explain this creature to me."

"Where do I start?"

"With the answer to a simple question. Why does he have a Roman numeral for a last name?"

"Actually, he doesn't. The number III means 'the third.' He's Horton Droney the Third."

Chiun's wrinkles smoothed in surprise. "You mean there are two more like him?"

"Not exactly. It means his father is Horton Droney II. Probably his grandfather was the First."

"How long will this go on?"

"As long as there are women willing to bear little Horton Droneys, I guess."

"Shhhh," Chiun said suddenly. "He speaks."

"Shouts," Remo corrected. Chiun's hand shot up.

"Now I know you're going to give these New Age hucksters exactly the welcome they so richly deserve," Horton Droney III proclaimed. A blood howl rose from the audience. "Here they come, Shane Billiken and—get this—Princess Sinanchu."

"Hey, did you catch that name? It sounded almost like—"

Remo's words were literally pinched off by Chiun's fingers. He tried removing Chiun's fingers from his lips. They were locked like pliers. Remo decided to sit quietly. Chiun would not let go until he was ready.

A square-faced man in black leather clothes and wraparound sunglasses stepped out. He led a small golden-skinned woman by the hand. She wore a short white costume and seemed frightened by the roar of the audience.

Even after they were seated, the man, whom an on-screen tag identified as "Shane Billiken, New Age Guru," continued holding the girl's hand, as if afraid she would bolt at any second.

"This, I take it, is Princess Sinanchu?" Horton Droney III sneered.

"That's right," said Shane Billiken. "And you can scoff all you want. But this woman is what I call a perpetual channeler. Unlike other channelers, she does not need to go into a trance in order to access her spirit guide. She is permanently locked into the consciousness of Princess Sinanchu, a warrior queen from prehistoric times, when technology was more advanced than ours."

Horton Droney III gave the studio audience, and the camera, an arched eyebrow look. The audience howled with laughter. A tomato splashed at the feet of Princess Sinanchu, who recoiled.

"No, not yet," Horton Droney told his audience reprovingly. "I'll tell you when to start throwing things."

"I can prove my claim," Shane Billiken insisted.

"I know, I know," Horton Droney said. "You've had language experts from all over the world listen to her, and they all agree that she's speaking in an unknown tongue."

"Exactly right."

"And we all know how infallible those ivory-tower geniuses are. I mean, if I wanted to run a scam like this, all I'd have to do is say, 'Yabbba-dabbo doo' a few times and I'd have them scratching their pointy little heads too."

"Why don't we let the audience judge for themselves?"

"Shoot."

Shane Billiken turned to the woman he called Princess Sinanchu and squeezed her hand hard. She began speaking in rapid bursts.

"*Mola re Sinanchu. A gosa du Sinanchu. Ponver dreu du Sinanchu.*"

"She says that she is Princess Sinanchu," Shane Billiken said carefully, "and she wants to warn us that we're letting our technology destroy us. We should eat more organic foods like cheese, clean up our water and our air, or the calamity that befell her civilization will fall upon ours."

"She said all that, eh?"

"That's correct."

"Then how come she said her name three times and you repeated it only once?" Horton Droney said savagely.

"I gave you the loose translation."

"And if this language is unknown to modern world, how come you speak it? Huh? Answer me that."

"Because in a previous life I was her husband."

"Oh, this is such crap." Horton Droney turned to the audience. "I say it's crap. What do you say?"

"It's crap!" yelled the studio audience. Security guards moved in when some in the front row started to rush the stage.

"They say it's crap," accused Horton Droney, turning to Princess Sinanchu. "And I'm going to prove it." He was shouting now, shouting abuse and invective in the frightened face of Princess Sinanchu.

"Come on, admit it. You're a fraud. This is an act. Who are you really? Some cheap stripper he picked up in a saloon? I'll bet right now there's someone in our television audience looking at you and saying, 'I know her. I went to high school with the little trollop. Come on, 'fess up, before someone else blows the whistle."

"*Dakka, qi Drue Sinanchu,*" said Princess Sinanchu.

"We know your freaking stage name, you smarmy fake. What we want is the truth. Who are you? How much is he paying you to work this little scam? Huh? Come on, admit it."

Horton Droney was spitting words in her face with relentless violence. His face was turning red. The studio audience was a mob.

"Shake it out of her, Hort," they yelled. "Make the bitch talk."

Horton Droney grabbed Princess Sinanchu by the hair and yanked her out of her seat.

"I know how to prove she's a fraud," he shouted, wrestling her to the front of the stage. "An old-fashioned spanking!"

Princess Sinanchu made a sound like a spitting cat and reached under her skirt. Her hand flashed up and Horton Droney suddenly backed away from her. He twisted on his feet until his knees started buckling. His mouth opened in a grimace. An ornate bone handle jutted from his chest.

He gripped it in both hands, and then, his face darkening even as his grimace widened, he fell on his face.

A "Technical Difficulties" sign was beamed into millions of homes across the nation.

"Enough," Chiun said abruptly, releasing Remo's numb lips. He arose and shut off the TV. "We are going to Moo."

"I realize television may have sunk to new depths here, Little Father," Remo protested. "But I think we can find some better way to entertain ourselves than by resorting to animal impressions."

"There is no time to explain," Chiun said, flouncing from the room like a fussy hen. "Pack."

"Pack? Why?"

"Because we are going to Moo."

Remo, seeing from the Master of Sinanju's body language that he meant business, shrugged and said, "I'd better inform Smith, then." He picked up the telephone and dialed the nonemergency number that connected him with CURE, the supersecret government organization for which he worked. A recorded message told him he had reached the Miami Beach Betterment League and that, at the sound of the beep, the caller had exactly thirty seconds to leave a message.

Remo waited for the beep and then, letting out his breath, let out with it a rapid-fire stream of words.

"Smitty. Remo. Chiun and I are going to moo. I don't know what exactly that means, but it involves travel, and from Chiun's look, it's serious. I'd explain, but I don't know any more than that, and besides, I have a hunch the explanation would take longer than thirty seconds. Next time spring for a longer tape. 'Bye."

Remo hung up with three seconds to spare and called into the other room:

"Smitty's taken care of."

"Good," called Chiun. "Are you packed?"

"One thing at a time," Remo grumbled, starting for his room. He stopped abruptly and ducked back into Chiun's room.

"Give me one good reason why I should," Remo demanded.

"I will tell you on the way."

"No, I think I deserve a straight answer right now." Remo folded his arms. "And if I don't get one, I'm not going to quack, bark, grunt, or whinny. Never mind moo."

Chiun stopped his packing. He straightened up from laying a traveling kimono in a bright red lacquer trunk with brass handles. His clear hazel eyes narrowed craftily.

"Because," the Master of Sinanju said carefully, "the women go bare-breasted."

Remo blinked as the significance of the Master of Sinanju's words sank in. He did not understand this moo business. He did not understand how it connected with this sudden urge to pack. Breasts, he understood. When Harold Smith had first subjected him to a battery of psychological tests before turning him over to Chiun, Remo had passed most of the tests handily. Except one. The Rorschach test. Smith laid down one inkblot and Remo looked at it briefly and pronounced it a pair of female breasts. That was the answer he gave for nine out of nine inkblots. Sometimes he saw only one breast. Once he saw three. When the worried look on Smith's parsimonious face made Remo fear he was about to be dumped into the grave bearing his name but which actually contained a nameless derelict, Remo announced that the tenth and final inkblot was an accurate depiction of the Indian subcontinent—even though it looked like the most colossal set of boobs he had ever seen.

Remo shook his head suddenly and straightened out of his leaning slouch against the doorjamb.

"Well, don't just stand there," he said. "Keep packing. I'll call a cab."

4

The doctor at New York Hospital wanted to say that Horton Droney III would not, could not, under any imaginable circumstances, see visitors.

Instead, a blood-curdling scream erupted in the room. It wasn't coming from the tiny Oriental gentleman in the colorful native costume. His companion, the one with the deadest eyes Dr. Alan Dooley had seen since medical school, stood tight-lipped. He was not the author of the blood-curdling scream either.

It might have been Nurse Bottomsly. Her mouth was open. But her throat wasn't pulsating the way people do when they scream. She looked more shocked than horrified. And she was looking directly at him.

It was then that Dr. Dooley noticed that it was he himself who had authored the mysterious scream. Imagine that. He was screaming and he hadn't even noticed. Before his fear-frozen brain synapses could begin the process of wondering why he was screaming, the answer shot up his arm, spread to the other arm, down both legs, up his screaming skull, and, most painfully, to his testicles.

He fell on the floor and clutched himself. He screamed louder. He coughed through the scream and the resulting sound was quite disgusting. As he curled up on the floor like a maggot that has been doused with lighter fluid and set afire, he noticed that his right arm hadn't joined his left in the necessary action of clutching himself at the point of maximum pain. It was hung up on something.

With tearing eyes, Dr. Dooley looked up. His wrist was pinched between the thumb and forefinger of the little Asian gentleman. The man's face was a thundercloud of wrath.

"I will ask again," the Asian said evenly. "Direct us to the room of Horton the Turd."

"Do us both a favor," the white man interposed casually. "He's in a rush and I'm in a hurry. Don't piss either of us off."

The thought, clear as a surgical needle going through Dr. Dooley's brain, penetrated with amazing clarity. If the Asian was inflicting this much agony before he was pissed, how much pain would he inflict when he crossed that terrible threshold?

Dr. Dooley decided not to find out. Better to risk a malpractice suit from the patient. Besides, he was not Horton Droney's personal physician. He was just the doctor on duty when the television host was rushed into the Emergency Room. Suddenly Dr. Dooley felt absolutely no obligation to his patient.

"Room thirty-seven," he groaned. His hand suddenly fell to the floor, landing beside his nose, as flaccid and lifeless as a dead tarantula.

"Thank you," a voice told him as he picked his hand off the floor. It was as if it was separate from his body. He couldn't even feel the arm that still linked it to his shoulder.

"Don't just stand there, nurse. Get a doctor!"

"Which . . . which one?"

"A good one, dammit."

"I hope he's conscious," Remo told Chiun as they approached the hospital room. "At the studio, they said he was stuck pretty deep."

"If he is not conscious, I will awaken him," Chiun promised.

"And if he's dead?"

"Then we will search out the poor unfortunate girl without his aid."

"I wouldn't call her unfortunate. She handled herself pretty well, especially in front of that bully."

"She was terrified. And that lummox refused to listen to her."

"What could he do? She didn't speak English."

"Yes, all the good languages are forgotten."

"Don't tell me, Chiun. You understood her gibberish?"

"I will not."

"Good."

"But I did."

"Sure," Remo said as he looked around.

The Master of Sinanju paused before the door marked thirty-seven and pushed it open. Remo followed him in.

It was a private room. Horton Droney III lay on an immaculate bed. Intravenous tubes led from his arm. A blood bag hung over his head. His eyes were half-closed dreamily.

"Excuse me," said the attending nurse, rising from a chair.

"You are excused," snapped Chiun.

"But—"

"He said you've been excused," Remo said gently, leading the nurse out the door. When she protested, he added, "Here, take my wallet as security. It contains my life savings and my ID. If we do anything bad, you'll know who to report to the police."

Then he closed the door after her. He held the doorknob in place while she vainly tried to turn it from the other side. Her poundings woke Horton Droney III.

"Who are you jerks?" he roared when he saw Chiun.

"I am Chiun and I would keep a civil tongue in my mouth."

"Hey, I don't take crap from Japanese. I haven't forgotten Pearl Harbor. So get lost, you Toyota-loving riceball."

"Now you did it," Remo said.

"Remo," Chiun said evenly, "would you excuse us?"

"Little Father, why don't you let me handle this?" Remo began, still holding the doorknob against the nurse's frantic struggling.

"Did he call you a Japanese?" Chiun demanded.

"No, but I don't think he knows any better."

"I know that if we don't stand up for our rights," Horton Droney screamed, spittle flying from his yawning mouth, "the Japanese are going to buy America out from under us."

"Remo," Chiun repeated.

"Okay, Little Father, I hear Security coming up the hall. Just, please, don't kill him. He's a television personality, for Christ's sake."

"Kill?" said Horton Droney III, looking at Chiun's wrinkled face. And then he threw his head back in laughter. He howled the word "Kill" in between spasms of hilarity.

The laughter stopped almost as soon as Remo closed the door behind him. The nurse landed on her white rump when the door she was straining against suddenly came toward her.

Two security guards came running up the hall.

"What is it? What's the trouble?" they demanded.

"She is," Remo said, pointing at the hapless nurse.

"I am not!" the nurse said indignantly.

"Who are you, buddy?"

"Horton Droney IV." Remo bared his teeth to the gum line, hoping to create the effect of a family resemblance.

The guards hesitated.

"The big guy's son?" one of them asked uncertainly.

"That's right. And it's a good thing I came along when I did. I found this nurse going through my father's stuff. And when I asked her what she was doing, she gave me a lot of double-talk and lifted my wallet."

"I did not!" the nurse cried.

"That's my wallet in her hand right there. Check it out."

"He gave it to me," the nurse protested.

"Hah!" retorted Remo. "A likely story." He hoped he sounded as self-important as Horton Droney IV would sound—assuming that there was a Horton Droney IV.

One of the security guards retrieved the wallet and was about to go through it when the Master of Sinanju glided out of Horton Droney's room.

"All set, Little Father?" Remo asked.

"I have what I want," Chiun replied.

"Good," said Remo, snatching his wallet from the guard's hand.

"Hey," the guard said. And suddenly he found himself on the other side of a closed door. He experienced a moment of profound disorientation. He remembered the hand snatching the wallet from him and then the guy's other hand hooking his belt buckle. Then he was in here. He didn't remember any intervening action. When he noticed the man with the caved-in mouth on the bed, he realized he was in Horton Droney III's room. Then he wasn't alone anymore. His fellow guard sprawled on the floor beside him. The nurse came running in on her own. She closed the door and leaned up again it, her skinny chest heaving spasmodically.

"What are you afraid of?" the guard asked her.

"Everything," she sobbed.

* * *

Out on the street, Remo trailed after the Master of Sinanju. Chiun was storming along First Avenue, oblivious of the crowds surging around him.

"Did you get what you wanted?" Remo asked.

"That, and more."

"Tell me about the 'that.' "

"The one known as Shane Billiken lives in a place called Malibu. We are going there."

"I'd better hail a cab," said Remo. He put two fingers into his mouth and whistled. A cab pulled up and Remo opened the door for Chiun.

The Master of Sinanju settled into the rear seat and the cab was in motion before Remo had the door closed after him.

"Kennedy International," he told the driver. And turning to Chiun, he asked, "What was the more?"

"This," said Chiun, pulling a huge set of false teeth from one voluminous sleeve. Chiun held it in a hospital towel to keep his hands clean.

"I guess his secret is out. What are you going to do with them?"

"I do not know," Chiun said casually, and balling the dentures inside the towel, he flipped them out the window. They hit the street, where a bus ran over them. The crack brought a satisfied smile to Chiun's face.

"That's a relief," Remo said. "I thought you were going to kill him."

"Another time, perhaps," said Chiun.

As they approached the airport, Remo suddenly remembered something.

"When do we get to the bare-breasted women?"

"Have patience. We are at least headed in the right direction."

"Anything I can do to get there faster? Like moo?"

"I do not understand this moo you speak of."

"Well, I don't understand the moo you keep talking about either."

"Obviously we are thinking of two entirely different Moos."

"Obviously," said Remo.

5

Dr. Harold W. Smith wore a lemony frown as he shut down the computer system in his office at Folcroft Sanitarium. The sun was setting, and darkness was enveloping Long Island Sound, which showed through the big one-way glass picture window directly behind his desk.

It was the end of a difficult day. He had made an inspection of the psychiatric wing of Folcroft. One of the inmates had been found missing. Not a routine matter in any asylum, for Smith it was fraught with potential serious ramifications. For Folcroft was a cover for CURE, a super-secret government organization, and under the guise of being Folcroft's director, Smith actually ran CURE.

Set up in the early 1960's when the tide of crime threatened to swamp the ship of state called the United States of America, CURE was the brainchild of a young President who had no idea then that an assassin was about to end his term in office prematurely. In those dark days, the handwriting had been on the wall. The nation was breaking down. Two roads lay ahead: anarchy, or a temporary suspension of the Constitution in order to set things right.

The President had come up with a third alternative. CURE. The Constitution would stand, but to root out the criminal elements that were using it to bury America under a mountain of legalistic red tape, CURE was set up to work outside of constitutional restrictions. If known, that would be a tacit admission that American democracy had ceased to work. And so CURE was sanctioned to operate in secret.

In those days, Smith recalled wistfully, CURE had been a sociological-research foundation, and its multiple banks of computers had functioned as CURE's information-gathering brain. But a crisis in which CURE had been nearly exposed forced a major change. Folcroft became a sanitarium in fact as well as name. And its many computers, thanks in part to the march of technology, went into a concealed basement where a small bank of them could do the work of a roomful.

With the change came new headaches. Medical staff. Patients. AMA oversight. Billing problems. And now this. A missing patient.

Smith's preoccupation with the missing patient forced from his mind two messages that had come in over the office tape machine. Two separate phone lines accessed the machine. One was a dummy line to be used by Remo and Chiun for noncritical contact messages, and the other was known only to his wife. Smith had balanced the additional six dollar-and-twenty-two-cent cost of an extra line against any possible security risk and erred in favor of frugality.

When he had returned to his office after a fruitless and frustrating search for the missing patient, whose name was Gilbert Grumley, Smith had replayed both messages. The first was from Remo. He had rattled off some breathless nonsense about mooing. Smith, not knowing the current whereabouts of Remo or Chiun, told himself that there was no problem as long as there were no assignments on the CURE agenda. And all was quiet there.

The second message was from his wife, Maude. It was brief. It ran:

"Harold, dear, could you please remember to bring home a package of those nice mashed-potato flakes you like so much? And by the way, I saw the oddest thing today. You know the—"

The tape had not caught the entire message and Smith made a mental note to get a longer tape cassette if he ever saw one on sale.

As he closed his briefcase and locked the office behind him, Harold Smith wondered what the odd thing Maude wanted to tell him was. Oh, well, he thought, he would know soon enough.

In the lobby, the guard informed him that the missing patient, Gilbert Grumley, was still nowhere to be found.

"It's just a matter of time," Smith said. He said good night to the guard, went to his personal parking space, and tooled his battered sedan out the gate.

He stopped off at a convenience store and bought an economy-size box of Flako Magic Potato Mix, first examining every box to find the one with the latest freshness date. The package cost exactly $1.37 and Smith paid for it with a dollar bill and exact change, which he took, one careful coin at a time, from a little red rubber change holder. It took longer to give exact change, but Smith had once been short-changed twelve cents by a careless clerk in 1955, and was forced to drive seven miles back to the store and argue for twenty minutes before the proprietor agreed to rectify the error. Smith had only caught it when he got home and went through his wallet to budget his spending money for the next working day. At any time, he knew exactly how much money he had on his person. A penny's difference was usually enough to depress him.

Maude Smith, frumpy and white-haired, greeted him with a perfunctory kiss at the door.

"Did you bring it?" she asked.

"Yes, of course," Smith replied, setting his worn briefcase on the table by the door. He settled onto the big stuffed sofa.

"Don't get comfortable, Harold. The roast is ready. And these potatoes will take only a moment."

Five minutes later, Smith had settled into his straight-backed wooden chair at the head of the dining-room table.

He tasted the roast first. It was very dry.

"Good?" asked Mrs. Smith.

"Yes, very," Smith said, taking a sip of ice water.

"And the peas?"

Smith took a knife and herded some peas onto his fork. The peas tasted like peas.

"Good," said Smith, who was indifferent to peas. Mrs. Smith beamed. She never got tired of cooking for her appreciative husband.

"And the potatoes, Harold. How are they?"

Smith tasted them. They tasted artificial. But of course, he wouldn't say that. As a matter of fact, after over thirty years of marriage to a woman who served mashed potatoes three or four times a week without fail, he had grown totally disinterested in mashed potatoes. But, of course, it would be the height of impoliteness to criticize his wife's cooking. When Maude Smith discovered artificial mashed potatoes, it was like going from bland to worse. But Smith consoled himself with the fact that at least these mashed potatoes were not lumpy.

"The potatoes are very . . . smooth," he told her. And with the tasting ritual done, Mrs. Smith dug into her own food. She thought the potatoes tasted medicinal, the peas tinny, and the roast beef too dry. But if this was the way her Harold preferred his food, she was going to be a good sport about it. But the man did have odd tastes.

Harold Smith got the potatoes out of the way as fast as possible. He mixed the peas into the white mush in a vain attempt to make them more flavorful. Then he washed them down with ice water.

Smith was working on the dry roast beef when Mrs. Smith perked up suddenly.

"Oh, what did you think of that strange thing I mentioned on the phone?"

"Actually, the tape ran out before you finished speaking. All I got was something odd that you had seen or heard about."

"We have new neighbors," Mrs. Smith said.

"Oh, did the Billingtons move?"

"The Billingtons moved out when Richard Nixon was in office. We've had two families in that house since."

"That's nice, dear," said Dr. Harold W. Smith, wondering what was so odd about having new neighbors. He knew his wife would get around to telling him. Eventually.

"There were the Reynoldses, who had too many children, and the Lippincotts, who had none. Well, Mr. Lippincott received a job offer in Tucson, so they had to move. Mrs. Lippincott was heartbroken."

"I don't think I ever had the pleasure of meeting them."

"With the hours you keep, it's no wonder. Really, Harold, does that office need you so much?"

"We had a patient turn up missing today."

"Did you find him?"

"Not yet. But we will. Our security is quite good. I'm certain he never left the grounds."

"That's nice," Mrs. Smith said vaguely. "But you know, I've been thinking of it all day and I still can't place him."

"Who?" asked Smith.

"Our new neighbor, silly. What do you think we've been talking about?"

"Oh," said Smith, who thought they were discussing Folcroft. "What about our new neighbor?"

"Well, I only caught a glimpse of him leaving. I waved to him, but I don't think he saw me. But he was someone I've met before. I'm sure of it."

Smith stopped with a desiccated slice of roast beef poised before his open mouth.

"Met where?" he asked. He forced his voice to be calm.

"Well, that's what I can't for the life of me figure."

"Could you describe this man?" Smith said in a voice he fought to keep steady. He did not know why he was suddenly concerned. Perhaps it was the unsettling matter of the missing patient. Loose ends always affected his nerves.

"Oh, he was tallish. His hair was dark. I didn't see his eyes very clearly. I would say he was handsome."

"Young or old?"

"Young. But not too, too young. In his late twenties, I would say. Maybe early thirties. It's so hard to tell these days."

"And you say he looked familiar?"

"Yes, definitely. I know I've met him before."

"Hmmm," said Smith. "When did they move in?"

"Well, that's one of the odd things. No one knows."

"What do you mean, no one knows?"

"I got on the phone to Mrs. Gregorian when I couldn't stand it anymore—you know, the nagging feeling that I knew the man—and she didn't even know anyone had moved in. There was no moving van. She told me that she could see their living room from her upstairs bedroom and there was practically no furniture."

"Maude!" Smith said reprovingly. "Snooping."

"I didn't snoop. It was Mrs. Gregorian. I just listened."

"To gossip," Smith said, but his lips thinned. Anything out of the ordinary was something that he, in his sensitive position, had to look into.

Probably the new neighbor was an ordinary person. But Smith knew that if there was a place he, as director of CURE, was vulnerable, it was not in his well-protected Folcroft office, it was in his modest Rye, New York, home.

And if there was a threat about to materialize against him, he must be prepared to move ruthlessly to eliminate everyone involved in it.

"Excuse me, please. There are some phone calls I must make," he said, dabbing his chin with a linen napkin.

"But you haven't finished your roast beef."

Smith looked at his plate. Two slices remained. He quickly wolfed them down, and drained the last of his ice water.

"Good," said Mrs. Smith, happy that her Harold had cleaned his plate. He always cleaned his plate. It was nice that tonight was no exception. She had worried that the roast beef was undercooked. She knew her Harold hated it rare. He so detested blood.

6

If the truth were to be known, Shane Billiken would have been perfectly content to chuck it all. The filthy-rich dowager clients. The best-seller book contracts. And the radio and TV talk-show appearances.

He was, as he saw it, an artist. But the world had kept slapping him down, and exploiting its wealthier inhabitants' world was his way of making up for past disappointments.

He meditated on it again after he hustled the girl he had dubbed Princess Sinanchu into his waiting limousine. He ordered the driver to take them to Newark International Airport, where his chartered Learfan jet awaited. With any luck, they'd be in the air before the police got organized.

After that, Shane Billiken had no idea what he was going to do. True, he told himself, he was not culpable for what had happened on *The Horton Droney III Show*. The whole nation could attest to that. But the police were likely to arrest Princess Sinanchu—or whatever her actual name was—and Shane Billiken wasn't about to let his meal ticket languish in jail.

Better to make a break for the Coast, where celebrity misadventures were swept under the rug every week. Let the lawyers handle it. New York was just too damn unevolved.

The Learfan was in the air less than thirty minutes after they had bolted from the Manhattan studio. Shane Billiken breathed a sigh of relief. Princess Sinanchu sat in the rear of the plane, her tawny face angry, her eyes blazing like dark jewels as they stared out into the night sky.

No, this was not what Shane Billiken had wanted to do with his life. There was another way, a better way. And if only his life had gone in that direction, he'd be happier, and probably still have the same Malibu beachfront home, fat bank account, and a hell of a lot younger groupies than he had now.

If only Roy the Boy would just lie down and die.

As Shane Billiken saw it, only a rock-and-roll dinosaur stood between him and a full calendar of yearly concert bookings.

Long before Shane Billiken knew a tarot deck from macrobiotic onion, he had been lead singer in a band called the Rockabilly Rockets. They had a meteoric career at the beginning of 1963. They crashed to earth like a bollid.

The Rockabilly Rockets had everything going for them. A sound, described by *Variety* as "doo-wop folk," trademark three-cornered hats, a hit single, and a record contract with a major label.

Then the Beatles hit New York and the Rockabilly Rockets' debut album, *The Rockabilly Rockets Live at the Hootenanny*, made recording history. It shipped tin. It went directly from the pressing room to the cut-out bins.

"What happened?" Shane Billiken had demanded of his personal manager. He kneaded his Paul Revere hat in nervous fingers.

"Look at it this way, Shane, baby, you made music history. Nobody's ever shipped tin before."

"You swore we'd go platinum overnight. I'd settle for gold. But tin!"

"Don't blame me, blame those shaggy-headed Brit pansies."

And Shane Billiken did. He held a bitter news conference, fired his band, and spent the early sixties bouncing around in restaurant dishwasher jobs. He was a poet with a broken heart.

It was in 1968 that Shane noticed the world was changing. The Beatles had gone psychedelic. Everyone was into astrology. And Zen. And higher consciousness. Especially the groupies. It was the Age of Aquarius.

Shane Billiken bought a stack of used books on mysticism at a head shop and decided that maybe he'd get in on the action. He worked carnivals and private parties in the beginning. It was a good life, and gradually he forgot his bitterness. Even the slump in the late seventies, when everyone suddenly decided the sixties were passé, was not so tough. Shane had put a lot of his money into stocks. He did well.

Then came the eighties. Suddenly the fifties and sixties were hot again. Old rockers were crawling out of the woodwork, working the nostalgia circuit. And Shane Billiken, energized from attending a Righteous Brothers reunion concert, returned to his Southern California home and dug out his old Ovation guitar.

Standing in front of the mirror, his ax hanging off one shoulder, and strumming an old I-VI-IV-V-I chord progression, he noticed that his pushing-fifty face had gotten puffy. He put on a pair of wraparound sunglasses to see if it would take the curse off him, and lo and behold, he made a wonderful discovery.

He looked almost exactly like the great Roy Orbison.

Especially when he combed his hair into a kind of Julius Caesar pageboy-bang effect.

Shane experimented with a few bars of "Only the Lonely," and inspiration hit him. The woods were full of Elvis Presley impersonators living off the bones of the King. Hell, almost every overweight singer who could curl his lip was cashing in. Why not Shane Billiken?

He convinced the owner of an Agoura discotheque to book him for a weekend as Roy Orbit Sun. Both nights sold out in advance, and Shane Billiken knew he had found his way at last.

The night of his first set, he waited for the warm-up act to finish. He was sweating so bad, even his Ray-Ban Wayfarer sunglasses were beading up.

"Relax," said the club manager. "You're gonna be dynamite. You sound just like the guy."

"I haven't done this in a few years. Are my shades on straight?"

"You'll do fine. In fact, there are a couple of suits in the front row. Look like talent scouts to me. What are you gonna open with?"

" 'Running Scared,' " said Shane Billiken, his teeth chattering.

"Good choice," said the manager. "Fitting."

"Then I'm gonna seque into 'Blue Angel,' shift up to 'Ooby Dooby,' and then do 'Oh, Pretty Woman.' "

"If you hit, I'm gonna want you to play every weekend for the next three months."

"If I hit, you'll have to talk to my agent about that."

"You told me you didn't have an agent."

"If I hit, I'm getting one."

"Don't get too big for your britches, pal. Try not to forget I'm the guy who's giving you your big break."

Shane Billiken was about to say something when the MC announced the world premiere of the hottest performer since the fifties, Roy Orbit Sun, and Shane Billiken clumped out on the stage.

He fired up a rocking rendition of "Running Scared," forgot the words midway through the soulful "Blue Angel," and switched over to "Crying Over You," which he was saving for the first encore. The crowd was with him from the third bar of "Crying Over You."

Unfortunately, so were the two suits who happened to be sitting in the front row. They jumped onstage and tried to hand Shane Billiken an official-looking envelope.

"It's over," one of them said.

"I'm saving that one for the second set," Shane Billiken hissed as he launched into an improvised guitar solo. "And I don't do requests. So get off the stage."

"We represent Roy Orbison. The original. And this is a cease-and-desist order. You can change acts right now, or you can see us in court."

"But, but—"

"Better decide fast, friend," the other man said.

"Screw you," snarled Shane Billiken. And then he was singing "Crryyiiiing Oooover Yooouuuuuu."

One of the suits snapped his fingers and a pair of plainclothes cops hustled Shane Billiken off the stage to a chorus of boos and catcalls.

Shane Billiken barely made bail that night. At the trial, faced with a battery of high-powered lawyers, his own attorney suggested that he plead no contest. Shane Billiken reluctantly agreed, and they made him sign a paper in which he promised that he would never steal Roy Orbison's act again.

Once more Shane Billiken's career in music had hit a brick wall.

If anything, he grew more embittered. A zillion Elvis

Presley impersonators were making individual fortunes and everyone knew that any warbler with a bay window and a spit curl could impersonate the King. But mimicking Roy Orbison, with his high, haunting bel canto tenor—that took skill.

For a time, Shane Billiken flirted with the idea of having Roy the Boy whacked. He went so far as to initiate contact with a hit man. But at the last minute he chickened out. It was too risky. Besides, how long could Orbison go on? Almost all of his contemporaries were dropping like flies from drugs or booze or some damn thing.

Shane Billiken decided to wait the guy out. How long could it take? And so he returned to his former trade. But by this time mysticism was no longer the province of dippy girls in tent dresses and guys with earrings. Now it belonged to the yuppies and the housewives. The Age of Aquarius was over. It was the New Age.

Once he got into the swing of it, Shane Billiken found that by working the exclusive-clientele angle, he could make ten times the money for one-twentieth the effort. Meantime, he practiced his singing in the shower.

A limo was waiting for him at LAX airport. Shane hustled the princess into the back. She spat at him. Some days she was touchy. Like the last time he tried to get into her pants. He hadn't been as much interested in that as he had been in getting another look at those silvery coins of hers. She guarded them jealously. She even slept with them, which was more than she did for the man who fed and clothed her and got her on talk shows all over the nation, thought Shane Billiken bitterly.

Even months after he had first taken her under his wing, after a battery of linguists had assured him to his own surprise that her language was not merely unidentified, but bore no linguistic resemblance to any tongue known to the modern world, Shane Billiken still had no idea where Princess Sinanchu came from. She resisted all his efforts to teach her English.

All he knew was that if no one could understand what she was saying, no one could possibly disprove his claim that she was the avatar of Princess Sinanchu of Atlantis.

For all he knew, it was true.

Returning to his house, Shane Billiken instructed Fernando, his Filipino valet, that he was not home.

"And I don't mean not home to visitors or callers, I mean not home. As far as you know, I'm in New York. Got that?"

"Yes, Mr. Billiken."

"And lock the princess in her room. She's been acting up again."

"Yes, Mr. Billiken," said the valet, gently but firmly taking Princess Sinanchu by the arm and escorting her to her room. He locked it, thinking that it was a shame that such an attractive woman should be a virtual prisoner in this house. But he dared say nothing to the authorities. He was an illegal alien himself and Shane Billiken constantly held the threat of deportation over his head.

When the doorbell rang hours later, Fernando was afraid to answer it. Mr. Billiken had ordered him to get his lawyer on the phone and then had ordered him out of the room while he took the call. Fernando was afraid that he had called the immigration authorities. He feared them.

But not as much as he feared his master. So when Mr. Billiken had yelled at him to answer the "freaking door," Fernando wiped the palm sweat on the side of his black pants and straightened his white housecoat properly.

They were not immigration authorities at the door, he was relieved to see. No unless they had an international force. The white man wore a T-shirt and slacks. There was an Asian man, very old, who wore a kimono. No, not Immigration, Fernando thought with relief.

"We're here to see Shane Billiken," the white one said simply.

"Mr. Billiken not home."

"I didn't say he was. We're willing to wait." And the white man breezed in. The Oriental started to follow, but Fernando tried to shut the door in his face.

The door, instead, kept on going. The knob flew out of Fernando's stung hand. It sailed over the tiny Oriental's head and hit the driveway like a fallen tree.

Fernando stepped aside quickly to let the Oriental pass.

"What's that noise?" demanded Shane Billiken from the den.

Fernando looked sheepish when the white man turned and shot an accusing glare at him.

"Not in, huh?"

Fernando shrugged.

Shane Billiken took one look at the fruity-looking man and the old Oriental's saffron costume and said, "If you're here for the Harmonic Convergence Open House, you're too late. That was last month."

"We're not," the white man said.

"Then who are you?" Shane demanded. "Not cops?"

"No, not cops," the white said.

"Lawyers, then. Process servers?"

"Interested parties."

"Yeah. What are you interested in?"

The old Oriental spoke up then. His voice was low and reserved. He was an Eastern type in a robe. Probably some fakir or something.

"We wish to speak with her highness."

"About what?"

"It is a matter that concerns her house and my house."

"Yeah, well, this is my house, and I have a right to know what your business is."

"Don't look at me," the skinny one said. "I've been trying to pry it out of him for hours."

"Fernando, get rid of them," Shane Billiken ordered.

Behind the two, Shane Billiken noticed Fernando pointing at the open door. He kept pointing. Shane blinked. He noticed the door was not there. Then he saw a corner of it lying out in the circular driveway. The corner was splintered.

"Hey, what'd you do to my door?" he demanded.

"Let us see the princess and we won't do a repeat demonstration on every door in the place," the white man said.

Shane Billiken hesitated. Then he said, "Okay, c'mon into the Crystal Room."

The pair followed him into a room adjoining the den. It was decorated in early psychedelic. The ceiling was a flat black. The walls were covered with astrological signs. Shane Billiken hit a light switch and black light tubes mounted flush to the ceiling made the astrology symbols jump into Day-Glo orange.

The old Oriental looked about the room approvingly. "You consult the stars?" he inquired.

"I'm one of the foremost astrological technicians of the New Age."

"Perhaps when we have concluded our discussion, you will cast my chart."

"Sure. I do it all the time. What's your sign?"

"Leo. I am a Leo by Western reckoning. But according to the ways of my village, I was born in the Year of the Screeching Monkey."

"Oh, yeah? That's a long time ago. I think."

"There are older things. I am Chiun, Master of Sinanju."

"Sinanju. Not Sinanchu?" said Shane Billiken suspiciously.

"In some lands, it is pronounced Sinanchu."

"Yeah, what lands?"

"Moo."

"Say again?"

"Moo."

"I guess this is where the animal impressions start," the white said. "My name's Remo, by the way, and I don't know what's going on any more than you do."

"Your ignorance, I am used to," Chiun told Remo. "But I do not understand how this enlightened one does not understand of what I speak."

"Him? Enlightened? This place looks like a sixties hangout."

"This is my Crystal Room," said Shane Billiken. "I do all my deep meditations here. If you look around you, you'll see that embedded into the walls are tiny crystal generators. They act to focus the odyllic energy that flows through the universe into this nexus room."

Remo looked. Embedded in the stucco wall were tiny shards. Remo touched one.

"These feel like glass."

"Crystals. Adventurine."

"Looks like glass to me. And now that I see you in person, you remind me of someone."

Shane Billiken puffed up his chest proudly.

"Is that so?" he remarked.

"Yeah, but I can't place the face. I used to be good with faces."

"This give you a hint?" asked Shane, strumming on an imaginary guitar. He threw his head back as if singing.

Remo rubbed his chin in thought. Finally he snapped his fingers and called out, "Elvis. Elvis Presley."

"No! Roy Orbison."

Remo frowned. "Did he die too?"

"I wish," Shane Billiken growled.

"Enough," Chiun said. "Let us get on with this. Explain to me, Shane Billiken, how you are ignorant of Moo when I saw you in the company of the Low Moo on television."

"Low Moo?" Remo and Shane Billiken asked in the same breath.

"Yes, the girl. Her highness. You spoke of her as the princess of a lost civilization. She obviously told you that."

"Yeah, she did. Sorta."

"Then you know her plight."

"Well, kinda."

"And even though she entreated you to take her to the Master of Sinanju, you forbore to do so."

"I for-what to do so?"

"He means you refused," Remo said, new interest in his face.

"What do you know about this?"

"Less than nothing," Remo said sourly.

"I demand to speak with the Low Moo," said Chiun. "Take us to her."

"You're not cops?"

"We represent the longest continuing line of true assassins in history," the old Oriental said proudly.

"Hey, it's cool," Shane said nervously. "I'm very nonjudgmental. It's like I always say: Be the best you can possibly be. But let's all get clear on one concept. Princess Sinanchu doesn't speak English. If I let you see her, I'm gonna have to translate every word she says."

"Not necessary," said Chiun loftily. "I speak her language as well as you."

"You do?"

"Yes."

The old Oriental sounded serious, and Shane Billiken hesitated momentarily. But if what he said was true, he'd probably be able to tell him who or what Princess Sinanchu really was. Not that Shane Billiken believed the old Oriental. He was acting pretty crazy, making barnyard sounds and spouting double-talk.

"Okay," he said at last. "Come with me."

Shane Billiken led Remo and Chiun to another room. It was a bedroom. He switched on the light and the girl blinked out of her sleep. She wore the same costume she had worn on TV. Her eyes were puffy—either from lack of sleep or tears, Remo decided.

"Princess Sinanchu," said Shane Billiken in a self-important voice, "I bring visitors who say they know you."

Princess Sinanchu sat up on the edge of the bed. Her eyes went to the old Oriental. He spoke. Her mouth opened like a surprised flower. She began speaking.

"Juilli do Banda Sinanchu?"

The old Oriental stepped up to the bedside and inclined his balding head in respect.

"Let me translate that," said Shane Billiken. "She said that she is Princess Sinanchu, of the lost continent of Atlantis."

The Oriental whirled on him suddenly.

"What lies are these? Are you deaf? She just asked me if I am the Master of Sinanju. Now, still your false tongue. This is a historic moment."

And Chiun faced the girl again. He spoke. To Shane Billiken's surprise, his words sounded very much like the girl's. The same inflections and accents.

"Do juty da Banda Sinanchu," he said firmly.

The girl rose from the bed and, sobbing, poured out a torrent of words. She pulled the leather pouch from under her costume and spilled the coins at the old Oriental's sandaled feet.

Shane Billiken drifted up to get a closer look at the coins. The guy named Remo got in his way.

"Like he said, this is a historic moment, Elvis."

"I thought you didn't know what was going on here."

"I don't. I'm just along for the ride."

Shane backed off.

As he watched, the girl and Chiun exchanged an excited volley of words in the same strange language. During the course of their talk, Princess Sinanchu fell to her knees and began to cry into her hands. The old Oriental laid a tender hand on her lustrous hair. He made sympathetic clucking sounds, like a father to a frightened child.

When at last the princess found her composure, the Master of Sinanju turned to Shane Billiken.

"The Low Moo has told me how you rescued her from the sea."

"We're Soul Mates. Did she tell you that?"

"And how you housed her and fed her."

"Yeah, I've been good to her. You see, she was my wife when I was King of Atlantis about seven or eight million years ago."

"And for those mercies," continued Chiun, "I will not slay you for the lies you speak to me now."

"What do you mean, lies? We were husband and wife in Atlantis. Disprove it if you can."

"Atlantis is a fraud, perpetrated by that Greek Plato to trick sailors into going to sea in search of it."

"Bull!"

"It is well known among my people that Plato had a relative who built boats. The story of Atlantis was but a scheme to drum up trade."

"That's ridiculous. She's a princess."

"That much is true."

"It is? I mean, I know it is! What I want to know is how come you speak her language when the best language experts in the world say her tongue is unknown?"

"Because truly it is a lost tongue. Or one believed to be lost. I know it only because my ancestors passed it down from generation to generation so that we, at least, would not forget."

"Forget what?"

"Moo."

"There he goes again," Remo sighed.

"Moo?" repeated Shane Billiken.

"Moo."

Shane Billiken looked at the little Eastern guy and at the white man named Remo. Then he looked at Chiun again.

"I'm not following very much here."

"Correct. You are not following us. We are leaving now."

"Well, nice of you to drop in," Shane Billiken said,

relief suffusing his puffy features. "Fernando will see you to the hole where the door was."

"Remo, gather up the coins. They belong to us now."

"No, they don't. They belong to Princess Sinanchu, and Princess Sinanchu belongs to me."

"Truly?" said the Master of Sinanju as Remo scooped up the coins and stuffed them into his pockets. "Have you told her that?"

"Yeah, actually."

"Then perhaps you should tell her again."

"Er, you can do it if you want."

"Thank you, I will," said Chiun. He turned to the girl and spoke a few words. She listened carefully.

Then Princess Sinanchu walked up to Shane Billiken. Her face was not pleasant. She slapped his once, hard. He fell back into a Japanese taboret and knocked over an ion fountain.

"Hey!" he said, coming to his feet angrily. "I could sue her for that!"

"Be grateful that she told me of your kindness, otherwise your transgressions would not be overlooked on this day."

And taking Princess Sinanchu by the elbow, the old man who called himself the Master of Sinanju led her from the room.

On his way out, the one named Remo waved good-bye. "See you later, alligator," he said.

7

Outside Shane Billiken's sprawling home, Remo put a question to Chiun.

"Now what?"

"We are going to Moo."

Remo shrugged. "Might as well get it over with." And raising his voice, Remo called, "Moo. Moo. Moo. Or should I give one long moo, like this: mooooo!"

"Are you crazed?"

"You said we were going to moo. I just did. Didn't I do it right?"

"You can do nothing right," Chiun snapped. "And you are embarrassing me in front of the Low Moo."

Remo glanced at the girl. She watched them with an openly quizzical expression on her oval face.

"Sorry," he said, "but I don't think she understands English."

"She does not. But she does understand Moo."

"She's one up on me, then. Not that I care."

"You should."

"Why? She's obviously not one of the bare-breasted women you keep promising me."

"They are merely a five-day sail from here."

"Sail?"

"Yes. The Low Moo's boat is nearby. Come."

His face gathering in confusion, Remo followed as the Master of Sinanju, the girl at his side, led him around to the back of the house. The girl cast several curious glances over her shoulder at Remo. Remo smiled at her. She smiled back. Maybe the night wouldn't be a total waste, Remo decided.

There was a boat set up on a wooden cradle on the dry beach sand. Chiun looked it over carefully, tugging at the rattan lashings and examining the drooping and tattered sail.

"It is too small," he said in a disappointed tone.

"Doesn't look very seaworthy," Remo agreed.

"Then we will build our vessel," Chiun announced, lifting a triumphant finger. "Come, Remo, let us fall to work."

"Build? Why not buy?"

"I will not be seen in an American boat. A thing of plastic and ugly metal. No, we will build our own."

"I don't know squat about building ships."

"Then it is time you learned. Ship-building is an honored skill."

"Especially if your relative writes stories about Atlantis."

Chiun's face contracted. "You are not taking this in the proper spirit," he fumed.

"Chiun, I have no idea what spirit I should be taking this in. I still don't know what is freaking going on."

"We are going to Moo, as I have told you."

"Oh, moo this and moo that. And moo to you too. I'm sick of double-talk and runarounds."

"Enough!" Chiun said, clapping his hands. "We will begin by felling some trees."

Remo looked around. There was a palm tree about a mile inland. Everything else was sand and ocean.

"When you get enough of them together, let me know," Remo said, lowering himself onto the sand. "I'll be catnapping." He folded his hands over his chest and shut his eyes.

"Remo," Chiun hissed, "do you want the Low Moo to think I have a lazy slug for a son?" He tugged on Remo's arm. "Up, up! She is a princess. A true princess."

"And I'm a Master of Sinanju, not a boat builder. You want to play Popeye the Sailor Man, fine. But you build your own boat."

Chiun stamped his foot angrily.

"Very well, lazy one," he said finally. "I will give in to your selfishness, but only this once. We will buy a boat."

Remo leapt to his feet. "Now you're talking," he said, grinning. It was a rare day when he won an argument with Chiun. The princess matched his smile with an infectious one of her own, and Remo thought it was a rare day indeed.

The salesman at the Malibu Marina wanted to know if Remo was interested in a racing sloop, a yacht, or a pleasure boat.

"Something fast," Remo said. "With dual motors."

"No motors," Chiun inserted quickly.

"No motors?" the salesman asked.

"A sail craft," Chiun added.

"You want something for pleasure trips, then."

"No," retorted Chiun. "We are going on a long voyage."

"We are?" said Remo. He was ignored.

"Then let me suggest something with auxiliary diesels."

"Sounds good to me," Remo said. "I want lots of chrome trim."

"I will have none of it," Chiun spat.

"Look, Little Father, I've strung along with you this far. I've traveled clear across the country, and now I'm agreeing to tag along while you and Yma Sumac there go off in search of Jacques Cousteau. I think you can bend just a little here."

"I am bending enough. I am not building a boat."

"Look," said the boatyard owner exasperatedly, "if you two could just get on the same frequency, I could help you, but—"

"There!" said Chiun suddenly, pointing past the salesman. The salesman turned. Remo looked. Even the princess followed the Master of Sinanju's quivering fingernail.

Remo groaned even before Chiun spoke the next words.

"There. That one. It is perfect," he cried.

"Not that!" groaned Remo. "Anything but that."

"The junk?" said the salesman.

"Good word for it," Remo piped up.

"It is authentic, of course?" asked Chiun.

"Yeah. Imported from Hong Kong. The previous owner lost his portfolio in the market crash. Couldn't afford the upkeep anymore. I took it on consignment, but I never expected to find a buyer."

"And you won't today," Remo growled.

"I must see it closer," Chiun breathed.

The salesman waved Chiun ahead.

"No way," said Remo, running after them.

"It's really a five-man craft," the salesman was saying. "You couldn't manage it with less than a crew of five. And it's difficult to handle. All those lugsails. It's not like manning a sloop or a ketch. By the way, how much sailing experience have you people had?"

"None," said Remo.

"Enough," said Chiun.

"It takes a skilled hand to pilot a Chinese junk."

"Did you hear that, Chiun? He said it's Chinese. And we all know how you feel about Chinese stuff. You despise them."

"Not as much as I despise American plastic," Chiun retorted. "Look at her, Remo, isn't she breathtaking?"

"Now that you mention it, there is an odor."

The junk wallowed in its slip like a three-story hovel with a keel. It had five masts, and the odd-shaped sails flapped like quilts in the wind. The junk creaked at every joint, like a haunted house. The name painted on its stern said *Jonah Ark* in green lettering.

"How much?" asked Chiun.

"The owner wants what he paid for it—seventy thousand."

"Fifty," countered Chiun.

"Sixty," offered the salesman.

"Wait a minute," Remo began.

"Sold," said Chiun triumphantly. "Come, Remo. Let us board our proud vessel."

"You take credit cards?" Remo asked unhappily.

"We can work something out. But you know, you're going to need a lot of training before you can risk piloting that thing out of dock."

"Twenty bucks says Chiun has us on the high seas within an hour."

"He's crazy."

"He's also determined," Remo said, digging for his wallet.

"I'll take that action," said the salesman.

Twenty minutes later, Chiun had single-handedly lowered the batten-reinforced sails, and they caught a shore wind.

"What are you waiting for?" Chiun called from the broad high stern. The Low Moo stood beside him. She waved Remo aboard.

"Thanks," Remo said, taking the salesman's money. "And wish me luck."

"You can't sail that thing with a three-man crew. It's suicide."

"That's what I said. Wish me luck," Remo called back as he pelted down the deck and leapt onto the groaning deck.

"Prepare to cast off," Chiun cried. "We sail with the dawn tides."

"Let's hope we don't sink with the sun," mumbled Remo, throwing off the stern lines while Chiun handled the port side. The wind, filling the quiltlike sails, seemed to grow stronger and the junk lumbered out of its slip like a fat dowager squeezing through a too-narrow door.

A piece of hull modeling caught on the dock and tore loose with a *rip-squeal* of a sound.

Chiun hurried to the tiller. He threw it to starboard. The junk pivoted slowly.

"Remo, why were you not at the rudder?" Chiun demanded querulously.

"I was casting off. And what do I know about rudders? I'm a landlubber."

"How much damage?"

Remo peered over the rail. "We lost some gingerbread," he reported.

"When we are at sea, it will be your responsibility to repair it."

"Oh, wonderful," Remo said sarcastically. "Just what I've always wanted—to learn a new trade."

8

Three days out of Malibu, Remo awoke in his bunk. The creaking of the *Jonah Ark* filled the hold like the sound of sick mice. Faint shards of morning sunlight came in through the chinks in the stained hull. The chattering of wind in the sails was noticeably absent.

Remo pulled on his salt-stiff pants and T-shirt, wishing that he had packed for the voyage. But he was too anxious to follow Chiun to the bare-breasted women to bother. He never stayed in one place long enough to acquire much of a wardrobe. With the many credit cards issued to him under a dozen cover identities by Harold Smith, it was more convenient to simply buy replacement clothes on the fly. He hadn't anticipated an ocean voyage.

During the early days of his work for CURE, when he was still bitter about the loss of his old life and identity, Remo bought a new pair of shoes every day, giving the old ones to people he met on the street. When Dr. Smith had complained about Remo's flagrant waste of taxpayer money, Remo had replied:

"Hey, you made me an assassin. Can I help it if I keep getting blood on my shoes? So make up your mind—more shoes or fewer targets."

And that had been the end of that.

As he walked up the creaking steps to the deck, Remo wished he had one of those extra pairs of shoes right now. But not as much as he wished for a change in underwear and a razor. He felt his beard growth, and he noticed his nails were getting longish, even though he had cut them only the other day.

On deck, Remo saw that the sails hung slack as shrouds. The junk was becalmed.

The princess was at the rudder. Remo shot her a smile and said, "*Ola!*"

"*Ola*, Remo!" she called back. "*Kukul can?*"

"*Nonda*," Remo said. When the girl frowned, Remo realized that he had replied "itchy" instead of "fine" to her inquiry.

"*Nah, nuda*," he said.

The Low Moo laughed. In three days, Remo had picked up just enough of their tongue to hold his own in simple conversations, but not enough to be really comfortable with the language. He suspected Chiun had fed him some imperfect translations just to be mischievous.

"*Dalka Chuin*?" Remo asked, joining her at the tiller.

"*Hiu*," the Low Moo said, pointing to the stern, which towered behind her.

"Yeah, I see him," Remo said in English. "Thanks."

"You're welcome," the Low Moo, whose name, she had told Remo, was Dolla-Dree, said in English.

The Master of Sinanju was seated on the high poop deck at the junk's stern. His pipestem legs dangled over the rail. He held a long bamboo pole in his hands. A string tied to the far end trailed in the water.

"How's the fishing?" Remo asked politely.

"Slow," said Chiun, twisting the pole so that the line coiled around the end. It lifted free of the water. There was no fish. As a matter of fact, there was no hook or bait either. He frowned. "I do not think there are any fish in this part of the ocean."

"Sure there are," Remo said brightly. "I can hear them laughing."

Chiun turned his head and glared. He spun the pole in the opposite direction, dropping the line back into the sea.

"Perhaps you will have better luck," he suggested sternly.

"Not me. I'm a city boy. Besides, I'm not hungry."

"But she is."

"I see. Gotta feed her highness."

"Do I detect a note of distaste in your voice, Remo?"

"No. I'm starting to like Dolla-Dree just fine. I'm just tired of you falling all over her like she's God's gift to Korean seamen. You gave all the food—what little of it there was in the larder—to her and none to me."

"You can go without food. So can I. Returning the Low

Moo to her father, the High Moo, intact and in good health, is more important than our stomachs."

"The High Moo?"

"Yes."

"Tell you what," Remo said, settling on the deck beside the Master of Sinanju. "You take the High Moo and I'll take the Low Moo, and whoever gets there first, wins."

"What are you prattling about?" Chiun demanded, staring at the water.

"It's a joke."

"To your feeble mind, perhaps. Not to mine. Please explain."

" 'Moo' is the sound a cow makes."

"No, Moo is the greatest client state in Sinanju history."

"You don't say," said Remo. "Well, since we're going to be here awhile, what with the lack of wind and the fact that you're fishing without hook or bait, why don't you tell me the whole involved story?"

"I do not need a hook."

"Tell that to the fish."

"And cows do not make a sound that resembles the name of Moo. Their sound is more like a 'looouuuwww.' " Chiun gave a creditable impression of a lonely cow.

"Not bad. But in America it's more like 'moooooo.' "

"Obviously American cows are inferior to Korean cows, just as Americans are inferior to Koreans. No self-respecting Korean cow would take the name of Moo in vain."

Remo shrugged. "I bow to you as the supreme authority on cows, both foreign and domestic. But can we get on with the legend?"

"How do you know I am about to treat you to a legend?"

"Your nose is wrinkled. It always wrinkles up when you are about to recite a legend."

Chiun looked at Remo as if to discern whether or not he was joking. Remo smiled impishly. Chiun turned his attention to his line, twirling it so the line cleared the water. He did it slowly, to heighten Remo's impatience. He returned the line to the water just as slowly. If Remo was going to make fun of the sacred traditions of Sinanju, he deserved a dose of delay.

When the line was back in the water, Chiun started to

speak. At intervals, he tapped the bamboo pole to make the line wiggle.

"The days of which I am about to speak are before those of Wang, greatest Master of Sinanju. Before the discovery of the sun source itself. In the days of which I am about to speak, Sinanju was not like it is now. Masters of Sinanju were not as they are now. The art of the assassin was known to Sinanju then, but it had not achieved the purity which you have been blessed to know, Remo. Masters of Sinanju used weapons—blades of iron, poisons—and not the natural tools of the body. And in these ancient days, Masters of Sinanju did not work alone. They were assisted by the young men of the village, who were known as night tigers. Of these night tigers, but one would be chosen to become the next Master. Thus, each night tiger fought hard and fought well, for only through his efforts could he hope to achieve full Masterhood. It is not like today, when even a white can achieve Masterhood."

Remo grimaced, but held his tongue. It had been a long time since Chiun had told him a story of the early days of Sinanju. Sometimes Remo thought Chiun preferred to sweep those days under the rug, because Sinanju was in such a primitive state.

"Now, the days of which I am about to speak were the era of Master Mangko. Have I ever told you of Mangko?"

"Nope."

"Mangko was the son of Kim, who was not a Master. For in the days of which I am about to speak, the line of Sinanju was not a bloodline. Instead, Masterhood was passed from generation to generation through merit and achievement. A worthy method, but now outdated, of course."

"Of course," Remo agreed. His eyes were on the horizon. He felt a strange peace out here on the still ocean, even not knowing where he was or where he was going.

Chiun smiled at Remo's agreement and continued in a low, dramatic voice. "Now, Mangko was the third Master of Sinanju. Young he was, and dark of hair and keen of eye. Tall he was, being by Western standards nearly five feet tall."

"A giant."

Chiun glared. "In those days, that was tall. Some would

say too tall. It is only the ridiculous modern Europeans who think five feet is not tall."

"Sorry," Remo said sheepishly.

"Now, these were prosperous days for Sinanju, although my lowly village was not then the jewel it is now, of course."

Remo started to snort in derision, but managed to turn it into a cough. The village of Sinanju was a cluster of mud-ringed huts clinging to the rocky coast of North Korea. It was cold and wet, and, even by the standards of a clam, inhospitable. But Remo didn't say that. He wanted to hear about Moo, and eventually the bare-breasted women he had been promised.

"Egypt knew of us in those days, although they were stingy with steady work. The Chinese knew of us, although they paid slowly and sometimes it was necessary to make an example of certain tribal princes in order to expedite payments."

"Business is business."

"But fortunately there was one client who was always on time with payments and who offered steady work, although it unfortunately involved extra travel time."

"Commuting is the bane of the workaday assassin, then and now," Remo remarked.

Chiun regarded him as if uncertain of Remo's meaning. His hazel eyes narrowed and he went on in a quieter voice, knowing that this would force Remo to strain to catch his every golden syllable.

"This land was known as the Kingdom of Moo."

"How do you spell that, by the way?"

"In the European alphabet, it is M, followed by two O's."

"That's what I thought," Remo said dryly.

Chiun rearranged his kimono skirts. "Are you making fun of Moo, Remo?"

"No, just holding up my end of the conversation. Go on."

"Now, Moo was a great land. Greater in area than Korea. It was an island, but larger in size and riches than all of the islands now claimed by Japan. It lay further east than Japan, in the ocean now called the Pacific. This ocean, Remo," Chiun said meaningfully.

Remo looked out over the water. Sunlight danced on the choppy waves.

"So great was Sinanju's fame that in the days of the first Master, whose name does not survive in any known record, the High Moo, ruler of the great land of Moo, sent a messenger to my village, requesting assistance. The first Master of Sinanju sailed to Moo and performed a great service for the High Moo, whose throne was beset by pretenders, and in doing this service, was richly rewarded for his efforts. And so Moo became a favorite client of Sinanju. And Moo also became a place beloved by my ancestors, for the rare coins of Moo were a currency more powerful than that of Egypt or China. And these coins enabled us to feed our young so that they did not have to be sent home to the sea. Have I told you how, when the food ran out in those days, mothers drowned their youngest infants, the females before the males, to spare them the slow death of starvation?"

"A million-zillion times."

"It is an important lesson, one you must never forget. For one day you will be in charge of my village."

"I won't forget the story of sending the babies home to the sea until the day I die. Maybe not even then."

"Good. But the occasional reminder does no harm."

"It does help pass the time, especially when the fish aren't exactly fighting to get out of the water."

The Master of Sinanju made his bamboo pole wriggle faster. He frowned. Surely there was at least one fish in this entire ocean.

"As I was saying," he went on, "Moo was good to Sinanju and Sinanju was good for Moo. It was a happy, fruitful association, blessed by the young gods of those early days. Then one cold morning, in the reign of Master Mangko, who was the third Master, there came a message from the High Moo. This was a different High Moo than the High Moo I spoke of earlier. For the High Moo is what a king would be to the English, or a pharaoh to the Egyptians."

"I figured out that part all by myself."

"And why not? I have taught you all you know."

"And I appreciate the continual subtle reminders," said Remo, trying to imagine where the bare-breasted women could possibly fit into this. He would have asked, but he knew that Chiun would probably save that part for the absolute end, just to annoy him.

"This message called upon the Master Mangko to journey to the land of Moo with urgent speed. It spoke of a terrible calamity, which only the Master of Sinanju could remedy. The messenger was of Moo, and like all men of Moo who ventured out into the world, his tongue had been cut off so that he would not reveal the true location of his emperor's domain if he were set upon by bandits, who were very common in those days."

"Unlike today."

"Exactly," said Chiun. He continued. "The message, which was written on tree-bark parchment, was very unspecific, and Master Mangko understood that it had been written in haste. So he slew the messenger and assembled his night tigers."

"Hold the phone," Remo said suddenly. "He slew the messenger! What for?"

"Because the messenger had delivered his message and was no longer needed."

"What was wrong with taking him back to Moo?"

"Remo! Have you no common sense? He was another mouth to feed and would require an extra horse. Men of Sinanju were great horsemen in those days. Did you know that?"

"Two seconds ago, no. Now, yes."

"You are never too old to be enlightened. And so the Master Mangko traveled from Korea through what would later be known as the kingdom of China. It was a hard journey, for they were beset by Chinese bandits and severe winter storms. But at last they reached the coast. But not without price. For one of the night tigers, whose name was Sako, had been wounded by the same Chinese bandits. It was a sad day for Master Mangko, for in his heart he had already chosen Sako to be trained as the next in line. Although, of course, Sako knew none of this."

Chiun paused in his recitation. His voice was hollow when he continued.

"It is a sad thing when a Master dies young, Remo. Sadder still when he does before achieving Masterhood. For who knows what great things Sako might have accomplished had he lived. Poor Sako. Alas. Cut down by Chinese bandits in the flower of his manhood."

"He died of his wounds, huh?"

"No, Master Mangko dispatched him."

"Why?" Remo demanded hotly.

"Because he was wounded and the bandits were riding hard after them. The Master and his entourage had a long sea voyage ahead of them and could not be burdened by a wounded man."

"That's awful!"

"The story gets worse," Chiun said.

"How is that possible? So far, the good guys are killing all their friends."

"Worse," repeated Chiun, his voice dropping to a hush. "They had to abandon the horses."

"So?"

"You do not understand. The Chinese got them."

"Is that bad?"

"Bad! It is a tragedy," Chiun screeched. "Beautiful Korean ponies left to big, brutish Chinese barbarians. Probably they were worked until their proud, straight backs were bowed and their strong legs crippled. It is sad." A single tear leaked out of Chiun's far eye. He turned his head so that Remo could not see, and brushed it away surreptitiously.

"Then what?" Remo prompted.

"With the Chinese bandits bearing down on them, the night tigers pushed off in boats. Those who remained slew the Chinese with their swords, taking care not to harm their horses, who were after all innocent brutes. For Sinanju never harms animals."

"Just messengers and potential Masters."

"If you insist upon distorting every word I utter, why do you not tell this story?"

"Because I don't know it."

"Exactly. Now, keep silent. The Master Mangko and his night tigers left many dead Chinese on their shores on that long-ago day. Sparing the horses, of course. Then they pushed off in the tiny boats that they had built, and sailed for Moo. Many days they sailed, through storm clouds—but no storm came to pelt their faces with hard rain or push their boats against one another. Lo, the entire earth had become a still place of deathly silent water. For seven terrible days, the future of my village was at the mercy of the great ocean we now sail on. A typhoon might have eradicated all of Sinanju's promise, just as Sako himself perished. Alas." Chiun brushed at his eyes again. His voice trembled with emotion when he resumed his story.

"Bravely, the Master Mangko sailed on. He watched the stars, seeking the configuration that would lead him to Moo. He followed it faithfully day and night. And still the storm clouds gathered, but no storm came."

Chiun was silent, thinking. His eyes grew inward and reflective, as if in his mind's eye he saw the very events he was relating.

"On the twelfth day," Chiun said, quavering, "the Master knew why the storm never swept over him. He understood why he did not spy the shores of Moo. He had sailed over the place where Moo should be. And the storm which was reflected in the sky, belonged not to the sky, but to the very ocean itself. This ocean, Remo."

"Moo sank?"

"Moo had perished, yes. The seas were the color of mud where Moo should have been. And where the very heart of Moo had lifted proudly over the waves, the flotsam of civilization floated and the seas bubbled green as with a sickness. And there were bodies too."

Chiun was silent a long time as he stared out at the white-capped waves. Remo was afraid to speak up. Finally he settled for clearing his throat.

"With a heavy heart," Chiun continued, "Master Mangko accepted the truth. He ordered the boats turned around, and they steeled themselves for the difficult return journey across water and bandit-infested China. He knew terrible days lay ahead for his village, and indeed, this was what came to be. The messenger had brought with him a bag of coins, each stamped with the head of the High Moo. These would be the last such coins, he knew. And when the Master Mangko returned to Sinanju, he himself chose the first female child to be sent home to the sea, because he knew that it would not be long before the coins ran out. For in those days of which I have spoken, the clients of Sinanju were only the slow-paying Egyptians and the stingy Chinese—and the great land of Moo, which was no more. That female child, Remo, was his very own daughter."

In spite of himself, Remo shivered. He was born and raised an American, and the ways of Sinanju were still alien to him. But sometimes he felt the tragedy of Chiun's stories almost as keenly as the Master of Sinanju.

"Since those days, there has been no word of Moo. Until now," Chiun said, removing a large flat coin from a pocket of his kimono.

Remo took the coin. It had obviously been hammered into shape by hand.

"Is this the High Moo?"

"The Low Moo's father, yes. for the coins of Moo are melted down and recast whenever a new High Moo ascends the Shark Throne."

"Shark Throne, huh? Sounds brutal."

"And today, after nearly five thousand years, Sinanju returns to Moo to fulfill the down payment accepted by Master Mangko—and earn the balance too, of course."

"I knew money had to enter into this somehow."

"A crass remark which I will ignore. You see, Remo, when I beheld the Low Moo on television, she was not saying what the charlatan white claimed at all. She was issuing a plea. A plea to the Master of Sinanju to journey to Moo to help the High Moo, whose throne was in mortal danger."

"So when you said we were going to Moo, that's what you meant?"

"All is clear to you now, Remo?"

"Not quite. If Moo sank nearly five thousand years ago, where does the Low Moo come from and where is she taking us?"

"Why don't you ask her? I have told you my story. Let her tell you her own. Besides, you will need the language practice if you are to get along on Moo."

"Why not? I'll be here all day waiting for you to catch a fish with that rig."

Suddenly the Master of Sinanju jerked his bamboo rod. The line arched up and a silver fish with flat eyes landed in Remo's lap.

"Hey!" Remo said, knocking the fish onto the deck. The

fish flopped and wriggled and Chiun speared him with a long-nailed finger. The fish gasped once and its tail ceased to move. Chiun lifted it up by the gills and examined it carefully.

"Ah, an excellent fish. Two more of these and we will dine very well today."

"Tell me, Little Father. How did you catch that fish without a hook?"

"It is simple. I dangle the line until I have the fish's interest. He thinks the line is a worm, and when I feel him bite, I whip the line up. I do it so fast the fish has no time to let go. A hook is not necessary. Besides, it is cruel. Sinanju does not harm animals, and it deals with those animals it eats as mercifully as possible."

"Sometimes I fail to fully grasp your philosophy," Remo said, climbing to his feet.

"It is easy to understand, Remo. For it is written in the Book of Sinanju that 'Death Feeds Life.' "

"Yeah, right under 'No Credit Issued.' If you want me, I'll be talking to the Low Moo."

"Do not dawdle. We will breakfast soon."

"I may pass. I checked last night and there are no matches left on this scow."

"Then we will eat them raw."

"Sushi isn't my thing. Besides," Remo said, scratching his bestubbled face, "I have this irresistible craving for egg-lemon soup."

9

Dr. Harold W. Smith had not played golf in years.

This was ironic, for in the days when CURE was being set up, Smith had bought his present home because it was virtually next door to one of the finest golf courses on the east coast. Smith, who had until then been with the Central Intelligence Agency, envisioned himself playing weekend golf. He had no idea of what he was getting into. The gravity of his new post was clear, but the sheer number of man-hours that would be demanded of him, first as the coordinator of CURE's vast network of information-gathering resources, and then later, when he was forced to admit that CURE would need an enforcement arm for situations beyond his operational reach, was not clear.

Smith had not touched his golf clubs in nearly a decade. He wouldn't be doing so now but for the fact that a few practice putts were the perfect cover for what he had to do.

Smith teed up and sent the ball skipping along the fairway. He pulled his wheeled bag behind him because today he did not want to be bothered with a caddy. He hit it again.

Smith had deliberately hit the ball out of bounds. When he found it, in the rough, he pulled out a small pair of high-powered binoculars and pretended to scan the fairway. His gaze drifted over to his house and then settled on the one next to it. Smith peered into the windows.

He saw bare hardwood flooring. He would need a different vantage point. He selected a driver and sent the ball in the general direction of the third hole.

The ball came to rest in a sand trap, and Smith, first checking to make sure that there was no one watching him, got down into the trap. He lay on his stomach, and peering up over the trap, directed his binoculars at the near side of the house.

The rooms were bare. In one he saw a big television but no other furniture. The open driveway was empty. It had been empty since his wife had first alerted him to the existence of the strange new neighbors.

It was the absence of a car that had caused Smith's initial disquiet to blossom into full-blown suspicion. He lived in an exclusive section of Rye, far from the bus routes. It was the kind of tree-lined peaceful suburban neighborhood he had once dreamed of retiring to, but now understood he could never enjoy because the only retirement from CURE would involve his death.

And if there was one absolute to living in suburbia, it was ownership of an automobile. The owners of the house next door did not own a car. Smith's wife had noticed this, and according to her, the neighbors had confirmed it.

No car, no furniture, no sign of habitation.

As Smith lay in the sand trap, attired in a short-sleeved pullover jersey and khaki pants, he tried to reason out who would buy a house and not furnish it.

More and more, it seemed to him as if the house were purchased, not as a home, but as some kind of blind. Or a staging area.

Grimly Smith climbed to his feet. Something was very wrong. It was time to stop pussyfooting around. He could no longer ignore the obvious. Replacing his driver and pocketing his ball, Smith pushed his golf bag back to the clubhouse.

"That was quick," said the caddy whom Smith had refused earlier.

"I'm more rusty than I thought," Smith muttered.

"Then you should stay out there. Work out the rust."

"Another time," said Smith, anxious to leave. He had attracted attention to himself by returning so early. That was a mistake. It was part of his job never to call undue attention to himself. But this had the earmarks of an emergency. Smith would bring all the awesome computer power of CURE to bear on the puzzle of learning who the new owner of the house next door was, and everything about his background.

As Smith drove off, every caddy and member in the

club surged to the windows. Everyone wanted to see the mysterious Dr. Harold W. Smith, who paid the annual membership fee on time every year, but who hadn't been seen on the golf course in a decade. A few of the older members, hearing of Smith's brief visitation, expressed surprise. They had assumed Smith had passed away years ago.

10

Tu-Min-Ka, High Moo of Moo, Lord of the Water Ocean, Wearer of the Golden Feather Crown, and He Whose Face Adorns the Coin of the Realm, ascended the worn stone steps.

Two guards, scarlet feathers dangling from their long shark-tooth spears, walked before him. Two others walked behind. Also following behind, ahead of the trailing guards, but a respectful two paces behind the High Moo, was the royal priest, Teihotu. He was cloaked in black, his narrow black eyes intent. Even the moonlight coming through the square openings cut into the passageway walls failed to light his pinched features.

The lead guards halted at the hardwood door, pivoted in place, and stiffened on either side, their spears snapping across their bare chests in the traditional salute.

The High Moo stopped. He turned to his royal priest.

"Teihotu, I would be alone."

"As you please," the royal priest replied. He gathered his cloak about him like protective wings.

"I have asked you to accompany me only because if I lose you too, I will have none to trust."

"I understand," said the royal priest. His eyes were small, like those of a bird.

"My guards will see to your safety. But I will pass the evening watching the eastern sky, for although my daughter has been gone far longer than I anticipated, I feel in my heart that she lives yet."

"So the stars tell me."

"You trust the stars. I trust my heart."

"As you wish."

And without another word, the High Moo passed through the door onto the roof of his palace, overlooking the low rice fields to the north and the mine-dotted slope to the east. He averted his eyes from the south, where the banyan trees grew thick and the Tall-Things-That-Were-Not-Men walked by moonlight. It was the place called the Grove of Ghosts, and for as long as he lived, only forty-one years, he had never dared to enter it. Although he knew some of his subjects were, even now, skulking there to perform who knew what obscene oblations.

It was to the east that the High Moo directed his kingly visage. His eyes were bold and proud. He was a squat, square man, thick of limb and well-muscled. He ruled this kingdom by dint of his mighty right arm, and he would die before he surrendered the Shark Throne.

But even he could not battle the things that walked by night and wore the faces of his villagers.

"Give me a skull to break, and I will prevail," he muttered to the unheeding wind. "But against the very spirits of evil, I am no match."

The waves to the east were dappled with moonglade. It was a beautiful sight, but it sent chills through the High Moo. For he knew that the greatest portion of his kingdom lay under those fantastic waters. The fishes had long ago ceased to feast on his great-great-great-grandfather's great-great-great-grandfather, but it still chilled him to look at the waters by night. Who could know when the Mighty Giver of Life might rise up to engulf them all? Even the royal priest said that the portents were back. The stars were moving into the position they had occupied when Old Moo, Great Moo, had fallen into oblivion.

But the High Moo did not truly believe the royal priest's portents. He believed in what he could touch and conquer and vanquish.

The wind caused the golden plume that stood up stiffly from the metal fillet that served as his crown to shiver. He folded his bronzed arms on his thick hairless chest.

Where was she? Where was Dolla-Dree, his daughter, Low Moo of Moo, and the only person he could trust to venture into the lost lands? Only she could be trusted to find the Master of Sinanju—if indeed there was a living Master of Sinanju. For had not the priests for centuries said that when Moo sank, so had China and India and Korea and all the other lands with which Moo had traded in those days?

But the High Moo did not truly believe that all was water beyond the horizon. There had been ships sighted. Some of these vessels were greater than a building. But all passed by without heeding this island far from any other land. There were tales of men with skin the color of a pale moon, who came from lands to the east. Such men had landed on Moo only three or four generations past. No lands to the east were known to Old Moo, just the western lands of Korea and China.

No, the land world endured, just as this speck of Moo had endured. And if life endured, so would the House of Sinanju. The royal priest had scoffed at the High Moo's assertion that this must be true, but he had held firm. Priests only wanted you to believe what they said was true. Else, how could they control you?

No, Moo endured. Sinanju endured. But to be certain, he had sent his daughter to the lands to the east, not to the west. She would learn there where to find the Master of Sinanju, if he still lived. Now he must wait for his daughter. He would wait until he was old and white-haired and the sun had wrinkled him like a turtle, and his kingly burdens had bent his spine. He would wait.

It was in the deepest part of the night, when the sea breezes seemed to hold their breath, and the High Moo's heart held the greatest loneliness, that the stillness of his sleeping kingdom was shattered.

The High Moo was leaning on the parapet, his arms folded, his eyes set on the eastern sky, when something sailed up from the courtyard below.

The High Moo's warrior-trained reflexes reacted instantly. He ducked the missile. He threw himself on the roof and rolled.

"Guards, to my side!" he called.

The object broke not five feet from him.

Two of the guards burst through the door.

"There!" he told them.

And their eyes fell on the clay jar. It lay in pieces, not flat, but completely shattered. Dark liquid drained from it in all directions. And from under the clay shards, something writhed and threw out ropy appendages.

"Slay it!" ordered the High Moo, coming to his feet.

But a single hooded eye peered out in a crack between

falling clay bits, and the guards let out a combined screech and fled the roof.

One of them had dropped a war club, and the High Moo dived to recover it.

He noticed that the stairwell was dark. There were no signs of the other guards, or the royal priest, Teihotu.

He returned to the roof. The thing was free of its prison now.

It was, as he knew it would be, an octopus. It was black, and the moon was reflected on his shiny hide. It flopped its tentacles weakly in the unfamiliar environment. The greater portion of the seawater had flowed into a drainage channel cut into the roof, and the octopus began to slide along it, desperate to cling to its true element.

The High Moo pounced as he slipped toward the roof's edge. He mashed one tentacle into jelly. Then, bringing the club up again, he struck the mortal blow.

It fell on water.

The octopus had slipped over the parapet with boneless fluidity. It struck the ground below with a wet smack that caused the hairs on the back of the High Moo's head to stand up.

Down in the courtyard, the royal priest came running from the palace, accompanied by the other guards—the two who had not run away.

"There!" cried the High Moo. "Below me. Kill it!"

"Do as your king bids," ordered the royal priest. And the two guards fell upon the octopus. They beat it into submission. A pulpy *pop* told that its boneless head had burst. They crushed the tentacles methodically. When they stood back after many more blows than were needed, the octopus was a black viscous puddle that did not move.

"The Enemy of Life is no more," said the royal priest solemnly.

"No," called down the High Moo wearily. "Only one of his children sent as a warning to me that nowhere am I safe, and no one may I trust, not even those closest to me."

"But, your highness—"

"Hold your tongue," said the High Moo. "You guards return to your stations. You, priest, find the guards who ran and punish them. I care not how you do it, just so that it is done. The sun comes up soon, and I will be here to see it rise." Then under his breath he added, "And the Sun God willing, it will bring my daughter, who alone is my only hope."

11

Dr. Harold W. Smith settled behind his shabby oak desk.

It was Saturday and his secretary was not at her desk in the reception area. That meant Smith would not be interrupted. He had told the lobby guard that unless the missing patient, Gilbert Grumley, who still had not been found, came to light, officially he was not on the premises.

Smith pressed the concealed stud that brought the terminal linked to hidden basement computers rising from a recess in his desk. It clicked into place like an obedient robot. Its glass face stared at him blankly.

He keyed in the password for the day. When the system was up and running, Smith began to key in a series of questions.

The problem was a simple one: to discover the identity of the new owner of the house next to his own. That information could not be found in Smith's data base, of course. Even after over twenty years of methodically collecting data—some gathered from anonymous field workers who believed they were really feeding their monthly reports to the CIA or the FBI or even the IRS, and some of it siphoned off America's burgeoning computer networks—there was just too much raw data out there, much of it trivia.

Ordinarily a change in home ownership would also be too trivial to note. Not this time. This time the strangeness was too close to home. Smith knew he was not being paranoid in suspecting the mystery of the empty house next to his own was a possible CURE problem. CURE security had been breached before. Even the Folcroft cover, as innocuous as it was, had nearly been compromised, most recently by a fluke of the last presidential campaign. That problem proved manageable, but it was not beyond the realm of possibility that this could be fallout from that incident. A leak or a slip of the tongue during the pressure of the campaign.

A pattern was forming. First the mysteriously missing patient. Then the empty house whose owner's face had triggered a memory in Mrs. Smith's mind. Something was going on.

It was time to put a name to that owner, and if he proved to be a security threat, then Harold Smith must eliminate him.

Smith logged onto the computer records at the Westchester County Registry of Deeds. The password was easy for a man as computer-skilled as Smith to break. It was simply a date code. He began paging through recent files.

After twenty minutes he was forced to admit defeat.

There was no record of the transaction. That meant one of two things: either the transaction had not yet been filed in the computer—which was reasonable, given the time frame—or the transaction might have been conducted illegally.

Before he could jump to that last damning conclusion, Smith would have to pay a call on the Registry of Deeds himself. If the house had changed hands legally, their books would contain the answer he sought.

12

"It is your turn at the rudder, Remo," laughed the Low Moo, Dolla-Dree. Just as Remo reached for it, she threw the tiller to one side. The *Jonah Ark* heeled sharply and cut away from the wind. Remo grabbed it and hauled back. The ship righted itself.

The Low Moo giggled, shaking her lustrous hair. It hung long and free. Remo noticed a natural wave.

"Very cute," he said dryly. "Sit with me?"

"Maybe," she said coquettishly.

"Please?" Remo said. He had to say it twice before he pronounced the Moovian word for "please" correctly.

"Only if you promise not to bore me," the Low Moo said.

"Promise," said Remo. He decided he liked her. Now that they were on the open sea, she had changed. Gone were her dark moods, her smoldering anger. She was going home, and the knowledge had liberated her spirit. Watching the Low Moo shake the windblown hair from her laughing face made Remo think of free-spirited island girls out of old Hollywood films. She had island written all over her. Remo decided he liked that.

"Tell me about Moo," Remo suggested.

"What do you wish to know?"

"Chiun said it disappeared thousands of years ago."

"Old Moo sank, yes," the Low Moo said sadly. "Our folk tales say that the sun looked down upon Moo and saw only greed. In punishment, he made the seas to devour Moo. But Kai, the Sea God, spared the highest portion of the empire and those who lived on it. That is where I come from, where we are bound."

"Is it big?"

"Oh, very big. It stretches from the north sea to the south sea, and there is the west sea to one side and the east sea to the other. There is a great palace and a city. My father is the High Moo, you know."

"So I gathered. But you don't act like a princess."

"And how many princesses do you know, Remo?"

"One or two. You don't act like either of them. You're more . . . down-to-earth."

The Low Moo's brow puckered. Remo's translation of "down-to-earth" into Moovian came out as "wallowing in dirt."

"Why do you say that? Why do you say I wallow in dirt?"

"I didn't mean it like that," Remo said hastily. "It's an expression. I mean 'regular'. 'Normal.' "

The Low Moo frowned prettily. As a member of the royal house, being called normal was an insult. Every man of Moo would gladly slay his brother for her hand in marriage.

" 'Nice'?" Remo ventured.

Her brow smoothed suddenly. "Oh, I am that. You are nice too—even if you are a slave."

"Slave?"

"You are the Master of Sinanchu's slave. I see him order you about and you obey. I do not mind that you are a slave. I like your white skin. It is so different. I wonder what you are like inside."

"I'm like I am. Like you see me. And I'm not a slave."

"Do not be ashamed. On Moo we have no slaves. In older times white men did come to our land. Some we made to be slaves, but not for long. Slavery is cruel and so they were set free."

"Really? Then what happened to them?"

The Low Moo looked away suddenly. She started toward the bow, and shaded her eyes from the sun. Seeing nothing, she looked back. She rubbed her stomach. "I am hungry," she said, sounding like a petulant child.

"Chiun's catching fish."

"I will go to him and see."

"Can't you stay a little longer?"

"I will return," the Low Moo said. She took hold of Remo's arm and stroked it gently. With her fingers she felt his hard muscles. "I like your nice white skin." She gave his arm a playful squeeze and jumped up suddenly.

Remo thought she was going to kiss him, but instead she bit him on the earlobe, not hard. It was more of a nip.

"What was that for?" he asked, taken aback.

"I like you. I will come back to you."

And with that she scampered up the steps to the afterdeck.

That evening an albatross flew along the horizon, making raucous sounds.

The Low Moo came up from the hold eagerly.

"A rugu bird!" she exclaimed. "Sail harder, Remo, we are almost to Moo."

"Are you sure?" asked Remo.

"There is no other land to be found under last night's stars. Only Moo. Oh, hurry. My father awaits us."

The Master of Sinanju, hearing those words, went below. He returned with a folded piece of white cotton. He laid it out on the deck and unfolded it until Remo recognized the parallelogram symbol that had been stitched into it with green sailcloth. The symbol of the House of Sinanju.

"Where'd you get that?" Remo asked.

"I made it. It will inform the people of Moo that the Master of Sinanju is coming. It will give them time to prepare a proper welcome."

"We're not there yet," Remo pointed out.

"Look again, O ye of little faith," Chiun retorted as he inserted the bamboo pole into a sleeve in one side of the cloth.

Remo looked past the complex of batten-stiffened sails. He thought he could make out a dark blue hump of land. From a distance it looked like an anthill with a flat top.

As Chiun raised the bamboo pole and the Sinanju flag began flapping and chattering in the crosswind, Remo said, "Looks awfully small for the huge island nation everyone keeps talking about."

"It is only your mind that is small," huffed Chiun as he marched to the bow, proudly waving his banner.

13

Trailed by his retinue, the High Moo hurried to the lagoon beach. He did not run, for it would be unseemly. But he walked with such alacrity that his Red Feather Guard were hard pressed to maintain a decorous pace.

"See?" said the little boy Mauu, the first to sight the great ship.

The High Moo drank in the sight. It was like no other ship he had ever seen. It was greater than the war canoes, bigger even than the ship in which his daughter had sailed. It had five poles for the sails, which were stiff and oddly shaped.

As he watched, the craft turned smartly to present its hull to the wind, and its sheer height astounded the High Moo. Sailing ships of such majesty were told of in legend. None had been seen in the lifetime of any living Moovian.

"What does it mean?" demanded the royal priest, Teihotu, as he hovered by the High Moo's ear.

"I do not know," said the High Moo, hope dying in his breast. Then the tiny figure in the bow moved to the rail and waved a banner. The wind tore at it, disturbing its emblem, but at last the High Moo discerned the age-old symbol of the House of Sinanchu.

"My daughter has returned!" he cried. "Go, priest, order the feast to start. You, guards, fetch women to beat a path from this spot to the Royal Palace. We will make my heroine daughter welcome, and treat with the Master of Sinanchu who returns to preserve my kingdom."

The priest padded off and set a runner to the village.

The High Moo turned his eyes to the ship. A massive thing he understood to be an anchor was thrown overboard. And after the sails were pulled up, a small boat was lowered over the side with two figurees in it. A third scrambled down a rope and joined them, taking up the oars.

One of them, he saw, was his daughter.

"Remo, you take the oars," commanded Chiun sternly.

"Why do I always get the scut work?" Remo demanded, one eye on the Low Moo.

"It is your responsibility to get the princess and me to shore. It is not scut work. It is a privilege. When I inscribe this day's events on a scroll, you may be certain that your honored role will be fully described."

"Yeah, pulling on the oars like a galley slave," Remo complained. "You know, she thinks I'm your servant," he added. He spoke English so the princess wouldn't understand their argument.

"If you would like, I will add a codicil to my records, assuring future Masters that to the best of my knowledge you were never at any time a slave."

"It's not future Masters I'm worried about. It's her."

"Then," Chiun retorted, turning from the bow, "you will bend your back to this task with vigor so that the Low Moo may admire your efforts on her behalf."

"Up yours," said Remo, who didn't like being thought of as a slave. But he pulled at the oars while Chiun returned to his proud stance at the bow. He stood with one arm on his hip and the other holding the Sinanju banner rigid. The princess sat behind him. Remo thought Chiun looked impossibly affected, like an idealized portrait of George Washington crossing the Delaware.

The Master of Sinanju was pleased. The High Moo stood surrounded by his retinue. Women busily swept the sand clear with straw whisks. An honor guard of warriors formed two ranks to meet them.

A bronze man clad only in a loincloth splashed into the water. He took the bow in hand and helped guide it ashore. The keel scraped sand. And the boat was quickly pulled up onto dry beach so that the sandals of the Master of Sinanju would not suffer being wet.

It was as Chiun always dreamed of being greeted. By a proper emperor in a proper kingdom. Let Remo see true respect, such as Masters of Sinanju had enjoyed in times when the world was ruled correctly and Sinanju was respected from pole to pole.

Chiun set the banner into the sand. It stuck, the fabric waving proudly.

"I am Chiun, Master of Sinanju," he proclaimed. And abruptly the retinue surrounding the High Moo parted and the High Moo strode forward. His face was broad and fine, a king's visage. But his garb was not as kingly as Chiun had imagined. He had expected more clothing than a feathered breechclout. But it was summer, so Chiun decided it was not an affront if the king greeted him bare-chested. Chiun was pleased to see the golden feather that signified the crown of the High Moo. True, the crown was not, strictly speaking, a crown, but more a band of metal. Probably the original crown had been lost when Moo had sunk.

Chiun placed his long-nailed hands into his joined sleeves and bowed once to the High Moo.

And the High Moo replied in a booming voice. "I am Tu-Min-Ka, High Moo of Moo. I am pleased that my daughter has brought you."

"Not so," said Chiun. "It is I who have brought your daughter. I found her in the thrall of an evil wizard, and recognizing her as of true royal blood, rescued her from this man."

"Then I am doubly grateful," murmured the High Moo, taking his daughter into his arms. He turned away from the Master of Sinanju abruptly.

Chiun's face wrinkled. An emperor did not turn his back on the Master of Sinanju during a formal greeting ceremony. Still, this was the man's daughter, whom he had believed lost. On the other hand, a daughter is only a female who happens to be a blood relation. This was the first meeting between the Master of Sinanju and a High Moo in nearly five thousand years. One would think that the man had more respect for history than to take his daughter aside to gossip. Chiun wondered what it was they discussed, but decided that eavesdropping would not be seemly. Besides, they were too far way.

Remo drifted up beside Chiun.

"What are they saying?" he wanted to know.

"I do not know. But he is probably thanking her profusely for finding me." Chiun noticed Remo's posture. "Straighten up! Do you want the High Moo to think I have trained a laggard?"

"Yes, Master," Remo muttered unhappily.

"Are you certain, my daughter?" the High Moo whispered.

"He alone of all I met spoke our language. He remembers Old Moo."

"But the Master of Sinanju is tall and powerful. This man is elderly. And he carries no weapons."

"I do not understand it either, but I am certain it is he."

"And where are the night tigers? Did he not think enough of my plea to bring his retinue? He travels with a slave, and a sickly pale one at that."

"He is a nice slave," said the princess. "I like him."

"If you are certain, my daughter . . ." the High Moo said vaguely. "But I fear he will not be able to help us. For he is very old and his limbs look as if a fever has withered them."

The High Moo turned to the Master of Sinanju. He forced himself to smile. In his heart he felt sick. The Master of Sinanju had been his last hope.

"I bid you welcome to Moo," he said. "And in honor of your landfall, we have prepared a feast. We have all the foods that in ancient times Masters of Sinanju enjoyed. There is roast pig, turtle, fresh eggs, and we have butchered a Korean delicacy—dog."

"No way, Chiun," Remo whispered in English. "I don't care what taboo it violates. I draw the line at dog."

"Hush, Remo." To the High Moo the Master of Sinanju said, "We are grateful for your thoughtfulness, O High Moo, but times have changed. Masters of Sinanju no longer eat meat."

"No meat?"

"Have you fish?"

"Yes, of course."

"We still eat fish. And rice."

"We have rice. But fish is peasant food."

Chiun winced at the implication.

"Here, perhaps," he said, "but in Sinanju it is considered a delicacy."

"Fish and rice are a delicacy nowhere on earth, Little Father," Remo whispered in English.

"What did your slave say?" the High Moo asked.

"He asked if you have lemons," Chiun replied.

"Yes."

"Good, he will have egg-lemon soup. But it must be prepared under my supervision."

"Very well," said the High Moo slowly.

"Thanks a lot, Chiun," Remo said sourly.

"I knew you would appreciate my suggesting it," Chiun replied.

"I don't mean the soup. I meant the fact that you didn't disabuse him of the notion that I'm your slave."

"This bothers you?"

"Slightly," Remo growled, looking at the Low Moo, who stared at him with a wild eager light in the depths of her black eyes.

Chiun suddenly shook his spindly arms free of his sleeves. He raised them to the heavens, and in a loud voice proclaimed, "In honor of this historic occasion, and knowing that the wicked practice of slavery has been long abolished by the enlightened rulers of Moo, I hereby set free my unworthy slave, Remo."

"Oh, you're a thrill," Remo hissed.

"He does not look happy," said the High Moo, taking note of Remo's expression.

"It is the shock," Chiun assured him. "He has been in my family for years. But he will get used to being free."

"And in honor of this meeting, joining the House of Sinanchu with the House of Moo," proclaimed the High Moo, "my royal priest, Teihotu, will bless you both so that no harm will come to you during your sojourn with us."

The priest padded out of the crowd. His dark robes rustled like serpents slipping through dry leaves.

"Please kneel," he intoned.

Chiun dropped to his knees. Remo did likewise. But only after Chiun pulled him down.

The royal priest laid his bony, long-fingered hands on their heads. Remo noticed that his hands smelled fishy. He held his breath until the man was through muttering incantations to the sky. Then he withdrew and they found their feet.

"Now, quickly, darkness comes," said the High Moo. "We must hurry to light the fires. For when darkness comes, *they* walk."

Chiun marched in the High Moo's wake. Remo stepped up alongside him.

"Moo looks pretty small, Little Father," he remarked casually.

"You have not seen the whole of it yet," Chiun sniffed.

"You spoke about an empire."

"I told you. Moo sank. This is all that is left."

"Where are the jeweled clothes, the golden shields? And that crown on the High Moo's head looks like an oversize wedding ring with feathers."

"It is his summer crown. I am certain that his winter crown is more impressive."

"I don't think they have winters in the South Pacific."

"And how would you know, O well-traveled one?"

"I remember my geography lessons."

"And did these geography lessons include a history of Moo?"

"No," Remo admitted.

"Then you have been taught by the ignorant and should not be surprised at your own lack of knowledge," Chiun said haughtily.

"Where are the women, by the way?"

"You did not see them because your back was turned as you rowed. They were here smoothing the sand for us. Then they left."

"Yeah? Were they bare-breasted?"

"I did not notice," Chiun said distantly.

"How could you not notice an important thing like that?"

"Because unlike you, I am not a lover of cows."

"Moo," said Remo.

"Is that another of your lame jests?"

"More like a prayer. If there aren't any bare-breasted native women on this sandhill, I've come a long way for nothing."

"You are very haughty for a newly freed slave," sniffed Chiun. He hastened his step so that he would not have to listen to any more of Remo's nonsense.

14

The world had done it to Shane Billiken again.

It was always this way. Just when success was within his grasp, some retro-case would snatch the brass ring away.

The Beatles hijacked his singing career. Roy Orbison's lawyers squelched his comeback. And now, two strange men had stolen the perfect channeler out of his own house.

Oh, sure, Glinda had been good. He'd never have gotten into channeling without her. Shane had met her in a Muscle Shoals bar, where she was waitressing. One drink led to another, which led to her apartment. They were reminiscing about the sixties—or Shane was. Glinda hadn't been born until 1967, so was lamenting that she'd missed out on "the good years."

"What was it, like, like?" she had asked.

"You want to experience the sixties?" Shane had replied, firing up a joint. "Try this organic time machine." It was in the smoky moments that followed that he made his discovery. When high, Glinda babbled. Not in English, but in some crazy nonsense baby-talk. That was what had given Shane the channeling idea.

And so was launched the career of Glinda Thrip, who, under certain conditions—usually a joint before a performance—became possessed by the spirit of Shastra, high priestess of Atlantis. Shane Billiken translated her babble into prophecies, for, as he repeated to anyone gullible enough to listen, the high priestess knew all and saw all.

Of course nothing was one hundred percent perfect. Sometimes Glinda muttered a few English words, which Shane covered over with a standard line about disruptions in the cosmic flow. And sometimes when she was high, Glinda giggled. That was worse. Atlantean high priestesses weren't supposed to giggle.

Which was why, when the Princess Sinanchu washed up on his beach, Shane Billiken realized he had struck true gold at last. Princess Sinanchu looked like a princess. Glinda looked like a silicone-augmented California waitress in Greek clothing. And Glinda did not have silver wires in her clothes or a pouch stuffed with strange coins.

It was the coins that particularly fascinated Shane Billiken. Coins were coins, but these looked authentic, historical. As artifacts, they might be worth a fortune to a museum. Millions, depending on who the girl was and where she came from.

Especially, Shane Billiken thought suddenly, if there were more of those coins where she came from.

The thought caused him to push aside the aluminum sun reflector on his chest and sit up.

It was the morning after Princess Sinanchu had left. He had slept fitfully all night, even after soaking in his hot tub, eating cheese and playing with the bath crystals he had brought into the tub. They were supposed to soak up negativity, but when he stepped out, wrinkled like a prune, he felt as frustrated as ever.

Even a joint didn't help.

Now Shane Billiken felt positively enraged. How could the world keep doing this to him? Why? Why him? He was evolved. He chanted every night. True, his heart wasn't always in it, but who knew how much of this New Age stuff really worked? It was not for nothing that his favorite off-camera saying was "You don't fuck with magic."

Shane paced his house fuming. He wandered into his personal library, which he had started with three battered paperbacks but which was now one of the most extensive collections of occult books in private hands. Maybe the *I Ching* had the answer to his problems.

Then he recalled the exchange between the old Eastern mystic and the skinny white man while they argued on his beach. Shane had listened through his cracked glass patio door.

They had talked about building a boat, then about buying one. The Asian kept babbling about going to Moo, like it was a place, not a sound effect. Why did that name sound familiar?

Shane went to the Atlantis section of his library. He ran

his thick fingers along the rows of spines until he came to the book he wanted. It was called *The Lost Continent of Mu*.

Eagerly he opened the book. Shane read three chapters straight through before he realized his feet were killing him. He was so mesmerized that he had forgotten to sit down.

According to the book, Mu was an island nation of great size which had dominated the Pacific Ocean before the dawn of recorded history. It had sunk during a fierce natural cataclysm that the book's author supposed was the Great Flood of biblical legend. Mu would have been forgotten, except when the Muvian race perished, they transmitted their thoughts to receptive survivors in other lands, who wrote of their visions and thus kept the existence of Mu alive despite skeptical nay-sayers.

"Makes sense to me," Shane muttered, reading on. When he put the book down, hours later, he thought he had it all figured out. Princess Sinanchu was from Mu. Somehow, Mu must have come to the surface again. As Shane Billiken saw it, this was perfectly plausible. After all, they were getting near the Millennium. Weird stuff like this was supposed to happen.

Why Princess Sinanchu had come to America remained a mystery, but Shane understood one thing: if that girl could make the trip one way, Shane Billiken, who was in tune with the universe, could retrace the voyage.

There was only one boat dealership in this area. Shane hopped into his Ferrari and drove for it at high speed.

The owner recognized his description of the unlikely pair.

"Sure, they bought that ratty junk, the *Jonah Ark*. Imagine that. Took off right away, too."

"Was there a girl with them?"

"Yep. Looked Tahitian or something like that. Didn't say a word."

"How long ago?"

"Ten, twelve hours."

"Is a junk slow?"

"Is Superman blue? It's one step up from a garbage scow."

"I'll take the fastest boat you have," Shane said suddenly.

"If you're thinking of following them, and I think you are, you'll want a deep-water craft, not some zippy little cigarette boat. They had long voyage written all over them."

"I'll take whatever you recommend."

"For sure," said the salesman. "But clue me in first: is there something I should know? I recognize you from *The Horton Droney Show* and that little Oriental lama looked pretty freaky. Is the world gonna end, or what?"

"Friend, we're talking a definite spiritual migration here."

"Oh wow, I knew it. Like I've been getting these really, really intense vibrations all week."

"Eat more cheese. It'll help you image better."

Once he had made the purchase arrangements on a two-masted schooner with twin inboard-outboard diesels—receiving a ten-percent discount in return for giving the salesman a biorhythmic polarity analysis—Shane Billiken returned home to pack. He didn't know what to expect, so he packed his entire wardrobe, ultimately filling seven medium-size suitcases, three large steamer trunks, an assortment of over-the-shoulder bags, and his electric guitar.

"Food!" he said suddenly. "I'll probably need food." He hurried into the wine cellar, where vats of natural cheese were hardening.

"Anything else would spoil, but cheese is good forever," he muttered, thanking his lucky stars that he had stumbled across the bioregenerative powers of cheese. He wondered if he should bring mineral water, but shrugged. What the hell, he thought, I'll just bring along a bucket and rough it on ocean water. It's probably chock-full of minerals and other healthful stuff.

When he had everything together, Shane realized that he would need help loading all these provisions on his new boat. Then he realized that he might just need help crewing the ship. Then he further realized he didn't know what to expect on the other end of the voyage.

I gotta think this through a little more, he decided, collapsing on a beanbag chair. He switched on his lava lamp. Watching the blue-green goop floating in the amber fluid always helped him to image.

Hours later, a thought struck him. He spoke it aloud.

"I'm thinking expedition when I should be thinking conquest."

He jumped out of the chair and ran for his bedroom. He rummaged through his dresser looking for that magazine clipping. He knew it was there somewhere. He never threw anything out. Not anything that important.

He found it wrapped around a copper antiarthritis bracelet with rubber bands. He pounced on the phone. After three rings, a hard voice answered.

"Yeah?"

"Mr. Eradicator?"

"Maybe." The voice was guarded.

"You probably won't remember me, but we had a meet three or four years back."

"You're right, pal. I don't remember you."

"Let me finish. I wanted a certain party taken care of. A certain famous party. A singer. Is it coming back?"

"Yeah. Sunglasses. Square face. Bangs."

"That's me."

"I meant the victim."

"That fits him too."

"If you've changed your mind, my rates have gone up."

"Yes and no. I don't want that particular party hit. Maybe later, if things work out. But your *Soldier of Fortune* ad said you handle military ops too."

"What have you got?"

"There's an island in the South Pacific. I want to take it over. You know, do a Marlon Brando."

"This island got a name?"

"Er, not yet," Shane said evasively. Better not mention Mu. Military types were notoriously unenlightened.

"I don't get you."

"It's a tiny island." Shane Billiken was talking fast, making up his facts as he went along. He needed this man. "Kind of a paradise. Just natives there. No army, no government."

"Don't discount native fighters. I've seen well-armed professionals gutted by fishbone knives. I'd rather take a dum-dum slug in the face anytime."

"I have a ship, but I need a team. They have to know sailcraft."

"How long a ship?"

"Actually, I haven't measured it yet. But the salesman said I'd need a five-man crew."

"I can deliver. But can you meet my price?"

"Sure, I'm loaded," Shane said enthusiastically. He regretted it a moment later when the man who advertised himself as Ed the Eradicator quoted a price that was five hundred dollars more than Shane Billiken's current bank balance. And that wasn't counting the money he owed on the boat.

Shane swallowed twice before he burbled, "No problem." What the heck, he'd make it all back soon enough if the cosmic flow went his way.

"When the money is deposited in my Swiss account, we have a deal."

"Give me the number. I'll do the transfer the minute we disconnect."

"Then you've got your invasion team. How soon do you want to move?"

"The ship is ready to sail. It's at the Malibu Marina."

"Give me a couple of hours to work out the details."

"Sure. One thing, though."

"Yeah?"

"Can you swing by my place? I could use some help with my luggage."

15

The High Moo led the Master of Sinanju and his freed slave from the lagoon to the very heart of Moo. They walked up the long mangrove slope where coconut palms waved above expanses of steaming turtle grass. He led them past the rice fields. The farmers were called from their work by the royal priest. Remo noticed that they were very young. Most of them were children. They laid down their hoes and adzes and followed, chanting one word over and over: "Sinanchu! Sinanchu!"

Chiun beamed with pleasure.

"See, Remo? Proper respect. You would never see this in America."

"You don't see bare-breasted girls in America. And I don't see them here either."

"Have patience."

They were escorted to high eminence on the far side of the island. Here and there, great bamboo-framed holes gaped from the dark slope like the sockets in a skull.

"These are my metal mines," said the High Moo proudly. "The greater number of them lie beyond the city where the ground rises sheer from the water. There, workers dig for the metal that makes the coins which bear my visage."

"I have seen these coins," said Chiun. "They are very fine coins, wonderfully cast. And the likeness is remarkable."

"Thank you," the High Moo said proudly. "I knew that the coins my daughter carried would bring you here."

"Truthfully," Chiun returned, "I was not enticed by your coins, fine as they are. I came to meet the High Moo, to join again my house with your house in the bondage of happy service."

"Liar," whispered Remo in English.

"What does he say?" the High Moo demanded.

"I said, I'm anxious to meet the young maidens of your village," Remo replied in Moovian.

"He speaks Moovian?"

"I taught him a few words," Chiun admitted.

"I also helped," added the Low Moo.

"I'm a quick study," Remo said. And everyone wondered what the freed white slave meant by saying, "I'm a rabbit lover."

"Does he mean that he eats them or mates with them?" the High Moo whispered to his daughter.

"I have seen him do neither," she replied, looking at Remo. He smiled at her. She smiled back, her eyes on his moon-pale arms. She had thought him too tall before, but now his long lean limbs interested her. She would ask her father later to grant her a special request about the former slave.

"Come, I hear the fires crackling," the High Moo called. "And the meat is on the spit. We must hurry, for the sun is dying."

They trudged up as they grew near the central hill that dominated Moo.

Remo noticed there were many mosquitoes and sand flies, but they left Chiun and him alone. It was a side benefit of the Sinanju diet that neither of them seemed to attract insects.

At length they reached the high plateau that was the heart of Moo.

"This is my city," the High Moo said proudly. He spread his well-muscled arms expansively.

Remo saw thatch huts on the outskirts. Snapping black eyes regarded him through the reed sides. He saw no women, much to his disappointment.

The inner buildings were stone. None were more than one story tall. But the palace was different. Made of some kind of kiln-fired brick, it reared up two stories. It had glassless windows and a flat roof with a gazebolike superstructure that Remo realized was the tallest point on the island. A vantage point.

"It's breathtaking," Remo said in Moovian. His sarcasm was lost on everyone except Chiun.

Chiun shot him a hard glance.

"Do not be so smug. I have seen your Newark."

"I'll take Newark over this jungle paradise."

"Wait until you see the women."

"I'm waiting. I'm waiting."

"Come," said the High Moo. And he led them to the courtyard of the palace.

In the stone-paved open area, fires burned in rows of rectangular earthen pits. A woman bent over a steaming pot. A man was singeing the body hair off a wild pig by hanging it over an open flame by its hind legs. There were carcasses on spits.

"There is your woman, Remo," Chiun whispered.

Remo craned to see over the heads of the escorting soldiers. He saw a brown-skinned woman bending over one steaming pot. She wore a long Hawaiian-style grass skirt. Her long black hair swished as she stirred the pot's contents.

When the sounds of their approach caught her attention, she faced them expectantly.

She smiled. She had three teeth. Her face was as wrinkled as a walnut shell and her bare breasts hung like goatskin bladders.

"There," Chiun said. "Go to her, Remo, and tell her that you have crossed a mighty ocean just to behold her loveliness. I am certain she will be flattered by your attention."

"Very funny," Remo fumed. "She's not my type."

"A breast is a breast," Chiun said flatly.

The High Moo motioned for them to form a circle around the fires. He signaled for Chiun to stand beside him and for his daughter to claim the other side. She motioned Remo to her side. The remaining villagers completed the circle.

The royal priest appeared inside the circle.

"Bring the throne," he commanded.

"It is a beautiful throne," Chiun told Remo. "Gold, with many jewels. And a footrest carved of a single block of white jade."

Two men in loincloths came out of the palace bearing a squat wooden box with short legs.

"Here comes the footstool," Remo said. "Doesn't look like jade to me."

"It is wood. No doubt it is your seat," Chiun said smugly.

The stool was set behind the High Moo.

"The Shark Throne," he said imperiously.

Remo looked closely. The top of the stool was covered in some kind of gray hide. At each end there were rolled protrusions resembling ornamental cushions, except that they were made of some cracked gray hide. Remo noticed flat, lifeless eyes at either end of these rolls, and suddenly realized that the stool was decorated with the heads of hammerhead sharks.

Remo grinned as the High Moo sat down. "Good thing they cut off the fin."

The royal priest motioned for the rest of the circle to sit.

"Before we eat," he intoned, "we will show our visitors the greatness of Moo."

"This is the ceremonial dance," whispered Chiun. "In its fluid motions are the entire history of Moo. We will learn much of what has transpired since the days of Master Mangko."

"Wonderful," Remo groaned. "I'm half-starved and we have to sit through a six-hour folk dance."

But then the circle parted at two points and Remo suddenly sat up very straight.

Two lines of native Moovian women slithered in and converged inside the circle. They wore skirts of grass or coarse black cloth low on their undulating hips. Colorful blossoms decorated their long hair and dazzling smiles split their happy faces. Their feet were bare, but Remo's eyes weren't on their feet, but on their exposed, jiggling breasts.

They began to sway in time to their clapping hands, which they held over their heads.

Remo's blank face broke out into a wide grin.

"Moo," he said.

"Do not stare," Chiun remonstrated.

"I'm sure not going to look away," Remo said. "Don't want to insult our gracious hosts."

"Watch their hands. They tell the story. And their hips."

"I'm watching, I'm watching."

"But not like that."

"I don't know any other way to watch," Remo said as a

line of sinuous hips undulated in perfect synchronization before his eyes. Firm young breasts bounced and swayed. The most dazzling smiles Remo had ever seen bathed him in a carefree radiance. Remo relaxed. All his cares seemed to ooze right out of him. He felt at peace.

The women were still dancing when the food began to arrive.

Chiun was speaking with the High Moo.

"My knowledge of Moo dance is not perfect," the Master of Sinanju admitted. "Does that shaking of hips mean that the Year of the Macaw was the same year that the volcanoes cooled?"

"No," replied the High Moo. "You must watch their fingers too. The snapping they make keeps the time. One snap means one moon. Ten snaps, and a year has passed."

"Oh, yes. Now I understand."

"Do you understand too?" the High Moo asked of Remo.

"Are you kidding? I was born knowing this stuff," Remo assured him, absently taking a wooden bowl from the old woman with the drooping breasts.

The aroma had to fill his nostrils before Remo realized what he had been offered.

"Hey," he said. "This is egg-lemon soup. Where did it come from?"

"I made it," Chiun told him.

"When? You were here all the time."

"During the break in the dance."

"What break in the dance?"

"The one where the maidens were not dancing, but instead formed two lines and swayed in imitation of the ocean at rest after Old Moo sank."

"I thought that was the best part. I was hypnotized."

"You would. Drink your soup."

Remo started in on the soup. He drank it straight from the bowl when no one offered him a spoon. He figured it was the native custom.

The Low Moo watched Remo drink down his third bowl, wondering what kind of a man found naked peasant girls so fascinating. He did not take his eyes off them. Unlike the others, she knew that Remo was not watching the dance, but the dancers. It was strange. But he was from a strange land, she told herself, where all women covered their breasts. The princess had thought that in America every woman was of royal blood, but the Master of Sinanchu had assured her such was not the case.

Still, why was Remo watching them when the Low Moo herself sat at his elbow? Could it be that he really did prefer rabbits to girls? But then why did he stare? Perhaps, she thought, he had never seen a woman naked before, being interested only in female rabbits.

"Is the soup to your liking, Remo?" she breathed in his ear.

"Yeah, yeah. Great soup. I could use another bowl," he said distractedly. His eyes did not leave the peasant dancing girls.

The Low Moo decided to experiment.

"Remo," she whispered.

"Yeah?" he said, not looking in her direction.

"Look, I will show you something."

"I'm seeing something," he replied dreamily.

"I will show you something you have never seen."

"Yeah?" Remo looked. "What's that?"

The Low Moo was smiling at him. His eyes were not fully focused. The Low Moo changed that when she pulled down the top of her costume.

Remo blinked. His eyes focused like a zoom lens.

"Are you going to dance too?" he asked.

"No. Not that way. I may dance for you in private."

And she quickly covered up, content that she had learned the truth.

At least Remo did like human females—even if he did have low tastes. Perhaps she would do something to elevate them.

She leaned over and whispered in his ear, "I want to *poon* you."

Remo grinned. He turned to the Master of Sinanju.

"What does *poon* mean?" he asked.

"Eat! Eat!" Chiun snapped, noticing Remo's nearly full bowl. "And stop asking foolish questions when I am conversing with the High Moo."

A splendid tropical moon lifted from the Pacific. It ascended into the sky, growing smaller and smaller as it sought the very pinnacle of the star-sprinkled heavens.

The fires grew dimmer, and the Moovian girls had given up their dancing. They took their places in the circle and began tearing chunks of meat off the roasting pigs and ate it with their fingers, laughing and giggling.

Many pairs of flashing black eyes looked Remo's way. He watched their bodies, tawny and impossibly smooth in the firelight. He decided he might like life on Moo after all.

The Master of Sinanju watched the fires die. He felt the eyes of the High Moo upon him. Good. The High Moo was doubtless impressed by the wise countenance of the Master of Sinanju as seen in profile. No doubt he was struck with awe at having come face-to-face with the ancestor of him who faithfully served the High Moo's earliest ancestors. Probably he was even now offering prayers of thankfulness to his many gods for the winds that brought Sinanju to him.

The High Moo regarded the profile of the Master of Sinanchu in puzzlement. The Master of Sinanchu described by the oral traditions of Moo was a tall sturdy man with thick black hair and smooth golden skin like a Moovian's. The Masters of Sinanchu wore strange leggings and loose shirts. This old man came swathed in something that belonged on a woman. And where were his weapons? The High Moo could stand it no longer. He had to ask.

"I have a question, Master of Sinanchu."

"I have the answers to your every question," the Master of Sinanju replied firmly.

"You carry no weapons. Are they on your ship?"

"They are not on my ship, for I carry them with me wherever I go," said the Master of Sinanju cryptically.

"I do not see them."

"These," said the Master of Sinanju, raising his long-nailed fingers in the firelight. "These are my weapons. In my language they are called the Knives of Eternity, for I enter the world with them and I take them with me when I at last go into the Void beyond the stars."

"Masters of Sinanchu in the days of Great Moo carried swords."

"Masters of Sinanju in the time of Great Moo did not

know the sun source, which enabled us to unlock the full potential of our minds and bodies. That era began with the Great Wang—not to be confused with the lesser Wang, of course."

"They were younger. Every Master I have heard of was young and strong of arm, the better to deal with the High Moo's enemies."

"Youth is not everything. Age has its benefits," Chiun said. "For with age comes wisdom. And wisdom sometimes reveals a path where force is not needed."

"I am the High Moo. I rule by the strength of my arm and the hardness of my war club," said the High Moo. He patted an ebony club that leaned against one leg.

Chiun sniffed. "A club can be broken or a blade taken away. But the mind is the mind."

"Brains can be clubbed out of a man's skull," returned the High Moo.

"If it is your wish to behold the color of your enemies' brains, I will undertake it," said Chiun with veiled distaste. "For, thousands of years ago, an unearned down payment of Moovian coin fed my village, and service is still owned Moo."

"I have enemies," said the High Moo conspiratorially.

"All rulers have enemies."

"Assassins."

"Pah!" spat Chiun. "Do not flatter them. They are mere killers. I am an assassin, and I speak the word with pride."

"They have tried to kill me three times. My guards have staved off two attempts. I myself have killed in my own defense."

"Point out the conspirators to me and their heads will be grinning at your feet," Chiun said boastfully.

"Not all my subjects are here. Some live apart from us. Each year, more are lured away. Women are stolen for their rites."

"Kidnappers?"

"A cult. An old cult, which is rising again. Old ways, old evils. They covet my throne. They covet my daughter. They want to plunge Moo into backwardness and ugliness."

"But point the way and they will be dust," Chiun promised. He sensed the High Moo's skepticism and desired to prove his prowess.

"They dwell in the Grove of Ghosts, at the west end of the island."

"Remo, listen to this," Chiun ordered.

"Huh? What?" Remo said, tearing his eyes off the feasting native girls.

"The High Moo now speaks of our task."

"I'm listening. Just tell him to talk slower. My Moo vocabulary isn't up to speed yet."

"What does he say?" the High Moo asked Chiun.

"He hangs on your every word," affirmed Chiun.

The High Moo nodded. "I spoke of old ways. Someone on this island has revived an ancient evil. They have failed to kill me three times. Now they hurl presentiments at me. Just last night, when I stood on the roof of my very palace, a wicked one threw a jug of ocean water at me. It missed, but from the shattered clay emerged . . ."

Chiun bent his old head. Remo leaned closer.

"An octopus," the High Moo breathed.

Chiun gasped. "No!" he said.

"Yes. Octopus worshipers!"

"Did you hear that, Remo? Octopus worshipers."

"Is that bad?" Remo wanted to know.

"Bad? It is terrible," Chiun said. "The octopus is the ancient Enemy of Life. Its servants are the most despicable cult of all."

"Worse than TV evangelists?"

"Worse than TV evangelists," Chiun said solemnly. "TV evangelists only want your money. Octopus worshipers covet the universe." He turned to the High Moo. "It has been many generations since the last octopus worshipers were thought stamped out."

"They have started up again in Moo."

"Then we will tear off their limbs and crush what remains," proclaimed Chiun. Everyone in the feast circle turned to look at him.

"I can trust no one. Except you," the High Moo said when the laughter and chatter started anew.

"The House of Sinanju owes service to the House of Moo. Of course, there is the matter of the balance," Chiun suggested.

"I will pay triple the down payment, for you have come

a long way. That is, if you are able to accomplish this task I set before you."

"Able?" Chiun squeaked. "I am the Master of Sinanju."

"But you are old. Past your prime years."

"Past! I am young by Sinanju counting."

"And you have no weapons."

The Master of Sinanju said nothing for a moment. He picked up a coconut that had been placed at his feet earlier. He had declined its sweet milk.

"Quadruple the down payment," said Chiun evenly.

"Too much! Too much!" cried the High Moo. "I do not have the coffers of Old Moo. This is a small island compared to the greatness of former times."

"If you cannot afford proper protection from assassins, you should have called upon a lesser house," Chiun returned coldly. "For although the glory of Moo has set, the power of Sinanju has waxed great in the modern world."

The High Moo winced at the pointed insult. And Chiun smiled thinly.

"Triple," repeated the High Moo stubbornly.

"Quadruple," said Chiun, "and I will deliver the perpetrators tonight."

"Tonight?"

"By dawn you will preside over a peaceful land," promised Chiun.

"And triple if it takes longer?"

"Agreed," said Chiun.

"Done is done," said the High Moo, getting to his feet. Chiun rose beside him. The High Moo placed a hand on the Master of Sinanju's frail shoulder and Chiun placed his on the High Moo's opposite shoulder to signify agreement.

"We will drink to our agreement," proclaimed the High Moo. "Fetch a coconut."

"No need," said Chiun, raising his right hand to the High Moo's broad face. The coconut was balanced on the uprights of Chiun's fingers. With his other hand he made a series of passes over the hairy shell, as if weaving a spell. When he knew the High Moo's attention was fixed on his hand, Chiun lashed out and sheared the top off the coconut.

The white meat lay exposed in a twinkling. Chiun offered the shell to the High Moo, who, to his disgust, spat into it. He offered it to the Master of Sinanju. Chiun sipped lightly. He spat the juice back into the husk and returned it to the High Moo.

The High Moo drained the husk greedily, milk spilling from the corners of his mouth.

"None for me?" asked Remo.

"Hush, slave," said Chiun. "I will now reveal the name of the chief culprit," he announced, stepping into the circle. Curious, Remo folded his arms.

"This better be good," he mumbled.

Chiun, his hazel eyes like steel, stamped around in a slow circle.

"The evil one is in our midst. I know this, for I am Chiun, Master of Sinanju, who came across a great ocean to bring peace to this troubled empire. I see all. I know all."

"Bull," whispered Remo in English. He was ignored.

"I know there are conspirators in this very feast. I do not know them all, but I know their leader."

The Red Feather Guard looked back at him stonily. The village women stared openmouthed. The Low Moo watched with tight lips. And the royal priest raked the crowd with his avid black eyes, as if to imply that he, too, knew and saw all, and was able to visit justice as well.

"I knew him on the beach," Chiun went on.

The High Moo looked at Chiun with steely eyes.

"I know him now," Chiun intoned. "And soon you will all know him for what he is—an octopus worshiper."

A hush fell over the feasters. The crackling of the fires alone broke the stillness. Cinders danced in the night air.

Chiun, his hands clasped behind his back, paced around the circle. Here and there he paused to look someone in the eye. Some flinched from his gaze. One or two of the children suppressed giggles.

Watching, Remo thought he knew what Chiun was trying to do. He hoped to smoke out the conspirator with psychology. It was a bluff.

Chiun continued his circuit. His face was hard, uncompromising. But no one broke and ran, as Remo expected.

Finally, on his third circuit, the Master of Sinanju went directly to one man.

"I accuse you, Teihotu," he screeched, one finger pointing with undeniable accusation, "royal priest to the Shark Throne, of being a secret octopus worshiper!"

"I . . . I . . ." sputtered the royal priest.

"Do not deny it. You reek of guilt."

And from the dark robes, Teihotu extracted a bone knife.

Chiun disarmed him with a twist of his wrist. He dragged the man to his knees and, clutching him by the neck, forced a horrible scream from his thin lips.

"No, no! I confess! I confess!"

There came a collective gasp from the Moovians.

"Who else, priest?" demanded Chiun. "Who else among this gathering belongs to your evil cult?"

"Goom. Googam. Bruttu. And Shagg."

At the sounds of their names, four of the Red Feather Guard broke and ran. Remo started after them.

"Hold," Chiun said. "Time for them later. This is the important one."

Out of the trees came a hurled object. It smashed, dousing the main fire. Moovians screamed. For in the embers an octopus sizzled and curled as the embers seared its tentacles. It died in a flopping, spitting agony.

"Fear not," said Chiun, "for this evil ends tonight." He dragged the priest before the Shark Throne and made him kneel.

"You have heard this man's confession," Chiun said loudly. "Now pronounce his fate."

"Death," intoned the High Moo.

"Death," the Moovians repeated.

"So be it," Chiun said. "I will give you a boon, priest. Reveal to us the name of every octopus worshiper, and your death will be swift and without agony."

Teihotu, royal priest to the Shark Throne, wept bitterly. He spat name after name until he had surrendered twelve names in all.

When he was done, Chiun nodded. The priest had spoken true. Abject fear was in his voice. Chiun passed his long-nailed fingers over the man's quaking head. On the third pass, there came a sound like the coconut shell cracking. Where the priest's hair had been was the open bowl of his skull.

Holding the corpse by the back of its neck, Chiun bent

the head forward so that the High Moo could see the yellowish curd of the traitor's brain. The High Moo nodded silently.

Chiun let the body collapse at the High Moo's feet and stepped back proudly. Remo joined him.

"Lucky guess," Remo whispered in English.

"No," Chiun replied. "I remember smelling octopus on his hands when he blessed us."

Remo thought. "Now that you mention it, I do remember his hands smelled kinda fishy."

"Not fish. Octopus."

"Same difference. I don't know why everyone's so petrified. I once watched a *National Geographic* TV special on octopi. They're actually gentle, harmless creatures."

"You will know the error of your ways by dawn."

The High Moo spoke up.

"You have done well, Master of Sinanchu," he said, his voice full of respect. "But dare you enter the Grove of Ghosts to complete what you have begun?"

"My servant and I depart now. Await us at first light."

"If you do not return, you will long be remembered for your feats of magic this night."

"Come, Remo," Chiun said.

Remo made a point of waving to the native girls as he left.

"Catch you later," he told them. They giggled, thinking that he meant he was going fishing.

16

Harold Smith pulled his car into an available space in the County Registry of Deeds office. He carried his worn leather briefcase with him through the glass doors and into the dim oak-paneled service area. He would not need his briefcase, but it contained his portable computer link and White House hot-line telephone. He never went anywhere without it, just as he was seldom seen wearing anything but a gray three-piece suit. Smith was a creature of rigid habits.

The prim woman in the white blouse, severe black skirt, and librarian's string tie pretended not to notice Smith's entrance. Smith walked up to the counter, straightening his Dartmouth tie. The close atmosphere reminded him of the Vermont elementary school he had attended. Municipal buildings always evoked a nostalgic reaction in Smith.

"Excuse me," Smith said, clearing his throat. "I would like to look up a deed. It's a recent sale, and I'm not sure how to go about this. Do I need to know the plot number?"

"No," the woman said. "This is, unless you don't know the name of either the grantee or grantor."

"Which is which?" Smith asked.

"The seller is called the grantor. The buyer is referred to as the grantee." Her voice was bored. The woman looked down her glasses as if to ask: who was this man who didn't know the most commonplace facts?

"I have the name of the grantor," said Smith.

"Come this way," said the woman, stepping out behind the flip-top counter. She led Smith to a book-lined alcove.

"These," she said sternly, running her fingers along a line of black-bound books, "are the Grantor Indexes. And these are the Grantee Indexes." She pointed to an opposite shelf of similar books. They were dated by year, Smith saw with relief. He had had visions of having to comb through countless volumes.

"You look up the name you know in either set," she concluded.

"I only know the grantor's name," Smith repeated.

"I am explaining the entire procedure in case you ever have to do this again. Now, do you understand the difference between the indexes?"

"Indices."

"I beg your pardon?"

"The plural of 'index' is 'indices,' not 'indexes.' "

"Sir, have you ever heard the expression 'close enough for government work'?"

"Of course."

"Well, it applies in this case." She went on in a lecturing like tone, "Now, if you will let me continue. You will find a reference number next to the name. It will probably be a four-digit number, unless of course you are searching records prior to 1889, in which case it will be a three- or possibly two-digit number. It will correspond to the number of one of these books." She indicated a bookshelf filled with worn black spines. They bore numbers written by hand in white ink.

"Select the correct book and look up the deed by the page number, which you will find next to the two-, three-, or four-digit number separated by an oblique stroke. These books contain sequential photocopies of all deeds within each serial."

"I see," Smith said.

"Good. Do you have any other questions?"

"Yes. Is there a photocopy machine on the premises?"

"Around the corner by the water cooler. Copies are fifteen cents. And I do not make change."

"Of course. Thank you," said Dr. Harold W. Smith.

The woman walked off without another word and Smith made a mental note to see if there was a nameplate at the counter. The woman was very efficient, no-nonsense. Smith liked that in a worker. He resolved, if he should ever lose his current secretary, to offer the position to this woman.

Smith went to the Grantor Index, found the name of his former next-door neighbor, and made a mental note of the serial and page number. The book was on a lower shelf. It was new. There was a red-stamped bindery date on the flyleaf that was barely two weeks old.

Smith flipped through the pages of photocopied deeds until he found the one he wanted. He gave it a quick scan.

The name of the grantee was James Churchward.

The name sounded familiar. Smith tried to place it. He could not.

Hurriedly he went to the photocopy machine and put in a quarter. He made a copy, and when his change did not come, he hit the change plunger several times without result. And so concerned was Harold Smith over the familiar name that he did something unprecedented for the frugal bureaucrat.

He did not stop at the counter on his way out to demand restitution.

In his car, Smith slid in on the passenger side and opened the briefcase on his lap. He dialed the Folcroft computer number and placed the receiver in the modem receptacle. Then Smith input the name of James Churchward and requested a global search of all CURE-sensitive files pertaining to past operations.

It was ten minutes and six seconds by Smith's wristwatch before the on-screen message showed. It said, "NOT FOUND."

Smith frowned. Perhaps he was wrong. Perhaps the name was not CURE-linked. He lifted the receiver and dialed his home.

"Dear," Smith said when his wife answered. "That man you saw leaving the house next door—the one whose name you couldn't recall?"

"Yes?"

"Was his name James Churchward?"

"No, I've never heard that name. Who is James Churchward?"

"I don't know," Smith said slowly. "It is probably nothing," he added. "Just a hunch. Excuse me. I must get back to work."

"On your way home, why don't you pick up another box of those nice potato flakes you like so much? The supermarket is having a two-for-one sale."

"If I can," said Smith, hanging up.

He stared unseeingly out the windshield for several

minutes, trying to make the puzzle parts come together. His wife recognized the face of a man coming from the house. And Smith recognized the name. The name did not match the face. Unless, Smith thought suddenly, Mrs. Smith never knew the man's name in the first place. Or this could mean that there were two of them. The man Mrs. Smith saw and this James Churchward.

Tight-lipped, Smith closed his briefcase and slid behind the wheel. He sent his car in the direction of Folcroft Sanitarium. The sun was going down, but there was much more work to do today. The Folcroft computers might not contain any reference to a James Churchward, but somewhere, he knew, there was a computer that did. And Dr. Harold W. Smith knew that his computers would find that computer and extract the information.

It was now, without question, a top-priority matter.

17

Remo raced into the benighted jungle, his eyes automatically compensating for the deeper darkness under tree cover. He glided like a phantom, his loafer-clad feet avoiding twigs and vines in an automatic way that Remo could not explain because his eyes weren't on the ground, but on the vine-choked path before him.

"Remo!" Chiun called breathily.

Remo halted, annoyed. He figured the chase for an easy one. And the quicker it was done, the sooner he could get back to the delectable Moovian maidens.

"What's the problem?" he demanded, hands on hips.

"Do not blunder ahead like a fool, Remo," Chiun warned, halting beside him. He looked up at Remo with a grave face.

"What's the big deal?"

"And what is the rush?" Chiun countered.

"I don't want them to get away," Remo said defensively.

"And where would they go? We are on an island."

Remo shrugged.

"And do not underestimate these people, Remo. They have dangerous weapons at their disposal."

"Come on, Chiun," Remo said, looking around. "Clubs and bone knives? I've been known to two-step between the bullets in a machine-gun crossfire, for crying out loud. No clown in bark briefs is going to get the drop on me."

"No?" asked Chiun. "Then what is that beside your left cheek?"

"Huh?" Remo said, turning. "It's a tree. So what?"

"And what is that sticking out of the tree?"

Remo looked closer. He saw a needlelike object projecting from the rough bark.

"You mean this thorn?" he asked, pointing.

Chiun shook his stern head. "It is not a thorn."

"Sure it is. It's growing out of the tree."

"If it is growing from that tree," Chiun went on, "it is growing backward. Look again, O brave and foolish one."

"What are you . . . ?" Then Remo noticed that the thick end of the thorn stuck out. The point was embedded in the bark.

"Booby trap, huh?" Remo said. "If we scratch ourselves on it, we die."

"You are beyond help, Remo. It is a blowgun dart."

"Blowgun! I didn't hear anything."

"That is why they are so dangerous. That one missed you by the span of one hand."

"Oh," Remo said in a small voice. He was looking around him.

"Now that you are enlightened, you will listen for the sound of the man who expels darts. You will be aware of the tiny tick of a sound as the dart embeds itself in a hard object."

"Fine. No problem." Remo started to go. Chiun restrained him with a firm hand.

"I have not finished my instruction, you who think dancing in the path of loud and large bullets is all there is in the world to know about preserving one's life."

"What else is there?"

"A question. It is this. What happens if you hear the expelling breath but not the tick?"

"I duck?"

"No, for by then it will already be too late."

"I look for darts in my skin?"

"If you live that long, you may," said Chiun with undisguised disgust, and abruptly took the lead.

"Guess I'm on my own," Remo muttered to himself. He took up the rear, his eyes questing this way and that. He moved with greater caution, his overconfidence gone.

"We will not follow them," Chiun said so softly it might have been the winds in the turtle grass. "We will go to this haunted grove where these devils in human form live."

Remo, surprised at the vehemence of Chiun's words, asked what he thought was a logical question.

"Business aside, why do you have it in for these cultists?"

"I suppose you were not taught about octopus worshipers in these schools where they knew naught of Moo."

"Not really."

"Westerners," Chiun mumbled. Then he spoke up. "There are many legends about the creation of the world, Remo. Every land has stories of how the Supreme Creator brought forth the universe and those who inhabit it. Of course, the Korean version is the only factual story, but in different lands, other stories are told."

They came to a clearing bathed by the full moon. Chiun crouched down, signaling for Remo to follow suit. Remo did.

As Chiun's hazel eyes raked the open area, he went on in a sonorous voice.

"Just as lands tell their tales of the Supreme Creator, they have stories of his opposite. Now, in some lands this opposite creature is ludicrously described as a man with a tail and the horns and hooves of a goat. Of course, this is beyond reason."

"The nuns who raised me didn't think so."

"They probably told you laughable stories about angels too."

"As a matter of fact—"

Chiun hushed him with a gesture. Then he waved Remo forward. Remo followed the Master of Sinanju through the clearing. He noticed that Chiun's eyes were on the ground. Remo looked down. He saw the disturbances—imperfect footprints and gouges in the porous black earth—that went through the clearing. Chiun was obviously following them. As he walked along, Remo saw that they veered off to one side. But Chiun continued in a straight line.

"Little Father, I think you—" Remo began. He never finished, because the trees over their head emitted a high keening sound. A skirling bird cry. In spite of himself, Remo froze.

The Master of Sinanju did not. With a countercry of his own, he twisted aside. His long-nailed fingers went up like predatory claws. There came a mushy cloth-ripping sound, and when Remo focused on the sound, he saw the Master of Sinanju holding the limp body of some sort of creature.

The thing was black and oily-looking. It had a pulpy

head and two legs. But from every point, tentacles grew. These quivered as they hung to the ground. The thing was big, larger than Chiun.

"Jesus H. Christ. What is that?" Remo asked.

"Dead," Chiun said. "It is dead." He held it over his head and Remo realized that he was not holding it in his palm. It was hung up on Chiun's long lethal fingernails. Impaled.

Chiun slowly tipped his hand, twisting his wrists so that the thing came off his fingernails without breaking them, like meat sliding off a fork.

The man-size thing sprawled on the ground. Gingerly Remo approached it. Its skin glimmered under the moonlight, glossy and quivering, like a sea creature. But here and there were greenish feathers, wet and drooping. There was some blood, and Remo was surprised to see that it was red.

"Is it real?" he asked.

"Yes and no," Chiun said. He reached down and Remo almost cringed. Chiun ripped off the thing's head. It landed at Remo's feet wetly.

"A mask?" Remo asked, picking it up. It was slimy. But where the head had been was the glassy-eyed face of a Moovian man.

"It is a disguise they use to spread their terror. An old trick."

"Not that old," Remo said. "When I was a Newark cop, I never had to deal with suspects who thought they were octopi."

"This is older than Newark, older even than Sinanju. An ancient evil long thought banished from the world. This man wore the mantle of Rangotango, the Plumed Octopus, one of the messengers of Ru-Taki-Nuhu."

"Any relation to Riki-Tiki-Tavvi? Or Rin-Tin-Tin?"

"Hush. Ru-Taki-Nuhu is the Enemy of Life. He was known by many people under many names. For as I told you, Remo, the Supreme Creator had an opposite. He was Ru-Taki-Nuhu to the Moovians. To the Koreans, he was Sa Mansang, the Dream Thing. Many are the legends, but their source is one: the octopus."

Remo's lopsided grin was fading. He searched the surrounding jungle for other assailants.

"In Old Moo," Chiun continued, "Ru-Taki-Nuhu was also called the Heaven-Propper. For it was said that Ru-Taki-Nuhu came from a place where there was no sun, no moon, no stars. In those days, the world was a barren rock. Until the coming of Ru-Taki-Nuhu. It is said he fell from a great height, and in falling, his ink sac burst, spilling its contents. What we call the sea is the ink of Ru-Taki-Nuhu. And when the Supreme Creator saw what had bespoiled his pretty world, he called upon the sky to fall and crush Ru-Taki-Nuhu. But the Enemy of Life was too swift. His tentacles reached up and arrested the descending sky. And when the Supreme Creator saw this, he poured a magic potion into the sea so that the Heaven-Propper would sleep and do no mischief. And so Ru-Taki-Nuhu sleeps, awaiting the end of the world, when he will awaken and drink all the ocean. Moovians believe that human life will continue only as long as the Heaven-Propper's tentacles continue to hold up the sky."

"And you snicker at angels," Remo said.

"In ancient times," Chiun went on, "there were men and women so evil that they sought through chants and rituals and other ways to pull down the tentacles of Ru-Taki-Nuhu. Others sought to awaken him before his time, hoping to produce the same wicked result."

"Not that I buy any of this," Remo remarked, "but what kind of idiot would be crazy enough to end the world?"

"Most of them were what you would call teenagers."

"Oh. Makes sense now," Remo said.

"The last of these cretins were thought to be extinct. And they weren't all Moovian. Some were Greek. Others Arab. There were even Koreans, believe it or not."

"I believe it."

Chiun made a face. "You would. Come, let us track the last of these octopus worshipers to their lair and stamp out their kind once and for all."

As they pushed on toward the southern shore, Remo thought of another question.

"Little Father, you don't believe all this octopus-demon stuff, do you?"

It was a long time before the Master of Sinanju answered.

"If we eradicate them all, then we will not have to worry about separating truth from legend."

"Gotcha."

"Until Ru-Taki-Nuhu awakens, that is," Chiun added.

Remo didn't have an answer to that.

The jungle path meandered between vines and banyan trees. At their approach, a monkey ran up a coconut tree. He chattered at them raucously. Chiun chattered back at him and the monkey scampered off.

"Wonder what made him run?" Remo asked idly.

"I insulted his mother," Chiun said. And Remo thought the Master of Sinanju wasn't kidding.

At last they came to the edge of the plateau that looked down on a declivity bordering the white sands of the southern tip of the island. Offshore, waves pounded a jutting blue coral reef. Closer inland was a shadow-clotted blot of foliage.

"There!" Chiun hissed, pointing.

Remo stared into the dark area. His eyes spied the brief starlike twinkle of a dying ember. Then it was gone. The wet smell that sometimes hung in the air around a burned building drifted up to their alert nostrils.

"Someone just doused a fire," Remo whispered.

"We approach without the advantage of surprise."

"Now what?"

And down in the grove, Remo heard a series of soft sounds. *Puff. Puff. Puff.*

"Darts," Chiun hissed.

Remo's eyes telescoped. He spotted them coming up out of the grove. They showed up as dull floating slivers, but when they reached the apex of their flight, for an instant moonlight painted them silver. Poised for instant action, Remo was astonished by how slowly the darts appeared to move. They reminded him of tracer fire rising up out of the Vietnam jungle as he helicoptered over enemy positions. Neither tracers nor darts appeared dangerous. Until they struck.

Remo felt something shoved into his hand.

"Here," Chiun said. "Protect yourself."

Remo saw that he held a huge rubber-tree leaf. He knew instantly what he should do with it.

As the darts descended, he shielded his face, feinting. The little ticks sounded, quick and vicious.

Out of the corner of his eye Remo saw Chiun dance

with the leaf over his head. His leaf quickly sprouted thorns. Remo caught a second volley. The ground in front of him took several hits as well.

Abruptly the puffing ceased. Remo turned over his leaf. It was peppered with darts. None had penetrated.

"Do you have respect for your enemy now, Remo?"

"Yeah," Remo said grimly. "I suppose these are dipped in some poison?"

"No. They are stonefish spines. They come prepoisoned."

"Brrrr," Remo said. He had faced death in back alleys and in bizarre situations, but on this isolated, demon-haunted island, there was something almost supernatural about how casual death could be. No sound of machine guns, no cries of rage. Just silent death from the darkness.

"Now what?"

"Do as I do," Chiun instructed. He flipped his leaf over so the needles pointed outward. Remo followed suit.

The Master of Sinanju drew his leaf back like a tennis racket and let go with sudden violence. Remo grinned and copied the action.

The silent darts rained down on the grove.

Remo listened for the cries of surprise. No sounds came.

"The poison works pretty fast, huh?" he said. "They don't even have time to yell out."

"They have probably left the grove," Chiun said unhappily.

"Impossible. We have the high ground. We'd have spotted them."

"Come," said Chiun, slipping down the sheer wall of the plateau.

Down in the grove, the wet smoky smell annoyed their lungs. The grove was choked with vegetation and Chiun was forced to cut a path into it with his fingernails. He did it with circling motions, like a man brushing cobwebs out of his way. Except that cobwebs broke apart silently. Here, jungle vines and branches cracked and flew off as if attacked by a thresher.

"You could help," Chiun called back.

"Mine aren't long enough," Remo said. But when he showed his hands, he had to swallow his words. His nails were much longer than normal. He shrugged and started to slice the thick growth.

"I'm going to have to find something to pare these down with," he muttered. "They grew a lot on the voyage."

Chiun said nothing.

Presently they came to something that Remo at first mistook for a huge dead tree. Then its hard outlines made him stop in his tracks. "Looks like a tiki god or something," he muttered.

"It is an octopus totem. A bad thing."

Remo walked around it. It possessed a big openmouthed face, six arms, and a serrated belly. The feet were short and stubby.

"This one is obviously male," he pointed out.

"Octopus worshipers are preoccupied with sex. They believe that by mating in certain ways, they can awaken Ru-Taki-Nuhu with their base cries."

"Speaking of sex," Remo said, "is it true what they say about Moovian girls?"

Chiun turned. "And what is it that they say?"

"That they're . . . you know . . ."

Chiun cocked his head. "Yes?"

"Er, loose."

"And what makes you say such a slanderous thing?"

"The way some of them were looking at me. And you know the reputation South Sea island girls have."

"If it is sex you want, I would stick with your American women. They do it less but enjoy it more."

"That's no answer."

"It is the truth you do not wish to hear. Now, come."

Chiun pushed ahead, hiking his skirts so they wouldn't snag on the snarled underbrush.

They came to the campfire. It was deserted except for the remains of a meal. The area was ringed with grotesque tiki gods. Here and there fallen darts feathered the ground. Chiun carefully harvested and buried every one.

"This is impossible," Remo said angrily. "They couldn't escape. We had the entire place in view all the time."

"Octopus worshipers are very tricky. Let us find their hiding place."

"You know where to look?"

"Of course. They are very predictable. Whatever a real octopus does, they do."

Remo followed, searching his memory for octopus habits as described by *National Geographic.*

He wasn't surprised when Chiun led him to a coral cave at the foot of the plateau.

"Think they're in there?"

"Not if I know octopus worshipers," said Chiun, striding in.

Inside the cave, they came to a coral-ringed pool.

"They went down this," Chiun explained. "It will lead to the open water. Are you prepared to follow?"

"Sure," Remo said casually. "What could be down there?"

"Ru-Taki-Nuhu, for one," said Chiun.

"Ha!" said Remo. But he didn't feel his bravado.

Chiun shrugged his long sleeves away from his arms and dived in. Remo kicked off his loafers and followed, thinking that at least a swim would get the salt stiffness out of his clothes.

The water was dark when Remo found his equilibrium. But he could see dimly. Chiun's skirts floated ahead of him, his feet kicking rhythmically.

Remo settled into a sweeping stroke that would keep him clear of the sharp coral outcroppings. The further they swam, the darker it got. But Remo knew that was temporary. They were heading for the sea. Moonlight would illuminate the open water.

But then Remo lost sight of Chiun. It happened so suddenly that Remo momentarily paused, thinking that he had blundered into a side tunnel. Then something wet and heavy brushed his wrist.

Must be Chiun, Remo thought. He reached out, and something cold wrapped around his arm.

Remo grabbed for it with the other hand and felt a slick length of sinew. He pulled at it, and his fingers encountered little flexible pads. And in that instant the image of an octopus' suckers flashed into his mind. His blood ran cold.

18

Smith trembled.

He lifted his long thin fingers from the Folcroft terminal keyboard and they actually shook. He cleared his throat as he reached into the upper-right-hand desk drawer for relief.

The drawer contained an assortment of antacids in tablet, liquid, and foam form, aspirin in regular, double-strength, and children's strength, and five bottles of Alka-Seltzer. After a few moments Smith decided his headache bothered him more than his ulcer. He shook out three pink-and-orange children's aspirin tablets and chased them down with mineral water from his office dispenser.

He returned to the screen, rubbing the spot between his eyes where his eyeglasses rested on his nose, and where the headache seemed situated. His hands were steady again.

The screen stared back at him. The word "BLOCKED" flashed on and off in glowing green letters.

In all his years of CURE operations, Dr. Harold W. Smith had never encountered such sophisticated methods of denying computer access. He had searched Social Security records for data on the name James Churchward.

The file existed. But he couldn't get into it.

He logged into the regional IRS computer banks around the country. He never learned if there was a file for the man because, somehow, his requests were transferred to another computer at an unknown location. A keyboard light flashed like an angry red eye, warning Smith that his probe was being back-traced. Smith logged off hastily.

All other attempts to access routine records on James Churchward met with similar rebuffs. It was incredible. As if the person, although plainly in several data banks, did not exist. Or was not supposed to exist. In all cases, there wasn't even an access code that would allow someone who was presumably authorized to access those files.

This left no doubt whatsoever in Smith's mind. Whoever he was, James Churchward was no ordinary man. These programs were too sophisticated. Smith recognized the probe transferral as a Moebius Siphon, a program he himself had devised years ago for CURE purposes. Obviously he was dealing with an operation as sophisticated as his own.

Baffled by his computer's inability to resolve the problem, Smith sent the terminal humming back into its desk well. Normal CURE resources had failed. Smith had only his own wits to fall back on.

He had to get into that house. Somehow.

19

At first the Master of Sinanju mistook the blackness for a cavern opening. Then he noticed that the edges were misty and cloudlike. The blackness was spreading.

Chiun found himself enveloped in a blackness that was beyond even the ability of Sinanju-skilled eyes to penetrate.

Chiun kicked around, looking for Remo. There was no sign of his pupil. He did not panic. Like Remo, he had enough oxygen in his lungs to survive over an hour underwater. But if the thing he suspected was lurking in these waters got hold of Remo, an hour might not be enough.

Chiun swam back to Remo's last position. His hands made sweeping patterns before his face. His stroke served him both as protection and as sensor. He prayed he would reach Remo in time, for Remo had been trained to battle many things, but not the minions of Ru-Taki-Nuhu.

Remo felt the constraining tentacles wrap around his legs, separating them. He struggled. Normally his strength was equal to just about any human foe. But underwater he lacked the leverage needed for most Sinanju defensive techniques. He floated in the grip of a many-armed monster. His free arm became entangled. In the blackness, which he understood was made by octopus ink, Remo couldn't tell if he was getting anyplace. He had no reference points. His only hope was to reach a coral outcropping.

But then Remo felt the unseen slimy bulk press closer to his chest and a thousand frightening images flooded his mind. In spite of his training, his ability to repress fear, this was a situation so primal that it triggered long-repressed phobias. Remo threshed wildly. The clinging octopus moved with him. But he couldn't shake it free. He felt the suckers gripping his bare arms like eager mouths. He sensed its dumb brain near him, thinking inchoate thoughts.

Then through the inky haze a dim something became visible. It looked like a shelled egg. Remo stared at it and realized it was staring back. Of course, the octopus' eye. Just the idea of that bloated, wrinkled head so close to his face was unnerving.

Remo shut his eyes. The memory of his too-long fingernails popped into his head. Remo raked at the afterimage of the eye that remained in his mind.

He felt something greasy collecting under his nails and raked again. The tentacles tightened and that was enough. Remo had something to work against. He jerked one arm suddenly. The tentacle clung, but he felt it go a little slack.

Then there was something hard and gritty cutting into his back.

Coral!

Reaching around, Remo grasped an outcropping. He steadied himself, and twisted sharply. He felt the octopus move with him. Sensing it strike with the coral, Remo struck again. Tentacles uncoiled and slapped his face and arm, but it wasn't enough.

Remo struck out with his hands. He felt them smash into the boneless head. He struck again and again, until the dark hide ruptured. The thing released him at last. Then Remo was kicking with all his might, not knowing or caring in which direction he was swimming—only anxious to get clear of the many-armed horror.

Chiun sensed rather than saw something glide past him.

He hesitated, his cheeks puffed out. At intervals he expelled air bubbles. After a moment's thought he reversed direction. Ahead, there was a faint lightening of the murk.

When he could see again, Chiun saw that he was swimming behind Remo. Remo's T-shirt was in rags, and there were red marks along his arms and chest. They told the story of Remo's encounter.

Chiun knew better than to touch Remo in his current state. Cocky as Remo was in even the most dangerous situations, this was a place alien to him. Chiun decided to swim under and show himself ahead to Remo, the better to reassure him.

But that stopped being an option when Remo suddenly reversed direction. He came at Chiun.

Chiun saw the look of terror on Remo's face. He swam to him and took his shoulder, mouthing the word "What?" silently.

Remo pointed back. Chiun pushed him aside to see.

There were a dozen of them. They filled the narrow tunnel, their mouths gulping and dribbling bubbles. Their black eyes were unwinking.

But it was not their fishy faces that concerned Chiun. It was the razorlike spines that covered their oblate bodies.

Stonefish. And they were heading in their direction. Behind them, Chiun saw two grinning Moovians swimming in place. A big rattan basket drifted beside them. It was clear that the Moovian octopus worshipers had released the stonefish from the basket and sent them on their deadly way.

Chiun pushed Remo to one side, signaling him to stay clear, and then arrowed for the stonefish like a speedy dolphin.

One stonefish swam a little ahead of the others and Chiun dealt with him first.

With an index finger, Chiun speared the fish through its open mouth. With the other hand he shaved the deadly spines with sharp flashing strokes.

In a twinkling the stonefish was as harmless as a guppy, its spines drifting to the tunnel floor like discarded toothpicks.

Chiun made quick work of the next three.

The effect on the remaining stonefish was remarkable. They turned around and wriggled their tails in the opposite direction. The Moovians saw them coming. They lost their pleased grins and climbed all over one another in their haste to get out of the way. One made it. The other got a stonefish tangled up between his legs. He struggled for a short time. Bubbles erupted from his open mouth, and he sank to the floor in slow motion.

Chiun signaled to Remo. Remo kicked off from the coral wall and swam after the Master of Sinanju. His face was calmer now.

Around a turn in the tunnel, the light increased. Moonlight. The tunnel turned vertical and Chin paused under the blue-coral well while Remo caught up.

When Remo arrived, he looked up in time to see two bare feet disappear from the water. Two more stonefish floated disconsolately.

Chiun pointed to Remo's long fingernails. Remo nodded a yes. It was not a very firm nod, but his face showed anger, which pleased Chiun. His fears were abating.

They went up.

Chiun performed his barbering trick on his fish, ran it through for good measure, and then looked to Remo.

Remo was like a man trying to catch a live mine in his hands. The stonefish twisted viciously. Remo dodged. In frustration, he grabbed its tail and smashed it against the coral. Stunned, the fish floated listlessly.

Chiun touched Remo on the shoulder and motioned for him to follow carefully. He led Remo up to the coral mouth of the natural well. He stopped under the surface and waited. Nothing happened for a long time. Then a Moovian face suddenly broke the still surface. The man looked down to see what was happening.

Chiun pinched the Moovian's nose between two fingers and pulled him into the water. Remo broke his spine with a chop across the back of the neck. The Moovian sank like a dead starfish.

Chiun then made a series of complicated motions that Remo interpreted as "Go take a look."

Remo gave the Master of Sinanju a "Who, me?" look.

Chiun nodded.

Reluctantly Remo went up. No sooner had he broken the surface than he felt hands wrap around his ankles and he was floating beside Chiun, his face furious.

Chiun's motions asked, "See anything?"

Remo shook his head angrily. Chiun smiled and went up. Remo kicked his feet angrily as he followed him up.

When he broke the surface, Remo demanded, "What was that all about?"

"I had to know it was safe."

"And I was the guinea pig?"

"You were in no danger. I had your ankles."

"And I almost had a freaking heart attack. Do you know what I went through back there?"

"You met a child of Ru-Taki-Nuhu. And why don't you speak up? Not all of our enemies may have heard you."

"We'll settle this later," Remo promised, pulling himself out of the well. When he stood up, his stocking feet made puddles.

Chiun shook his kimono skirts of excess water. Then he began to wring out the hem.

They were on the coral reef they had seen earlier. It was a mad jumble of blue outcroppings and hollows streaked with white lying about thirty feet from shore. They stood on one end, the sea to their backs and coral ridges before them.

"When this is over I'm going to have nightmares for a week," Remo said in a bitter voice.

"Now you know why the octopus is called the Enemy of Life."

"Yeah, and remind me to write the *National Geographic* people a nasty letter."

"Hush, Remo," Chiun said quickly. Remo froze. His ears became attuned to their surroundings. The slosh and suck of waves on coral predominated. But through selective attuning, Remo focused those sounds out until they became distant background noise.

Other sounds surfaced. Lungs respirating. Hearts beating, measured, but loud. There was a gurgle that Remo recognized as a man's bowel contents shifting.

"I count nine of them," Remo whispered.

"No, three."

"Listen again. Nine. Nine hearts. Nine pairs of lungs."

"But three opponents. Trust me, I know."

And the seriousness of the Master of Sinanju's tone made Remo feel a thrill of supernatural disquiet. Flashing afterimages of his underwater fight with the octopus came back to him. He shook them off.

Then came the scrape of sandals against coral. It was all around them. They were surrounded.

"I have never trained you for this, my son. For that, I am sorry. But I had thought these octopus worshipers were no more."

"We can handle them," Remo said gamely. But his eyes were nervous.

"Remember that they will use fear to conquer your spirit before they attempt to conquer your body."

"We're Sinanju. We can take them," Remo repeated woodenly. And the pad and scrape of sandals inched closer.

A head appeared over the top of an outcropping. It was gray and bulbous with frighteningly large orblike eyes. It was the head of an octopus. Remo wondered what it was doing out of water, when a hardwood club appeared next to the head. It was being held by a human hand. Remo figured it for another octopus worshiper climbing along the top of the coral ridge. But it moved more swiftly that a man should be able to crawl.

It stepped out from behind the ridge. It was over twelve feet tall.

Then, seeing what made it so tall, Remo laughed out loud.

"Look at those fools," he yelled, pointing. He laughed again. It was with relief.

For the thing with the head of an octopus was a Moovian man. He was riding the shoulders of another man, who rode atop a third, who in turn carried them both with surprising agility.

"What is this, the Moo circus?" Remo chortled. "They look like acrobats."

"Have respect," Chiun warned. "For you face a foe twice your height, with three minds to outthink you and six arms with which to fight. In olden days, this was the feared octopus pyramid."

"If they're trying to be a human octopus," Remo pointed out, "they're two arms short."

"They use their feet as well."

"I stand corrected. Now, you stand back. I want this one for my own."

"I have two others to deal with."

Remo peered over his shoulder. Another octopus pyramid was striding up behind them. A third clambered up from the sea, dripping water. They waved their many arms and made hooing sounds that reminded Remo of owls. Each hand clutched a weapon—a bone knife or war club or blowgun.

Remo went for his man—or men. A blowgun puffed from the middle component in the human octopus construct. The moonlight silvered its path. Remo dodged it with ease.

He twisted around the thing in a series of eye-defying steps. Once behind it, Remo kicked out. The bottom man's knees buckled and the three-man pyramid wavered. A hardwood club swiped at Remo's head, but he avoided it. A knife sliced at him and he danced out of the way. The puff of a dart came on its heels, and Remo had no time to spot it. He dropped and rolled.

When he came up, Remo blinked. The bottom man was now on top. He hadn't seen it happen, but he knew it was true. He had recognized the bottom Moovian as one of the traitorous Red Feather Guard.

Remo cursed his mistake. He should have kicked the front of the kneecap to shatter it. He had clipped the man in the back of the knee where the natural buckling reflex had absorbed the blow. And now the man had somehow changed places so that his damaged knee didn't matter.

Well, Remo wasn't going to make that mistake again. Chiun was counting on him. A hasty glance showed the Master of Sinanju poised between two lumbering totemlike groups. Silhouetted against a full moon, it was a fantastic sight. As if the tiki gods of the Grove of Ghosts had come to life.

Remo circled his foe, but the creature—Remo had already started to think of it as such—kept shifting with him. The occasional dart puffed out. Remo was forced to keep his distance so he could maneuver. Every time he shifted closer, they tried to nail him. Already Remo was beginning to feel respect for these octopus worshipers.

The Master of Sinanju let them come. No fear touched his heart. Not for himself. He was concerned for Remo. The last Master of Sinanju to vanquish an octopus attack was Lu. He had used the Bursting Seed attack. That would not do here. And these octopus worshipers might know of that famous battle and have devised a defense. They had had centuries in which to consider the matter.

Chiun let the demons come for him. They were easily evaded in the clear light. The things made their ridiculous hooing sounds.

A hardwood club smashed down. Chiun's hand intercepted it. The club shattered. The shock traveled up in the low man's arm. He howled in his agony, and the sound was fearsome.

"*Aiiee!*" Chiun cried, adding a fearsome sound of his own. The octopus pyramid behind him froze. That was enough. Chiun moved for the group with the injured limb.

His leap carried him to the height of the second man's head. Chiun's sandal touched the head and found purchase. The other sandal kicked one way, his arms slashed the other. The middle limbs suddenly let go of their weapons, and another howl came forth. Chiun floated up to the top man, who was hooing forlornly.

Chiun caused him to drop his blowgun with a slashing of fingernails. The hand came off at the wrist, pumping blood. A chopping blow shattered the opposite shoulder.

Chiun leapt to the ground and whirled.

The octopus man was howling and screeching in pain. Its limbs waved feebly. Chiun added to their symphony of agony with a brutal groin kick.

The lowest man collapsed in pain. The octopus fell apart on the coral, and, once more facing mere men—injured ones at that—the Master of Sinanju went among them, liberating their brains from their skulls with quick, bone-crunching blows.

Proudly Chiun turned to the remaining octopus man.

"Come," he taunted in Moovian. "You think you are one mighty creature, but I will make of you three corpses."

Remo decided that the heads were the creature's weak spots. This time he would take out the man on the bottom and then the others would fall into range of his hands—like pulling down a sand castle.

If only they would stop making that eerie sound. It was starting to get to him.

Remo feinted to the left. The thing shifted with amazing speed. It was as if all three brains were hooked together. He moved right, and went for the bottom head.

Suddenly the thing split into three men. Remo felt his reflexes react automatically to deal with the new situation. A mistake. But he couldn't help himself. Whoever these guys were, they had a way of fighting that took Sinanju training into account.

Remo was suddenly surrounded by three club-waving Moovians all staring like owls. He looked for the one with the blowgun. He was the only one who concerned Remo.

Remo sidestepped a speeding dart. He moved in. Then the blowgun was tossed to another hand, and another dart came from that direction. Remo shifted, and one of the clubs came at him.

He ducked under the blow and took the man's wrist, using the force of the Moovian's attack to flip him.

The man skidded along the coral, but found his feet with the agility of an acrobat. He suddenly leapt onto the blowgun man's back and the third scampered atop them. They stood joined again and resumed their frenzied octopuslike gesticulations.

Remo dodged behind a coral ridge. He needed time to think. And he wouldn't get it while he was preoccupied with avoiding darts.

Behind the coral, Remo considered the ridiculousness of his predicament. In his time, he'd weaved through heavily armed hordes of killers. But these circus-freak Moovians had him on the run. Remo had been trained to deal with opponents either singly or in groups—but not freaking octopus worshipers. He'd have to find a different approach.

The octopus head of the tallest Moovian suddenly topped the ridge above him. It went "Hooo-hoooo."

And Remo had an idea.

He went up the ridge until he was in the Moovian's face.

"Boo!" Remo said. And he jellied the man's face with the flat of his palm. Remo knocked the top man off the human pyramid and took his place.

It happened so fast that the middle Moovian didn't know how to react. While he was giving it thought, Remo staved the top of his head in and pushed him aside.

The man on the bottom found himself surrounded by the dead bodies of his comrades. Then whose legs were those wrapped around his neck? he wondered. He looked up.

"Hoooo?" he said.

"Me," the foe with the face like milk said. And then a

double fist came at his face and the world turned first red, like blood, and then black, like octopus ink. Or like death.

Remo jumped off the man's back. His feet hit the ground just ahead of the Moovian's pulped face. Remo dusted his hands off with pride.

"Nothing to it," he said, "once you get the hang of it." He looked around for Chiun. The Master of Sinanju stood framed against the silvery-black water. He was in a defensive crouch, an octopus pyramid of men stalking him. They hovered over the edge of the water, many feet below. Remo saw three other Moovian bodies sprawled nearby.

The Master of Sinanju knew that his pupil had succeeded in vanquishing his opponents. His heart swelled with pride. Now, together, the two of them would make short work of his last pyramid of octopus worshipers.

"Remo, to me!" he called.

Remo came up at a trot. And Chiun decided that here, the last battle between Sinanju and the octopus cult of Ru-Taki-Nuhu would take place. It would be best, and read best in the Book of Sinanju, if both the Master Chiun and his white pupil vanquished it. He would show Remo the correct attack method and they would do it together.

"Hurry, Remo," Chiun called, considering how to word this last skirmish in his scrolls. Perhaps it would be better not to mention that Remo was white.

"What's the rush?" Remo asked as he casually joined the Master of Sinanju.

Chiun looked at him.

"Are you mad? There is one of these monsters left. Here, I will show you the best way to defeat him."

"Hold your horses, Little Father," Remo said.

The octopus pyramid suddenly stopped waving its many limbs. Its hoooing sound began to die like a failing wind through a hollow tree.

Remo walked up to the thing, not bothering to raise his arms to ward off the blows that would surely come.

"Remo!"

"Yes?" Remo asked, turning casually. It was unbelievable. Had Remo learned nothing from his battle? Turning his back on the evil thing like that.

Chiun flashed into action, his sandals beating the ground, his hands reaching out to yank Remo from harm.

Then Remo turned back and waved good-bye to the octopus pyramid. The silent thing waved its arms back. They were feeble little shakes. Then, stepping up to it, Remo pushed the lowest man in the chest.

The entire octopus man fell back like a fallen tree.

It struck the edge of the coral cliff, and without breaking into individual men, splashed into the ocean below.

The Master of Sinanju peered over the edge into the water.

"They did not fight you," Chiun said in disbelief.

"How could they?" Remo asked. "They were already dead."

"Already . . . ?"

And from a back pocket Remo pulled out a blowgun.

"I took this from my guy. One of them, anyway."

"You . . . you . . ." Chiun sputtered.

"Neat, huh? I figured, why screw around with them? Well, aren't you going to say something? Aren't you proud of the slick way I handled my end?"

"Proud?" Chiun screeched. "Do you know how this will look in the Book of Sinanju? This was the last battle with these creatures."

Remo's face acquired an injured look. "Why should I care how it will look? I got them. Dead is dead."

"It was ridiculous. And you used a weapon. What will the High Moo say?"

"He'll say it's about time. He thinks you forgot your weapons."

"I am mortified," Chiun said huffily.

"You're just pissed because when you write in your dippy scrolls how Sinanju conquered the last octopus worshiper, I'll get all the credit."

"Glory hound," Chiun spat.

"I knew it," Remo laughed. And laughing felt pretty good after all he had been through.

20

Remo finished lashing the bamboo poles together.

"I think it's long enough now," he called to Chiun.

"Then bring it here," Chiun said testily.

Remo hefted the pole onto his shoulder. To his surprise, it held.

The sun was coming up. Pinkish rays tinged the Pacific. There were birds calling now. Not the twittering birds of the States, but the cacophony of jungle birds. Mynahs. Parakeets. Terns.

The Master of Sinanju finished lashing the hands of one of the octopus worshipers behind his back with a vine.

"Give it to me," Chiun said.

After Remo had handed over the pole, the Master of Sinanju ran it up under the man's bound feet. It passed up his back, under his tied hands, to the next pair of bound ankles, and then to the next lashed wrists.

Remo lifted the hands as necessary, until the pole's end bumped the shattered skull of the topmost man.

"This is ridiculous," Remo said for the twelfth or thirteenth time as he examined the monstrosity that lay on the ground.

All nine octopus men had been joined into one huge octopus man. Remo had been harangued into retrieving the group he had knocked into the water. They had been easy to handle because they had stiffened into position from the effects of the poison darts.

But the others had to be reassembled one by one and their limbs set and then broken so they were locked into place. Chiun had done that. He knew how to crush bone and joints so that they fused.

"Now what? As if I can't guess," Remo asked.

"Take your end. I will take mine."

"On a count of three," Remo said, bending down. "One, two, three. Lift!"

The bamboo pole groaned, but it held. The bodies hung off it like slaughtered chickens. Tongues lolled. Some of the eyes stared glassily.

"Now, carefully," Chiun said, "back to the palace."

"The mighty hunters return, huh?"

"Say nothing about the blowgun," Chiun said in a sour voice.

They trudged down to the water, sloshing inland and through the jungle. Dead Moovian heads bounced like overripe fruit. They stopped to pick up the other bodies they had vanquished along the way, piling them unceremoniously atop the others. When they neared the village, Chiun suddenly called a halt.

"Lay it down," he ordered.

"Tired, Little Father?" Remo asked solicitously.

"Do not be ridiculous," Chiun countered, joining Remo in front of their burden. "I am reigning Master. To me goes the honor of entering the village first."

"Oh," said Remo. "I guess that means the back of the bus for me." And without another word he took Chiun's place at the end of the bamboo pole.

When they entered the village outskirts, Chiun began to call out in a loud singsong voice.

"Arise, O children of Moo. See what Sinanju has brought you. No longer need you fear the darkness. For the last of the spawn of Sa Mansang, known to you as Ru-Taki-Nuhu, has been vanquished! Arise, O children of Moo, to greet a new day and a golden era."

The children were the first to poke their heads out of the grass huts. Then the adults. Runners were sent to the palace, and Chiun smiled.

Amazed voices lifted at the sight of the round red sucker marks that decorated Remo's chest and arms.

"Ru-Taki-Nuhu!" they whispered. "The white one has fought Ru-Taki-Nuhu and lives!"

When they at last came to the feast circle in front of the Royal Palace, the High Moo stood waiting with folded arms. His daughter hovered at his side.

Red Feather Guards stepped forward as Remo and Chiun

set down their burden. They poked and stabbed at the corpses with spears, seeking signs of life.

"All are dead," one reported to the High Moo.

The High Moo strode up to the Master of Sinanju.

"You have brought me twelve kills, and twelve is the number the traitor of a royal priest swore served Ru-Taki-Nuhu. The octopus cult is no more. You have lived up to your word, Master of Sinanchu and have earned the full fee due to you."

"Payable on demand," said Chiun.

"I will be glad to store it for you in the royal treasure house for the length of your stay," the High Moo suggested.

"And I accept," Chiun said with a quick bow.

"The full hospitality of Moo is yours."

"My . . . slave and I are weary. We have had a long journey and ate much this evening. We require rest. A few hours only."

"Come, rooms have been prepared in my palace. Dolla-Dree, show Remo to his room. I will escort the Master of Sinanchu to his quarters personally."

"Hello again," Remo said when the Low Moo came to take him by the arm.

"Will you tell me how you vanquished them before you sleep?" she asked, admiring the red marks on his arms.

"Sure," Remo said.

"Do not believe all he says," Chiun warned. "He will try to take more credit than is his due."

"No, I won't," Remo said, winking at the Low Moo. "Chiun helped. Some."

And Remo hurried into the palace ahead of Chiun's flurry of invective.

21

It was raining when Dr. Harold W. Smith's flight landed at Boston's Logan Airport.

He waited ten minutes at the underground exit of Terminal B for a free MBTA bus to the Blue Line subway stop. He rode the rattling train five stops to Government Center, walked upstairs, and switched to a Green Line trolley, riding it one stop to Park Street. The rain had tapered off to a sullen sprinkle when Smith emerged on the corner of Tremont and Park streets at the edge of Boston Common. He walked down Tremont.

The office of Michael P. Brunt was above an antiquarian bookstore on West Street. Trudging up the dingy steps, Smith found an empty reception room.

He stood for a moment, uncertainly clutching his briefcase. He wiped rainwater off his rimless glasses. He cleared his throat.

The inner door opened and a square-faced man built along the lines of a refrigerator in a blue serge suit poked his unshaven chin out.

"You Mr. Brown?" he demanded.

"Yes," Smith lied.

"You look more like Mr. Gray. But come in anyway. Sorry about the secretary. I sent her out for some bullets. I kinda ran out on my last case."

The office was cluttered, Smith noticed, as he entered. Papers overflowed a wastepaper basket. The window was a film of grime that looked out over row of graying buildings so nondescript they might have been painted on the glass by an indifferent artist.

Mike Brunt dropped behind his desk. His wooden chair squeaked loudly. The set looked as if it had once seen service in a high school. He leaned back and set size-thirteen brogans on the desktop, showing Smith the color of his left sock through a hole in the sole. It was white.

On the wall behind him was a framed cloth saying: "When in Doubt, Punt, Bunt, or Shoot to Kill." It was done in needlepoint.

"I will come right to the point," Smith said, seating himself primly on a vinyl chair, his briefcase on his knees.

"I don't charge for the initial consultation," Brunt said, running a toothpick under his nails. He made a little pile of grayish ash on the desktop. "Unless you hire me. Then I try to sneak it into the expense sheet somewhere." He grinned disarmingly.

"Yes. Well, I have a matter that only someone in your profession can handle."

"You got the crime, I got the time," Brunt sang.

"I have had an important personal item stolen from my home. I know who stole it and I know where this person lives."

"And you want it back?"

"Yes. It is quite important to me. The police say they can do nothing. My suspicions aren't enough for them to question the man."

"Okay, I'll bite. What's missing? The family jewels? Gorbachev's birthmark? The Bermuda Triangle?"

Smith hesitated, wondering if he shouldn't feign a weak smile. He decided not. He was growing uncomfortable with this man, who seemed to take nothing seriously. Doesn't he want work? Smith's computers had spit out his name as one of the least prosperous private investigators in the Northeast. Certainly such a man would be desperate for clients.

"It's a tea service," Smith said at last.

Brunt cocked a skeptical eye at Smith. "A tea service?" he said dryly.

"Sterling. It's been in my family for over a hundred years. It has great sentimental value."

"At my prices, you'd be better off switching to coffee."

"It's an heirloom," Smith said stubbornly.

"Takes all kinds," Mike Brunt said laconically.

"The man's name is James Churchward. He lives at 334 Larchwood Place in Rye, New York. I happen to know he is away on vacation this week, but I do not know where. This would be the ideal time to search his house for my property. I have taken the liberty of writing out a check for your usual one-day fee." Smith started to rise, the check in hand.

"Whoa! Did I say I was taking this case?"

"No. But it is not a difficult task. A simple break-in."

"Break-ins are illegal."

"Yes, I know. But I have nowhere else to turn. And I understood that people in your . . . ah . . . profession do this type of work all the time."

"Yeah, but that doesn't mean Mike Brunt stoops that low. Hey, you may not know it from his office, but I have scruples. Somewhere. Maybe in that filing cabinet. Under C, if I know my secretary."

"Well, then, I won't waste any more of your time," Smith said, starting to rise again.

Mike Brunt put up a hamlike hand.

"Slow down, sport. Let's see the color of your money."

Smith passed over the check. Brunt examined it.

"A money order?" he said doubtfully.

"Naturally I do not want to give you anything that could be traced back to me."

"This must not be the first time someone walked off with your teapot. You really ought to hide it when company comes." Brunt took his feet off the desk and sat up. "Okay. So what happens if I'm arrested?"

"I will take care of you in that eventuality."

"Connected, huh? I had you figured for Mafia the minute you walked in."

"I have political connections," Smith said testily.

"This is a lot of potential fuss for a lousy tea service."

"It has sentimental value," Smith repeated, thinking that perhaps he should have made up something more elaborate than a tea service. But anything too valuable might tempt a man such as Brunt to consider pilfering the house of other valuables.

"That so? Come on, Brown. Spill it. Nobody lays down cash in advance over a tea service. What's in it? Diamonds? Gold? Is the exact location of Blackbeard's treasure worked into the filigree? You can tell me. The office cockroaches have taken a vow of silence."

"It is a tea service," Smith repeated stiffly. "And if you are not interested in the matter, we are wasting each other's time."

"Tell you what, Brown. I'll take this little caper. Strictly for chuckles, you understand. Maybe I'll get lucky and your friend will come back while I'm in the house."

"Why would that be lucky?" Smith asked, his voice filling with horror.

Just then the outer door banged open and the click of high heels announced the entrance of Michael Brunt's secretary. A thirtyish blonde in a beehive hairdo stuck her head in the office.

"Here you go, shamus," she said, tossing a box onto the bare desk. Mike Brunt grabbed it and shook it apart. Shiny brass cartridges spilled over the desktop like wayward marbles.

Michael Brunt unholstered a worn .38 revolver and began stuffing slugs into the cylinder. When he was done, he answered Smith's question with a cracked grin.

"Maybe I'll get into a shoot-out."

"You wouldn't," Smith croaked.

"Suuuure, he would," the secretary said wryly, closing the door.

"Perhaps I should see someone else," Smith began. "I do not want any unnecessary complications. This must be done in such a way that the homeowner is unaware of the entry."

"Too late, pal," Mike Brunt said, pulling open a desk drawer and plunking a bottle of Old Mister Boston in front of his face. Two shot glasses came up next. "I've already spent your money. Why don't we just drink a toast to our new business relationship."

"No, thank you," Smith said. "I must be going. The number at which I can be reached is on the check."

"Good," said Michael Brunt, pulling the top off with his teeth and spitting it onto the desk. "I hate drinking with clients. It usually means less booze for me." He then proceeded to drink straight from the bottle. When he was done, he belched.

Smith left the office feeling very ill. It was raining when he got out on the street. It was a three-block walk back to the subway, and Smith hunched his shoulders against the rain. Taxis drove by in each direction, but Smith disdained them. A cab would cost several dollars, and the subway ride back to the airport, even with two changes, was only sixty cents.

22

Remo woke to a strange rustling sound.

"Arise, you lazy slugabed," a familiar squeaky voice said. And Chiun entered the room.

"Did someone steal your clothes?" Remo asked, propping himself up on one elbow. "Or have you just gone native?"

Chiun puffed up his thin chest. "You do not like this gift from the High Moo?" He spread his skirts. They were made of rattan strips woven together with vegetable fiber. He wore a blouse of rough-weave wheat-colored cotton over it. Belled sleeves copied from his kimono design rounded out the ensemble.

"It's a new you," Remo said, sitting up on his bed mat. He pulled on his stiff trousers. He left his rag of a T-shirt. "What time is it?"

"Time passes differently on Moo, but you have slept nearly six hours. Are you ill?"

"No," Remo said evasively. "I just felt like sleeping."

"We are summoned to the Shark Throne. Come."

Remo reached for his shoes, then realized that he had left them back at the Grove of Ghosts. He pulled on his socks. They would do for now. When he stood up, he noticed his fingernails were even longer than before, almost twice as long as he remembered from the previous night. He rubbed his face. He needed a shave too. He reminded himself to ask Chiun about getting the Moovian equivalent of a barber.

Bare-chested, Remo followed Chiun down a maze of stone corridors to a central room.

Guards stood outside the open door, on the inside, and at every corner of the room, Remo saw as he entered.

Chiun bowed before the High Moo, who sat on his low Shark Throne. The Low Moo sat to his right, on an even lower stool. There was an empty stool on the left that Remo assumed belonged to the late royal priest.

"My Red Feather Guard has returned from scouring the island," said the High Moo without preamble. "Emboldened by the trophy you have laid at my feet, they even ventured into the Grove of Ghosts. They found no living men, there or anywhere else. I hereby proclaim today the Dawn of the Era Without Octopus Worshipers."

"Sinanju is pleased to serve," Chiun said simply.

"Full payment will be tendered to you upon your leave-taking of Moo. A leave-taking I and my daughter beg is not soon."

"I have not discussed this with Remo as yet," Chiun said.

"Actually, we can't stay long," Remo said in Moovian. The High Moo frowned. The Low Moo gasped.

"What Remo means," Chiun inserted hastily, "is that we have responsibilities elsewhere. Other clients. None so generous as you, of course. But it does not mean that we cannot pass the span of, say, one moon on Moo."

"So be it," said the High Moo, mollified. "The full moon saw the end of the octopus cult. The next moon will see your going—unless you change you mind before then."

"All things are possible on Moo," Chiun said, bowing.

"Have you any requests?"

"My son has not yet breakfasted. I would like to prepare for him his favorite. I will need lemons and eggs."

"And I could do with something for my nails and beard," Remo added, showing his hands.

Chiun looked at Remo's hands curiously.

"You should have cut them before we left America," he said under his breath.

"I thought I did," Remo shot back.

And Chiun allowed himself a tiny smile of satisfaction.

They were in the royal dining room, a roofless cubicle in one corner of the palace, when a steaming kettle of egg-lemon soup was brought in by a topless cook. Remo was relieved to see it wasn't the old woman from the feast this time, but a comely maiden.

He said, "*Ola.*" The girl smiled shyly and began to fill a wooden bowl.

Another girl came in with a handful of objects. Remo saw a couple of bone knives and a fist-size stone.

"What's this stuff?" he asked, tasting the soup.

"You asked for these," the girl replied, kneeling at his feet. She took one of Remo's hands and examined the nails critically. The cook took one of the other knives and approached Remo from the other side.

"Looks like I'm in for the Moovian version of a shave and manicure," Remo said, pushing his soup aside.

Chiun frowned. "Do not forget your soup," he said evenly, pushing the bowl back under Remo's nose.

"It can wait," Remo said, eyes on the sinuous bodies hovering over him. They smelled nice too, he noticed. Like coconuts.

"No," Chiun said suddenly. "The other thing can wait. Shoo, shoo!" he said to the maidens. "Come back later. My son has fought a hard battle and needs to replenish his strength."

The native girls fled the room on bare feet.

"Hey! What's with you?" Remo demanded.

"You must eat first. Keep up your strength."

"I like to set my own priorities," Remo growled, his unhappy face watching the girls scurry down the corridor.

"Eat," said Chiun.

Reluctantly Remo started in on the soup. After a few tastes he was greedily devouring it, the girls of Moo forgotten.

"I can't seem to get enough of this stuff," he said.

"I will tell the hens to continue laying," Chiun said blandly, "so that you do not run out for the duration of our stay here."

"We can't stay here a whole month," Remo protested.

"We are due a vacation. This will be it."

"What if Smith needs us?"

"Then he can summon us, as always."

"How? There aren't any phones here."

"How is that my fault?" Chiun squeaked. "According to my contract, I am permitted to vacation where I will. Nowhere does it say that the Master of Sinanju is obligated to call ahead to see if there are telephones at his chosen retreat. Besides, I did not know the number of the High Moo."

"Smith is going to be very upset," Remo cautioned.

"Let him be upset. If he complains, I will tell him that he is not the only worthy emperor in the world. He has a rival, the High Moo."

"I don't think he'll appreciate that. And what happens after the thirty days?"

"Who can say?" Chiun said mischievously. "Thirty days is a long time from now. We live in an uncertain world. Anything is possible. Moo sank once. Perhaps America will be next. Then you will thank me for bringing you to this lovely land."

"Dream on," said Remo, starting in on his second bowl.

After he was done, Remo said, "Okay, call back the girls."

"For what?"

"For these," Remo said, showing his nearly half-inch-long nails.

Chiun took Remo's hands in his. "If you let them grow, soon they will curve inward like mine."

"Not interested," Remo snapped, withdrawing his hands.

"Why not? We are on Moo now. You no longer have your lame excuse not to grow them long."

"Chiun, I'm supposed to be an agent for my government. I gotta blend in with the natives, so to speak."

"Now that you are on Moo, you can blend in with Moovian natives."

"I don't see any long-nailed people on Moo either."

"Nor do I. But where we are now, Emperor Smith's absurd secrecy mania is not in effect. We walk this land known for what we are, admired for our work, and honored for our skills. Wear your nails with pride, Remo. Who knows, you might come to like them."

"No chance," Remo snapped, grabbing up a sharp knife. He attacked his left hand with the serrated edge. The blade dug in and Remo made furious sawing motions. Dust rose up. Remo paused. To his chagrin, he saw the nail was intact. And the knife had lost its edge.

"Hey!" he said, looking up. He noticed that Chiun had been bent over his shoulder, watching intently. "Look at this."

"Ah, wonderfully strong."

"Are you kidding? This knife's a joke."

"I meant the nail."

"Maybe I can find a metal knife."

"Not on Moo. All metal is saved for coins and jewelry. And you have ruined a knife of the finest bone."

Remo looked at the knife. It was white and polished. And over a foot long.

"Wonder what kind of animal they have on the island to make a knife this long?" he wondered.

"The fiercest, most dangerous one," Chiun said.

"Yeah?"

"Man."

Remo dropped the knife. "This is a *human* bone?" he asked.

Chiun picked it up. "Yes, and from the freshness, I would say it was made from the femur of one of the octopus worshipers we vanquished last night."

"They use human bone for knives?" Remo said in a dumbstruck voice.

"Hush, Remo. How many times have I told you never to criticize another empire's way of doing things?"

"But human bone. It's barbarous."

"That is easy for you to say, you who come from a land where everything is wasted. Do you know that I have a steamer trunk full of perfectly good toothpicks that careless waiter persons tried to throw out simply because they had been used once?"

"They were made to be used just once. It's unsanitary to reuse toothpicks."

"They are washable. On Moo, toothpicks would be handed down from generation to generation by people who know the value of property."

"I give up," Remo said. "If you'll excuse me . . ."

"Where are you going?"

"I left my shoes back at the grove."

"You can retrieve them when we leave—if we leave."

"No ifs about it. We're leaving. In a month."

"Before you waste your time, examine your feet."

"For what? Athlete's foot?"

When Chiun didn't answer, Remo sat down and pulled off a sock. His toenails were very long. Too long to accommodate his shoes.

"Damn!" he said. "How'd you know that?"

"Perhaps I am psychic," Chiun said with a smile.

"I'm going after my shoes anyway," Remo said, pulling on his sock and storming out the door.

"I will join you."

"Suit yourself," Remo growled.

23

Remo stepped into the blinding tropical sun of the palace courtyard. The courtyard was empty. The ashes of the feast sifted in the breeze. The smells of meat clung to the air. They offended Remo's sensitive nostrils.

Chiun materialized beside him.

"Where is everybody?" Remo asked.

"Working, of course."

Remo frowned. "I thought islanders lived the life of Riley."

"Who is Riley?"

"A figment of someone's imagination. Why do people have to work here? They have the sun, all the fruit and fish they could want. This place is a paradise."

"Come," said Chiun.

"I want to get my shoes back," Remo said.

"What I have to show you is on the way to your precious shoes."

Remo shrugged. He followed silently as Chiun began speaking. The jungle all around them steamed with a pleasant warmth.

"I have heard you speak of Moo with ill-concealed mockery in your voice. You think Moo is small?"

"It *is* small."

"Once it was larger."

"I'll bet Old Moo was nothing to crow about either, otherwise why wouldn't anyone have heard about it?"

Chiun stopped and whirled.

"Sinanju has heard of it. And the nation that is looked upon with favor by the House of Sinanju needs nothing else—especially the approval of a nation that is only two hundred years old."

Remo sighed. "Point taken. Shall we just try to keep up the pace?" he suggested.

Chiun turned and stalked off. It was a while before the dark flush left his face and he resumed speaking.

"Once, Moo was the great seafaring empire in the world. Before Egypt it was. Before Greece it was, and before the oldest settlements in Africa."

"Okay, it's old. So's the moon. So what?"

"Before Sinanju it was," Chiun continued. Remo's face registered surprise. It was rare that Chiun gave anything credit that dimmed the shining beacon that was Sinanju.

"Yeah?"

"For in truth, when Moo became a client of Sinanju, Moo was old. Its glory days were waning like the moon that we will behold tonight. It had withdrawn its mighty fleet from the world's seas. Moo had turned inward, beset by octopus worshipers and internal strife. But strong it was still. And its coins were the most prized of all currencies."

They walked along a winding jungle path. On either side, Remo saw rice and sweet-potato fields tended by young boys and girls. They stood in the rice fields, ankle-deep in brown water. Their bare brown backs were bent. They paid Remo and Chiun no heed.

"The rice did not grow itself in the days of Old Moo, either," Chiun remarked dryly.

"They could live off the coconuts."

"You could live off egg-lemon soup if you wished. But variety is preferable."

"I wouldn't mind a steady diet of it."

"Good," Chiun murmured.

"What's that?" Remo asked.

"Moo was strong because it produced abundant food," Chiun went on as if he hadn't heard. "It is a tradition that the current High Moo holds dear. Each year, they grow more rice than necessary. This way they never want."

"How come I see only boys and girls? Where are the adults? Fishing?"

"Some fish. The women do that."

"What about the men?"

"Have you forgotten the coins of Moo?"

'Oh, right," Remo said as the path began to dip toward the lagoon. "The mines."

"Moo had the most powerful currency because Moo had

the greatest treasury. Its treasure house held stack after stack of the great round coins. For the Moovians were great miners in those days."

"These days too," Remo said, jerking a thumb at a shored-up hole in the side of a creeper-overgrown hillock. It was the third abandoned mine they had spotted during their walk.

"They have fewer mines, but they work them very hard. So the High Moo told me."

They came at last to the lagoon where their junk lay anchored.

"Still there," Remo said.

"Of course. Why should it not be?"

"No reason. I was just thinking it's our only ticket home."

"Assuming that it does not sink," Chiun said.

"Don't even say it out loud."

Chiun turned. He allowed himself a gentle smile.

"I merely jested. Can you not take a joke in return, O teller of Moo jokes?"

"Touché," admitted Remo. He jerked his thumb to the right. "The grove is over that way."

"Soon, soon. For now look to the east."

Remo shielded his eyes from the sun. It was at its apex. High noon. Remo wondered what time it was back in America.

"I see water," he said.

"Do you see the far water that touches the very sky?"

"You mean the horizon? Sure."

Chiun nodded. "Now look to the south. Do you see that horizon?"

"Sure."

"And north? And west?"

"That's a lot of water."

"If you could see twice as far in all directions, still your gaze would not encompass the whole of the Empire of Moo."

"From where I stand, Moo is about three square miles," Remo said flatly. "Most of it vertical."

"I feel like a swim," Chiun said brightly. "Will you join me?"

"Is that an invitation or a command?"

"Did it sound like an invitation?"

"Yeah, but I'm wondering what will happen if I decline."

"Do not decline and you will forever have a mystery to ponder," Chiun said.

Remo considered. "Lead on," he said. "I don't know where this is going, but obviously it's going somewhere."

Without another word, Chiun waded into the water. When it was up to his chest, he slid onto his stomach and began striking out for open water. Remo dug in after him.

Three miles out they had left the junk behind, and Chiun paused, treading water.

"Come, Remo. I want to show you something."

And Chiun disappeared as if something had pulled him down by the leg. Remo jackknifed in place. The water closed in over his head. It was cool, and clearer than he had expected.

Remo homed in on the trailing air bubbles left by the Master of Sinanju. A hammerhead shark cruised into view, but left them alone. Other, more colorful fish scattered out of Chiun's path. Remo kept his eyes out for octopi, but he saw none. For as far as the eye could see, the ocean floor was a fairyland of multicolored coral formations.

Hundreds of feet below, Chiun alighted on a sprawling pink coral outcropping. Remo settled beside him, his stocking feet touching the sandpaperlike coral.

Remo faced Chiun. Sea shadows dappled their faces. Remo made a question mark with a finger.

Chiun bent over and chopped away a chunk of coral with his hand. Under the coral, a flat gray surface was exposed. Chiun continued chipping away. Finally he had a man-size place on which to stand. He stamped his foot once and disappeared. There was only a hole in the gray surface to show that he had stood there.

Remo hesitated, thinking of octopi. Then he dived into the hole.

Inside, Remo found himself in a square room. Dead seaweed clung to what he recognized were stone benches. There were murals on the walls. They were made up of colored tiles. There was just enough sea-filtered light coming in that Remo could make out scenes of a great city with tall towers and golden domes. People dressed like

Greeks, in togas and short skirts, were visible on the depicted walkways.

Remo realized he was inside a sunken house of Old Moo. Chiun disappeared into an adjoining room. Remo swam after him.

Though not impressive by the modern standards of Western architecture, for buildings that were thousands of years old, they were magnificent.

Remo touched pottery jars, wooden chests that had fallen in from the eroding action of the sea. They swam down a long tunnel with muraled walls. The light grew dimmer.

Eventually they came to a huge vaulted room. Remo sensed the expanding space. He kicked himself up to the ceiling, and touched stone blocks. He started pulling them loose. The mortar was brittle. He got through to pink coral. A series of rapid straight-fingered blows brought the coral floating down in chunks.

Greenish light flooded the room. Pushing off, Remo joined Chiun.

The Master of Sinanju floated like a jellyfish. His legs scissored, keeping him upright. With spread arms he indicated the distant walls.

Every wall was the same. Row upon row of glass vessels. They were huge. Each wall had been built up with shelves so that the vessels covered every available square foot of wall.

Remo swam for one of them and floated before it.

He touched it. It was like a jug, stoppered with a glass plug. The edges were sealed with clay or tar to make them waterproof. Inside, a man floated. He was shriveled into a near-fetal position. Remo saw a wizened face, the eyes closed as if in sleep. He went to the next vessel. A woman, young and peaceful of face, hung up against the glass. Her feet touched the bottom, but the narrow base kept her from slipping into a pile of inert flesh. Her shoulder leaned against the wall nearest Remo, and Remo felt as if he could reach out and touch her.

Every vessel contained a body floating in a reddish fluid.

Remo paddled away from them, suddenly horrified by the great number of dead people.

He found Chiun searching among the vessels. Remo had started toward him when the Master of Sinanju suddenly darted away like a frightened fish.

The walls trembled. The water stirred. Remo felt a sudden current. He saw wood particles swirl up from a top shelf. The shelf began to tilt. Remo moved, impelled by an unexplained fear. He got under the shelf, took it in both hands. His kicking feet sought purchase. They touched a glass stopper and, in fear of upsetting the jug, recoiled.

Chiun swam into view. He made quick lifting motions with his hands. Remo nodded. He understood. He was to hold up the shelf. Chiun would do the rest.

One by one, Chiun wrapped his frail-appearing arms around the vessels and carried them to the floor. He made an arrangement of them until the shelf was bare. Then Remo yanked the shelf free and sent it floating away.

Chiun began making hand signs toward the roof opening. Remo nodded. Then a wall cracked. The shelving held, but one vessel teetered. Remo darted for it. He was too late.

The jug broke apart soundlessly. Red fluid billowed and spread like a bloody cloud. Remo kicked into reverse. He tasted alcohol. Wine. The bodies had been preserved in wine. He spit furiously, knowing that alcohol was dangerous to his system.

The body—it was that of a middle-aged man in a toga—lay covered in glass. One foot floated away, severed by glass. It looked as if it were trailing blood, but Remo knew that the dead didn't bleed.

Chiun was suddenly tugging at his bare forearm and Remo floated for the ceiling opening. Chiun squeezed through easily. Remo had to break off more coral before he made it.

Emerging from the outcropping, Remo was suddenly aware of the vast falling-away of the ocean floor on this side of the encrusted building. For miles to the east, there was rank upon rank of the strange coral formations. Not all were coral. There was a shattered tower not far away. A dome like an inverted cracked bowl expelled a string of blue-green fish. Silt kicked up from the ocean floor.

And Remo felt a coldness that had nothing to do with

the ocean temperature. He was looking upon Old Moo—what was left of it.

When his head broke the surface, Chiun was already there, taking measured breaths.

"It's all down there, isn't it?" Remo said. There was moisture on his face that wasn't seawater. His voice was twisted.

"Yes, my son," Chiun said sadly. "You have been privileged to visit that which no man—not even Moovian man—has seen since the young sun of earth's past touched those buildings. Old Moo."

"We shouldn't have disturbed them. Look what happened."

"Have no regrets, Remo. We did not cause that disturbance. It was a shifting of the ocean floor."

"Moo really sank. The whole thing. And it stretched forever in all directions."

"Think not that any empire is forever. Even your America exists only at the whim of the universe."

Remo was silent a long time. "What was that place? With the bodies?"

"The Royal Tomb of the Line of Moo. The High Moo told me that it would be found there."

"You led me there on purpose. Why?"

"You were just along for the ride," Chiun said. "I wished to behold the face of the High Moo whom Master Mangko knew."

"Why?"

"Call me sentimental," Chiun said. And Remo laughed.

They struck off for land. Chiun paused at the junk and climbed aboard. Remo waited at his command. Chiun threw over a bag. Remo caught it. It jingled. He didn't have to open it to know it contained the coins given to Chiun by the Low Moo.

"Planning a shopping spree, Little Father?" Remo asked when Chiun splashed to his side. Chiun had donned an emerald-and-gold kimono.

"The High Moo kindly offered to store the entire payment in his treasure house while we sojourn on his island."

"I wish there was someplace we could store this junk."

"The typhoon season is months away," Chiun assured him.

They made land at the coral reef where the night before they had fought the octopus men. Remo passed the coins to Chiun while he plunged into the Grove of Ghosts. He found his shoes where he had left them and, sitting on the ground, tried to put them on. They wouldn't fit. His toenails were too long.

Cursing, he carried them out, past the totems. He knocked one off its base out of pique.

"Don't say you told me so," Remo said when Chiun saw him carrying his shoes.

"I won't."

"Good."

"But I did."

Remo's retort died in his mouth. Plunging through the jungle was a bouncing-bosomed maiden.

"*Wiki-wiki!* Oh, come! Men of Sinanchu!" she cried. "An assassin has struck down the High Moo. Hurry! *Wiki-wiki!*"

24

Shane Billiken recognized that people had different tastes. He could get next to that concept. It was real. People were individuals, after all. We shared the same planet. We were all connected, all part of the dao, but human diversity was one of the universal constants too.

"Okay, so you don't like cheese," he said. He tried to keep his voice even. It was hard when you were facing a half-dozen mercenaries armed with automatic weapons and there was no place to run. Unless you counted a hundred square miles of ocean. "But you could get used to it," he added hopefully. He smiled under his Ray-Bans.

"Cheese gives me gas," said Dirk Edwards, AKA Ed the Eliminator. He had decided that since they were over a hundred miles out of Southern California and the wind was good, it was time to chow down.

He had gone below to the larder whistling. He came up like a rogue elephant. When the word passed through the crew that the provisions aboard the newly christened *New Age Hope* consisted of three kinds of hard cheese and two soft, Shane Billiken, taking his turn at the wheel, found himself surrounded.

"I once wrote a whole book about cheeses," Shane went on quickly. "Do you know it's the perfect food? It provides calcium and iron, reduces stress, and is a natural anticarcinogen. Best of all—and I know you guys will appreciate this—when you apply it to boils and wounds, it promotes healing."

"Sounds like Southern California bullshit to me," growled Dirk Edwards.

"Maybe you heard that penicillin was first discovered in moldy bread. They used to apply moldy bread to wounds. It helped. It really did. My discovery is like that."

"That will come in real handy if we decide to shoot you," Dirk Edwards said.

"You wouldn't do that."

"We will if we don't eat."

"I'm sure there are other kinds of food on the island."

"We can't wait that long. Okay, men," Dirk said, turning to his people. "Keep an eye out for pleasure boats. Maybe," he laughed, "we can arrange a swap. In the meantime, we eat cheese."

No one looked happy. Their stony expressions darkened when they heard Shane Billiken answer Dirk's next question.

"Where's the water supply?"

"The bucket's down with the cheese," Shane told him.

"Bucket?"

"Yeah, and I brought a rope. You can help yourself," Shane said, flinging his arms out to encompass the entire Pacific with its cool sweet water.

Dirk Edwards blinked. In a too-low voice he said, "Excuse us a sec."

As Shane watched, the contingent retired to the bow. They formed a circle and conferred. Some of them began to shout. Others waved their arms. Angry glances were flung in Shane's direction and he went into an immediate mental calculation of the swimming distance back to Malibu. He decided it was N.G. Maybe, he thought, this would be a good time to get back into astral projection.

Finally the argument subsided and Dirk joined him at the wheel.

"My men and I have decided."

"I noticed you were getting in touch with your feelings back there."

"If we come across a pleasure boat or island where we can get food before dawn, we won't shoot you in the belly, dump you overboard, and sail for Central America."

"What's in Central America?" Shane asked in an attempt to redirect the conversation.

"A lot of good fighting."

"I brought binoculars," Shane said suddenly. "Why don't I go up the mast and see what I can find?"

"You do that," said Dirk Edwards, taking the wheel.

Two of the others worked the rope that sent the boatswain's chair up the mast. Shane Billiken searched the sea in all directions. He decided that he had made a mistake paying those men in advance. It took away their motivation. Imagine battle-hardened guys that talked mutiny just because the water was a little salty. Some of them looked like they drank carbolic acid.

The sun went down, the moon came up, and the seas remained as bare as newly laid asphalt.

But hours before dawn, Shane spied running lights on the water.

"Ship off the port bow!" he cried.

Everyone surged to the port rail.

"No," Shane called. "The other direction."

They surged to starboard and Shane winced at the looks being thrown up at him.

It was a cabin cruiser. Music floated across the water. A party boat. Or maybe night fishermen.

"How many aboard?" Dirk called up.

"I count five."

"Okay," Dirk said. "Tex. J.D. Go below and get them on the radio." He kicked the engine into idle. The *New Age Hope* settled in the water and described a lazy circle.

As Shane watched, the cabin cruiser abruptly heeled and came in their direction.

"Someone want to let me down now?" Shane asked as Tex and J.D. came up from below and gave Dirk the thumbs-up sign.

"Better not," Dirk said laconically. "You might catch a stray."

"Stray what?" Shane asked as the sudden eruption of automatic-weapons fire drowned out his words.

Across the water, the cabin cruiser began spitting splinters. The man in the wheelhouse corkscrewed into a pool of his own blood. The partiers dived under the gunwales. But the gunwales were methodically chewed down to deck level by a fusillade of bullets. One man jumped overboard. Bullet tracks crisscrossed the water in front of him. Unwittingly he swam into them. He bobbed like a cork when they hit him, and floundered briefly before going down.

When Shane Billiken pulled his hands away from his Ray-Bans, Dirk was lowering the dinghy over the side. He rowed for the cabin cruiser. Minutes later he returned with several coolers filled with beer and raw steaks.

After the *New Age Hope* got under way again, the cabin cruiser exploded. Bat-size splinters rained from the boiling fireball that lifted over the place it had been.

"Time-delay fuse," Dirk remarked as they lowered Shane to the deck. Shane's legs collapsed under him.

"Beer?" asked Dirk nonchalantly.

"No, no," Shane croaked. "Did you have to kill them?"

"Hell, you hired us to kill, didn't you?"

"But that was different. Those were real people."

"Hell," Dirk Edwards chortled, hoisting a can to the burning patch of water, "we do real people too. No extra charge."

25

They found the High Moo seated on his Shark Throne. It stood in the open courtyard. The High Moo clutched one muscular bicep. Blood trailed crazily from an unseen wound. Moovian maidens came with pestles of hot ash, which they carefully applied to the wound.

The Low Moo paced distractedly, pulling at her hair.

"Not all the octopus worshipers have been purged," the Low Moo complained. She stuck out her sensuous lower lip like a pouting child.

"Impossible," said Chiun. "The priest did not lie."

"He was a traitor," growled the High Moo, wincing as the cauterizing hot ash stung him. "Of course he lied."

"The priest could not lie, O High Moo," Chiun went on stubbornly. "No man is capable of untruth when the iron hand of Sinanju squeezes from him his inmost thoughts."

"I was attacked on this very spot. I did not see the traitor. But I struck him with my war club. I drew blood. I would have slain him had I not been felled."

Remo's eyes went to the war club resting against the High Moo's muscular calf. The dark wood was crushed in one spot, and flecks of skin and blood clung to the patch.

"A man of royal blood should not raise his hand in combat," said Chiun. "Leave such distasteful chores to us, your assassins."

"No man who is a man runs from combat," spat the High Moo.

Chiun winced. He composed himself and pressed on. "For twenty coins I will bring you his carcass."

"Bring me his head and I will not keep the coins you falsely earned when you claimed to have rid my island of octopus worshipers."

Chiun's hand went to his wispy beard. His mouth opened as if to speak. What manner of emperor was this, who sullied his hands with weapons and did not understand the inviolateness of the word of the Master of Sinanju? Chiun stroked his beard in silence. His eyes narrowed. When he spoke, his words were like pearls sinking into a jar of thick honey. Slow but clear.

"I will bring this wicked one to you alive, that he may tell you the truth of my words himself. And if his words please you, I will ask again for twenty coins."

"I have ruled this island for all my adult life," the High Moo said. He seemed to be speaking to the Moovians surrounding him and not to Chiun. "And my father before him and his father before him, back to the days when Ru-Taki-Nuhu first closed his slumberous orbs. No High Moo ever faced such ingratitude for the gifts he has bestowed upon his people. No High Moo was ever less appreciated."

"I know how it is to be unappreciated," Chiun said proudly. "And I vow that once this matter is settled, I will see to it that henceforth no Moovian will fail to pay proper respect to his liege." And Chiun fixed the gathering crowd with his steady gaze while Remo stood aside, his arms folded, trying to follow the rapid stream of Moovian words.

The High Moo waved the Master of Sinanju away, as if to dismiss his protestations of loyalty as trifling.

Chiun's kimono skirts swirled with the force of his sudden about-face. He marched off.

Remo caught up a few minutes later.

"The High Moo's in a bad mood, huh?" he offered.

"He is entitled. For he is surrounded by ingratitude. A common problem among those who are heir to long lines of honorable ancestry. Some believe that distinguished parentage is not earned."

"Really?"

"Orphans and the lowborn are especially susceptible to this fallacy," Chiun said pointedly.

"You can't mean me," Remo said ironically. "Being an American, I was probably born on the upper floor of a hospital."

Chiun did not reply. Remo noticed that his eyes had fixed upon the ground, Chiun led him off the foot-beaten path and into the jungle. Remo saw a drop of blood glisten on a leaf. Another darkened the soil many feet beyond it. Chiun was following the blood spoor of the failed killer.

Like malignant rubies, the drops led to one of the many mines which dotted Moo like empty eyes. This mine had fallen into disuse. Foliage had overgrown its bamboo-shored mouth. A few branches were broken and trampled.

"How do you say 'Come out, come out, wherever you are' in Moovian?" Remo joked.

The Master of Sinanju brushed past him and stormed into the dark tunnel.

Remo had to duck to get through the entrance. Ahead of him, Chiun walked tall and defiant. The High Moo's accusation had stung him, and Remo knew that the would-be killer faced a terrible fate once Chiun laid hands on him.

Remo crouched as he walked. His hands brushed the loose tunnel walls. They were dry and gritty like pumice. Probably volcanic residue. The tunnel meandered like a snail track, as if the burrowing Moovians had followed the metal deposits as they found them rather than systematically working the mine. The moisture increased the deeper they went, and Remo realized they were below sea level.

The tunnel ended in a cul-de-sac of mud. The floor was a brown puddle and the lower walls were mud. And squatting in the water was a young Moovian with hunted eyes.

He bared his teeth at Chiun's approach.

"You have committed a foul deed against the House of Moo," the Master of Sinanju told him.

"I will no longer work the mines," the Moovian spat. "All my life I have worked in the mines. And all the coins end up in the High Moo's treasure house. None for his workers. None for the people." He felt his hair. His hand came away sticky with blood.

"You are not an octopus worshiper, then?" Chiun asked.

"No," he sneered. "I am Ca-Don-Ho, slayer of kings."

"The High Moo lives, and after you have repeated your words for him, you will die," Chiun promised gravely.

"Wait a minute, Chiun," Remo put in. "Let's hear this guy out. I think he has some valid complaints here."

"He is a hater of royalty. I know his ilk. I will listen no more." And so saying, the Master of Sinanju stepped into the mud to retrieve the man for his emperor.

Ca-Don-Ho uncoiled like a spring. His hands sought the Master of Sinanju's wattled throat. But the Master of Sinanju was quicker still. He struck the man in the side of the head. Ca-Don-Ho went down. He shook his head angrily.

And then, reaching for a knife tucked in his loincloth, he attacked the mud wall. He threshed and splashed, causing the Master of Sinanju to withdraw hastily—but only to avoid having his kimono soiled by mud.

"He is mad," Chiun whispered in English.

"I don't think so," Remo said, jumping for the man.

Remo was too late. The muddy wall suddenly crumbled and a torrent of water surged over the man. He went down, laughing wildly.

Remo backpedaled. Chiun was already ahead of him. They ran swiftly, whipping around twisting corners just ahead of the wall of water that chased them all the way to the surface.

Remo and Chiun shot out of the mine as if propelled. They kept moving. The water crested and collapsed. The ground soon drank it up. The body of the would-be king slayer floated out with the last blurp of water and was deposited on the wet turtle grass.

Remo walked up to him.

"Guess he won't be telling the High Moo anything."

"You were witness to his words," Chiun said. He gave the dead man's ribs a vicious kick. The splintery sound that it brought was muffled.

"The High Moo may not buy it, you know."

"And why not?"

"Because he thinks I'm a slave."

Chiun said nothing for a long time. He kicked the dead man's ribs again. "Bring this bag of meat."

As Remo stopped to pick him up, something glinted in the water-disturbed soil. He plucked it up.

"Hey, I found one of the High Moo's coins."

"Good. We will return it to the High Moo."

"Why? I found it."

"All coins belong to the High Moo. This is why his face adorns them."

"That's what this guy said. But what good is money if you don't spread it around?"

"It is power," said Chiun, putting out his hand.

"I say it's mine," Remo countered. He looked at the coin again. "Check this out, Chiun, It's got a different High Moo's face on it."

Chiun snatched the coin away. "All the more reason to return it promptly. All coins are melted down and recast when a new High Moo ascends the throne. This one bears the face of an earlier High Moo. It will soon bear the profile of the High Moo we serve . . ."

Chiun's voice trailed off. He lifted the coin to the light.

"Don't tell me it's counterfeit," Remo said.

Chiun frowned. The coin disappeared up one voluminous sleeve.

"Pick up the dead one," he said, starting off. "And say nothing about this coin to anyone."

"Yeah?" Remo remarked lightly, hefting the body over his shoulders. "Do I smell a mystery?"

"It is probably your socks," Chiun said haughtily. "They reek."

26

The High Moo would have none of it.

"He confessed to being lazy," Chiun insisted. "He did not like to work in your mines, the ingrate. But he was no octopus worshiper. He told us so. Tell him, Remo." Chiun pushed Remo before the High Moo like an idiot child about to recite an important school lesson.

"It's true," Remo said. "I heard him say so."

"You bring me a dead body and the word of a mere slave?" spat the High Moo.

"Told you so," Remo whispered to Chiun in English. He couldn't resist throwing in a knowing grin.

"He is dead. The last octopus worshiper is no more," Chiun went on in an agitated voice.

"He is not dead enough," said the High Moo, who then took up his hardwood club and proceeded to beat the body into a shapeless bloody lump. He took his time about this, working around the body methodically. He saved the head for last.

Remo, watching the High Moo at work, said, "I'm cutting out. This isn't my thing."

Even the Master of Sinanju was sickened.

The Moovians watched stonily. They neither turned away nor seemed ill-at-ease. They looked, if anything, resigned. Only the Low Moo looked away. She was plucking hibiscus blossoms. She discarded them carelessly until she found one she liked. Then she put it in her hair over her left ear.

When the High Moo was finished, he stood on bowed and sweaty legs.

"Take this thing away," he ordered his Red Feather Guard. "Boil the traitorous flesh from his leg bones and I will have them for swords. They will remind all plotters of their fate."

The body was carted off by four guards, each lugging a wrist or ankle.

"I speak the truth," Chiun told the High Moo after he had sunk back onto his Shark Throne. The High Moo wiped sweat off his brow. His underarms exuded a sweaty stench that made Chiun's nose wrinkle distastefully.

"We will soon know," said the High Moo. His chest heaved from his exertions. "For if no one harms my person between now and the next moon, I will allow you to take away your full payment."

"One who is protected by Sinanju need fear nothing," Chiun said flintily.

"I look around me and my stomach is uneasy," the High Moo said pointedly.

Chiun clapped his hands. The thunder sent birds winging from distant trees.

"Why are you all standing around?" he cried. "Your emperor is safe. Get you to your work. The rice fields need tending. The mines are empty. Be gone, you lazy sons and daughters of the greatest empire of ancient times."

Moovians scattered in all directions. Children fled for the safety of their mothers. And Chiun, seeing the effect of his words, turned to the High Moo and bowed once, formally.

"See that my kingdom runs smoothly," said the High Moo through heavy-lidded eyes, "and I will reward you handsomely upon your departure."

The Master of Sinanju did not observe the cunning smiled that wreathed the High Moo's face as he took his leave.

Chiun found Remo walking along the eastern shore. The sun beat down on Remo's bare chest and the Master of Sinanju noticed that the red sucker marks on his arms and chest were very red. Remo's face was tight and troubled.

"Nice emperor you serve," Remo remarked acidly when Chiun padded up beside him.

"*We* serve," Chiun corrected. But his bell-like voice was subdued.

"Not me. I'm just a lowly slave. And an orphan."

Chiun said nothing. The sun was setting and the shadows lengthened along the white beach. They walked together, Chiun's hands inside his belled sleeves. Remo rotated his thick wrists unconsciously. It was a habit that surfaced when he was preoccupied.

"A month is too long," Remo said, breaking the silence.

"I have been making a list," Chiun said, as if not hearing. "I have been listing all kings and princes who still rule kingdoms in the modern world."

"Maybe next time you'll remember the crossword puzzles."

"It is a very short list."

"Life goes on," Remo said in a bored voice.

"And my life has gone on longer than yours. Perhaps in the next century, as Westerners reckon time, the world will right itself and sane statecraft will prevail once more. There may again be kings and princes aplenty in the years to come. But I may never know them. You may, Remo, but I will not. Not that I am old."

"No, not you."

"But I live a dangerous life. And the future is unknowable, even to a Master of Sinanju."

"But you've got the past locked down tight."

"The High Moo may be the only true emperor my Mastership will know. I have a month. A month to savor true service. Would you begrudge me that month, Remo?"

"No. But we both have to answer to Smith. And he pays better. He pays in gold. Not silver or platinum or whatever those coins are."

Chiun separated his sleeves to reveal the coin Remo had found in the ground.

"This is more precious than silver. Rarer than platinum. Any patch of dirt will yield those metals. But coins such as these were thought lost when Moo was lost."

"I'll bet we have a time figuring out the exchange rate when we get back," Remo joked.

Chiun regarded his wavering reflection in the coin's polished surface.

"Come," he said abruptly.

"Where?"

"I must compare this coin to those in the High Moo's treasure house."

"Why not? It'll kill an afternoon."

As they picked their way inland, they passed the mines.

Men were hauling coconut shells heaping with dirt out in fire-brigade fashion and making a pile. In the fields, the children toiled. No one looked happy, and Remo remarked on that observation.

"For islanders, they're a pretty morose lot."

"You first saw them at their best. At the feast. Do you really believe your fantasies of happy brown people basking in the sun indulging in free love all day and night?"

"Oh, I don't know," Remo said airily, rubbing the red marks on his arms. "Some myths might have a kernel of truth."

Chiun eyed him doubtfully. He went on: "You see the Moovians as they are in their ordinary life. Would you judge Americans by their behavior during the festival of the Nazarene?"

"I might if I knew what that was."

"The feast's name escapes me. Jesus Time, I think it is called."

"You mean Christmas?"

"Possibly. The exact names of unimportant pagan festivals are not worth memorizing."

"That sounds really convincing coming from someone whose national holiday is the Feast of the Pig," Remo said dryly. "Where are we going, by the way? I don't remember having the treasure house pointed out to us."

"It is no doubt in a secret location. But we will find it. We have only to go to the source."

Chiun led Remo into the village proper. He walked with his head cocking to each side, listening. Chiun homed in on the sound of metallic clickings and hammerings. It came from a one-story stone hut behind the palace.

Chiun entered.

"Greetings, metalsmiths to the High Moo."

A circle of bronze faces looked up from their work. The men squatted before a stone oven. They were beating lumps of coin metal into the proper shape. In a corner one man, with skin like dried and stretched beef, was etching the High Moo's profile into the finished coins. A neat stack of newly minted coins sat beside him.

No one reacted to Chiun's intrusion. Their faces were sullen.

"By order of the High Moo, I have come to escort the

newest coins to their proper place," Chiun said in an important voice.

The old man gathered up his coins in a square of cloth. He tied the four corners into a knot and presented himself to Chiun, the coins clinking in the makeshift sack.

"I will be your guard," Chiun told him.

The old man muttered something out of the side of his mouth that Remo didn't catch.

"What did he say?" Remo asked in English.

"Something about foreigners taking away all the coins."

"Meaning?"

"I think he resents that we will one day leave Moo with some of the fruits of his labors."

"What's it to him?" Remo asked. They followed the men into the forest. "The coins all belong to the High Moo anyway."

"Some people grow intolerant as they get along in years."

"No!" Remo said in a mock-aghast voice.

Chiun nodded sagely. "Indeed. Wisdom is not always the end result of long life."

"My last illusion is shattered. I have met my first emperor-in-the-raw and he looks like a Hawaiian wrestler, and his wise subjects aren't wise at all, only bigoted."

"Do not judge all Moovians by one cranky example," Chiun warned.

The old man brought them to the center of a cleared area. Lightning had blasted a banyan tree and it had toppled across the stump of another tree that had been leveled by hand. The old man set down his bag of coins and pushed the tree aside. The easy way in which he accomplished that feat indicated that it was hollow.

The old man took a bone knife and inserted it into the tree stump. He levered the flat top upward and set it aside.

Remo and Chiun gathered around. As they had expected, the stump had been hollowed out. Coins glinted in stacks directly beneath the opening. They stood in nearly three feet of water.

"Some treasure house," Remo said. "A tree stump."

"Which coins are mine?" Chiun asked anxiously.

The old man shrugged. "Whichever the High Moo decrees."

"But the coins presented me by the Low Moo are special coins."

"They are all the same. I know. Of all others, I know."

"No. Those are historic. They are artifacts of the first contact between our two houses in generations."

The old man shrugged as if to say that Chiun's excited protestations were as important as the distinction between grains of beach sand.

"What's the big deal, Chiun?" Remo asked. "Gold is gold. Silver is silver."

"They were special coins," Chiun squeaked, peering intently. The stacks were closely packed. None stood apart from the others.

The old man knelt beside the stump and lowered his arms into the water, setting the coins atop different piles.

"He is covering every pile!" Chiun snapped. "He is mixing the coins. This is terrible!"

When the old man was done, he replaced the stump lid. Remo put the shattered tree back. When he was done, he noticed that the old man had left without a word of farewell.

"Get what you came for?" Remo asked.

"I saw the coin faces. They were minted in the Fifth Year of the Third Cycle."

"Yeah?"

"That is the year the current High Moo ascended the throne. Fix that in your memory, Remo, for it is important."

"I'd write it down, but at the moment I'm strangely bereft of crayons."

"This coin," Chiun went on, holding the other one up, "was minted in the Fifth Year of the Third Cycle also."

"So? The High Moo is dead. Long live the High Moo. Isn't that the way it usually goes?"

Chiun's papery lips thinned. He replaced the coin in his robes.

"Say nothing of this to anyone." And Chiun marched off.

"My lips are sealed," Remo said to the surrounding forest. "Even if I knew what the heck you were talking about—and I don't—who would I tell? Every time I try to speak two sentences in Moovian, everyone for three miles around breaks out in hysterics."

27

The credit-card bill went to a post-office box in Lander, Texas, where a postal employee, who thought that monthly supplementary check came from the CIA, was under instructions to send it to a mail-forwarding service in Chicago, which relayed it to Folcroft Sanitarium in Rye, New York, by express mail. With the current state of the U.S. Postal Service, this system took a minimum of six weeks and sometimes as long as nine.

Thus the bill was already overdue when it finally crossed Smith's desk. He put it aside for the moment as he tried once again to contact Michael Brunt in Boston. Brunt's secretary informed him that Mr. Brunt was out of town. Smith distinctly heard the sound of gum cracking as he hung up in distaste.

Then the blue-and-orange express envelope caught Smith's eye. He opened the nearly indestructable Tivek envelope with shears.

Inside, there was an American Express credit-card bill made out to Remo Robeson, one of the many fictitious identities and accounts Smith had created for Remo's use. This was the name on his American Express card. Smith examined the bill.

It listed a variety of purchases, including a tractor lawn mower and a big-screen projection TV. Smith couldn't imagine what Remo would need a lawn mower for, but in years past, odd items had cropped up on his expense accounts, the most puzzling of which was an industrial ice-scraping machine whose only purpose was to clear the ice between hockey games. Smith never asked what Remo had needed with such a thing. Not after the time five refrigerators showed up on the account and Remo had informed Smith, when asked, that he had given them away to deserving families who had been burnt out of a split duplex apartment house in Detroit.

The other charges were an airline flight and something purchased from a concern called Malibu Marine. Smith blinked.

"Can't be," he muttered. "This must be in error."

The charge was sixty thousand dollars. Smith called the airline first. He was informed that the flight originated in New York City and terminated in Los Angeles, with no connecting flight booked on that airline. Was there a problem with the charge?

Smith said no and hung up. The Malibu Marine charge was dated one day after the airline flight. He called Malibu Marine.

"I am calling about a charge on my American Express card," he told the manager. "Can you verify that price? Sixty thousand dollars."

"That's right. Is there a problem?"

"I'm not certain. Exactly what was purchased?"

"It's your card. Don't you know?"

"I am co-signatory. My nephew also has use of this card."

"Well, I hope you have deep pockets. He bought a junk. Right now, he's somewhere out where the buses don't run."

"Junk," Smith gasped, envisioning Remo purchasing the contents of an entire junkyard for some frivolous purpose. "He spent sixty thousand dollars on junk!"

"No, not *junk* junk. A junk."

"Beg pardon?"

"He bought a Chinese junk. Sailed off in it right away, too."

"Oh. Did he say where he was going?"

"No, he and this elderly Chinese guy just hopped aboard and sailed off. They had a gal with them."

"Did they say anything that would lead you to guess at their destination?" Smith inquired.

"Nope. Once the charge was verified, they went out with the tide. Say, you *can* cover these charges, can't you?"

"Yes, of course. Thank you for your time." And with that, Dr. Harold W. Smith hung up. His face was an etching. The title might have been "Pain." Without looking, he reached into his desk drawer and brought out a bottle. He needed an aspirin badly.

Smith was so intent on his thoughts that he failed to notice that he was chewing on an Alka-Seltzer tablet and not aspirin.

Remo and Chiun had left the country. They had gone without a word. What could have happened? Had he offended the Master of Sinanju somehow? And would Remo have gone with him if he had?

All that Dr. Harold W. Smith could imagine was that Remo and Chiun had returned to the village of Sinanju on the West Korea Bay. And he was alone against whoever had bought the mysterious house next to his own.

Suddenly realizing that he had eaten an entire aspirin without benefit of water, Smith drew a paper cup of mineral water from the office dispenser and drank it. For the remainer of the day he wondered why his headache persisted and he kept belching uncontrollably.

28

Remo heard the scream and reached for his pants.

"Excuse me," he said as he darted from the room. It was night. The Royal Palace of Moo was dark except for the odd places where moonlight cast geometric patterns of light.

Chiun emerged from his bedroom, his face grim. Together, without a word, they ran down the corridor leading to the High Moo's bedroom, their bare feet slapping the cool stones.

The High Moo confronted them at the door. He waved his war club angrily. It was spattered with blood, as was the High Moo's greasy chest.

"There were three of them," he thundered, gesticulating wildly. "Two have gotten away."

Groans came from behind the High Moo. He stepped aside to show a Moovian sitting on the floor. The man was holding his red-splashed arm. His forearm was bent below the elbow joint. A jagged spear of bone stuck out. It was broken.

"They forget. How easily they forget." The High Moo grinned.

A Moovian girl slipped up behind Remo. She held her bare breasts in fear. Her mouth gaped open.

"What is that peasant girl doing in my palace?" the High Moo thundered. "Is she another traitor?"

"No, she's with me," Remo said evenly.

Chiun turned on Remo. "With you?"

"We were together," Remo said. "You know."

"We will speak of this later," Chiun warned.

The Low Moo crept out from an adjoining room. She took one look at the peasant girl, and the girl retreated in fear.

"Are you safe, my father?" the Low Moo asked.

"Traitors. I am beset by traitors," he said bitterly.

"Let's round up the usual suspects," Remo said in English.

"Allow me to dispatch that base traitor," Chiun said, pointing to the broken-armed assailant.

"He is nothing. The ones who roam free are the threat," the High Moo said. His Red Feather Guard showed up at that moment.

"We could not find them," the captain of the guard reported.

"Then it is up to Sinanchu," the High Moo said pointedly. "If they hope to leave Moo with their full measure of coins."

Remo and Chiun left the palace. Out in the courtyard, Remo said, "He's sure getting a lot of service for payment that was supposed to be in the bag."

"That man was not an octopus worshiper. He will admit that later. At this moment we must get the other two."

"Want to split up?"

"No. Stay with me." And Chiun flashed through the foliage. People were stirring at the sight of them; faces retreated into doorways.

"Reminds me of when I was a cop," Remo said unhappily.

"Their fear will vanish once we have eliminated the plotters."

"At the rate we're going, we're on our way to depopulating all of Moo."

Chiun was following tracks in the dirt. The tracks veered off into the jungle, and from there the trail was one of broken stems and crushed grass that slowly straightened.

The trail led down to the south beach and into the water.

The Pacific sparkled. No shadows dotted its surface.

"Looks like we lost them. Octopus worshipers or not."

Chiun watched the water. When he was certain no swimmer would surface, he spoke.

"I do not think they were octopus worshipers, although they fled into the ocean. Come, we must inform the High Moo."

As they walked back, Chiun spoke up.

"That girl. What was she to you?"

"I don't know. I'd only known her ten minutes when the trouble started."

"Ten?"

"She came in through the window."

"Obviously a tramp," sniffed Chiun.

"If she was, that's how they grow them on Moo."

Chiun stopped. "There were others?"

"Yeah," Remo admitted. "A few."

Chiun's eyes became slits. "How many?"

"Oh, five or sex—I mean six."

"So many!" Chiun demanded hotly. "You have lain with five or six maidens in three nights?"

"Actually, I'm just counting tonight. I don't know how many there were on the other nights."

"*Aiieee!*" Chiun screeched. "Are you mad? Have you given no thought to the diseases these girls may carry?"

"Little Father," Remo said gently, "we're on an island with maybe two hundred inhabitants, tops. And with the way these girls behave, one sexually transmitted disease would have wiped everyone out long before we got here."

"I cannot believe you."

"Hey, this is an island. No radio. No TV. No place to go that doesn't look like every other place here. I'm bored. Besides, it was their idea. They keep sneaking in through my window."

"You could have turned them away," Chiun huffed.

"I'm entitled to a little fun."

"And did you have it? This fun?"

"Well, I'm not sure. It's interesting, but you know how it is with sex when you're a Master of Sinanju."

"Yes, you do it properly and get it out of the way so that you can go on to important things."

"That's been my problem with it, all right. I get up to step two in the thirty-seven steps to sexual fulfillment and the party of the second part has been to cloud nine and back twice while I'm left waiting for the fireworks that never come. So to speak."

"Sex is a drug. It is better to be the supplier than the imbiber."

"I used to like imbibing. But you know what's strange, Little Father?" Remo's voice sank into a hushed tone, no longer testy.

"Many things are strange, you most of all."

"These island girls are just like I always imagined they would be. Except for one thing. Sex is like chewing bubble gum to them. Once it's over, zoom, they're out the window. Wham, bang, thank you, Remo. I don't even get to ask if it was good for them too."

"I told you American women would be more to your taste. Unlike Moo girls, they are raised to think of sex as a forbidden riddle. They spin webs of magic and mystery around the simple act itself. No wonder they spend more of their time talking about it than doing it. No wonder all your Western songs are dirty."

"That's a gross generalization. Which songs are dirty?"

" 'I Wanna Hold Your Hand' is a prime specimen."

"That's not dirty."

"It always starts with hand-holding," Chiun snapped. "Come, the High Moo awaits. Say nothing of your night escapades to him."

"I was hoping I could ask him a few questions about Moovian courtship practices."

"Such as?"

"Why the marks on my arm, for one thing."

Chiun skidded to a stop. He examined Remo's extended arms.

"These marks are redder than before," he murmured. "They should be fading."

"The octopus-sucker marks are fading," Remo pointed out. "These are fresh marks."

"I do not understand."

"They're . . . uh . . . bite marks."

"Bite?"

"That's what I'm talking about," Remo said excitedly. "They don't kiss. They bite. I can't figure it out."

"Who bites? Which has bitten you?"

"The girls. All of them. They don't seem to know what kissing is. I hope this isn't some kind of savage engagement ritual, because if it is, look out, I'm betrothed to half the female population of Moo."

"The peasant girls bite?" Chiun repeated. He turned Remo's arms over. The rose-colored marks were everywhere. Even under Remo's armpits, he saw with revulsion.

"The Low Moo does it too," Remo told him.

"You slept with the Low Moo!" Chiun demanded, his nails digging into Remo's arms.

"Not yet," Remo said, extricating himself from Chiun's clutch. "I mean, no, I haven't. But when we were on the junk, she nipped me a couple of times. I think she likes me."

"There is no mention of biting in the records of our house."

"Must be new."

"Come," Chiun ordered curtly.

"If only," Remo sighed.

"Must you turn everything into a dirty joke?"

"Let me remind you, in case it's slipped your mind, that I wouldn't have come along on this one if you hadn't dangled the promise of a bevy of bare-breasted maidens."

"I did not promise you the use of them. Only the sight."

"That's how it always begins," Remo said. "Even before the hand holding."

"And do not let me catch you making eyes at the Low Moo, Remo. You must respect the royal family. Marriage is another matter. But dalliance creates problems. She is, without doubt, a virgin."

"No wonder she's so revered," Remo remarked dryly. "They're practically an extinct species around here."

They found the High Moo in his bedroom, straddling the injured assailant. He was twisting the man's broken arm cruelly. The man screamed. He was crying over and over that he knew nothing more.

The High Moo twisted again, and the screams would have scraped rust off an old tin can.

Finally the High Moo gave up.

"He says he knew not the other ones," the High Moo told Chiun. "He admitted his intent to slay me. The others also desired my life, but he claims he was not with them. Obviously he lies."

"He speaks the truth," Chiun intoned. "I can tell by the fear in his voice. And the pain was enough to impel truth from him, but I will try."

The man cringed and whimpered as Chiun approached him. To his surprise, the Master of Sinanju touched a wrist nerve and the pain fled from his broken arm. Chiun knelt beside him. He carefully forced the protruding bone into place. He set the bone with sure fingers.

As relief flooded the man's face, Chiun pinched him by an earlobe. The man knew true pain then. He bit back his screams.

"Speak! Speak!" Chiun called. "The quicker you speak, the sooner the pain goes away. Who were the other plotters?"

"I did not see their faces. They were not with me. I do not think they were together." His face was a grimace of agony, and tears leaked from his squinched-shut eyes.

"Lies!" spat the High Moo.

"No," said Chiun. "Not lies. One more question. Are you an octopus worshiper?"

"Never. I swear by Kai, god of the holy sea."

Chiun let go of the man's earlobe. He rose grimly and faced the High Moo.

"I have proven to you that the octopus worshipers are not behind this."

"Perhaps," the High Moo said grudgingly.

"But the danger to your throne is greater. Other plotters are at work. And they are not working together. Your enemies are many, and therefore more difficult to deal with."

"Double your payment if you expose them all," the High Moo suddenly roared.

"Done," said Chiun. "Now I will dispose of this carrion."

"No!" said the High Moo.

"No?" Chiun was aghast.

"I have lost many subjects since your arrival."

"Enemies all."

"But still my subjects. I need every hand to work my mines. And to tend the fields. This one will be put to work when his arms heals."

"A serpent that is not crushed knows no gratitude. His fangs are forever a danger."

"You have performed good service for the night. Now leave me. All of you. I will sleep."

"Remo and I will stand guard outside your door."

"Ixnay, Chiun," Remo hissed. "I haven't had a wink of sleep since I got here."

"Is that my fault?" Chiun said in English. He reverted

to Moovian and told the High Moo: "We will be without your door should you require us."

But the High Moo was no longer listening. He had lain back on his sleeping pad and was already snoring.

The Red Feather Guard dragged the assailant out of the room by his ankles. The last to leave, Chiun closed the rattan door behind him.

When they were alone, Remo asked, "Mind if I pop back into my room for a second?"

"Have you forgotten something?"

"My socks," Remo said, wiggling his toes. The nails stuck out like talons.

"They will be ripped by those nails."

"I'll wear them loose. Like a Moovian girl." And Remo grinned when Chiun shooed him on his way. With luck there would be another delectable maiden waiting for him in the room. Maybe this time he could take it past step two. It wasn't much, but in a land devoid of TV and newspaper comics strips, it was the only diversion Remo had.

29

It had been over a week without any word from Remo and Chiun.

Dr. Harold W. Smith replayed the tape of Remo's last message. He played it twice.

"What could he have meant by 'moo'?" Smith said aloud. His dry words bounced off his office walls. He replayed the sentence wherein Remo spoke of "going to moo" several times.

Sliding over to his desk terminal, Smith called up the geographic atlas data base. In it was contained the name of every town, city, and locality in the entire world. He typed in the name Moo, because although Remo had made it sound as if he were going to imitate a cow, that made no sense in the context of their disappearance. Smith hit the Search key.

Several minutes later the screen read out a scroll of names that began with the letters "m-o-o." There was a Moore, Oklahoma, a Moorhead, Minnesota and others. But no Moo, USA. The only possibilities left were in exotic places like India and Tibet. But none were known simply as Moo, either. Smith considered this inconclusive because his information-gathering ability was next to useless in underdeveloped countries where the pencil and index card still ruled.

Smith paused. On a hunch, he input a phonetic equivalent: Mu.

The search produced a seemingly endless string of names. Smith frowned as he recalled that the letter M was one of the commonest when it came to personal and place names. There was, however, one place name spelled simply Mu. Eagerly Smith called up the file. His face fell when he saw that it contained data on a mythical island nation believed by pseudo-scientists to have existed in the Pacific Ocean before the dawn of recorded history, but which had sunk during a natural cataclysm.

Obviously that was not the Mu Remo had meant. It had never existed. And even if it had ever been a reality, which Smith thought improbable, all that remained of it was an additional layer of sediment at the bottom of the Pacific.

30

The sun kissed his face through the open window and Remo awoke. It was mid-morning. He had slept late again. All night, there had been a steady stream of Moovian maidens who had slipped through his window. He had counted eight, a new high. Remo wondered what had caused the increased traffic and, between bouts, put his head out the rough-hewn window.

His discovered several maidens crouching and talking in whispers. When they saw him, they flashed identical easy smiles.

"It is Oahula's turn next," one remarked casually.

"You're taking turns!" Remo had said in surprise.

When it was pointed out to him that he had only one male organ, Remo apologized for being so silly and added that of course if it was Oahula's turn, who was he to disrupt the orderly procession of Moovian events.

After he woke up, Remo felt his enthusiasm for Moovian maidens cooling. He decided that this was it. No more nocturnal interruptions. It had been fun for a while, but now the luster had worn off. Especially now that he understood he was being regarded as the island's free stud service.

Besides, they were biting even harder now.

Remo pulled on his now-frayed pants and walked barefoot out of the palace. The courtyard was deserted except for a handful of children who were lazily sweeping it clean with straw brooms.

When they saw him, the children pointed and giggled. They had never done that before. Must be my fingernails, Remo thought, looking at his hands. They were now half as long as Chiun's. And there was nothing he could do about it. The knives were too brittle. And even the densest rock wasn't hard enough to file them down. He couldn't understand it.

As he walked from the village, the children called after him. Their childish words were hard to understand, but they were calling him Hokko-ili. "Hokko" translated as "yellow," but "ili" was less clear. It sounded like "ilo," the Moovian word for "pineapple."

"Why are they calling me 'yellow pineapple'?" Remo asked as he drew near Chiun. The Master of Sinanju stood atop one of the largest mines in Moo. Men popped in and out at regular intervals, hauling coconut shells full of gritty black soil. They made a huge pile. Others spread the soil over stretched bolts of coarse cloth to sift out the metal.

Chiun turned at Remo's approach. His face lost its stern, commanding appearance.

"What has happened to your face?" Chiun wanted to know.

Remo reached up. "Got me. Is it still there?"

"You have a beard," Chiun snapped.

"Tell me about it," Remo said, feeling the thick stubble.

Chiun climbed down and motioned for Remo to bend at the waist. He picked through Remo's scalp in silence.

"Cooties?" Remo asked.

"Worse."

"Worse?"

"Your hair is turning yellow at the roots."

"Yellow?"

"The sun must be bleaching it. Perhaps the salt water is also responsible."

"I never had this problem when I was young," Remo remarked.

"It is strange. The yellow is in the roots, not the tips. Although your beard is yellow throughout."

"Is that why they're calling me names?" Remo asked, straightening.

"They were calling you 'yellow pineapple,' 'yellow head'."

"I've been called worse."

"I see you have had a strenuous evening," Chiun sniffed, looking at Remo's forearms and chest. They were covered with tiny inflamed blotches. Bite marks.

"I'm swearing off Moovian girls. They're practically drawing straws to see who gets the next crack at me. And I've gotten so used to bare breasts, I hardly notice them anymore."

"That is good, because the Low Moo has been looking for you."

"Is that so?" Remo said vaguely. "She's been cool to me ever since it got around that I haven't exactly been spending my nights counting the stars."

"It is good that you have come to your senses. For the Low Moo has that look on her face," Chiun said conspiratorially.

"What look?"

"You know."

"No. Spell it out."

"That sex-hungry look."

"Oh, *that* look. Don't look now, but isn't that her coming down from the palace?"

"I will leave you to deal with her. I must go to the rice fields. The peasants have been slacking off. Do not let these miners rest. Their break is not for another hour."

"They get breaks?"

"Naturally. The High Moo is an enlightened ruler."

"That wasn't what I meant," Remo said, watching the Low Moo's languid approach out of the corner of his eye. "You know, Chiun, this isn't the kind of gig I envisioned when you first started training me. I'm an assassin, not an overseer."

"Today you are an overseer," said Chiun. "And a good assassin protects his ruler's empire as his ruler expects it to be protected. It has been a week since the last attempt on the High Moo's life."

"That's because we've been riding herd on these poor people so much, it's all they can do to crawl off to sleep at day's end."

"It worked for Simon Legree too," Chiun remarked as he walked off.

After the Master of Sinanju had left, the miners watched Remo as if to measure him. When Remo turned his back on them, they slowed their work. A few sneaked off into the brush.

"*Ola!*" Remo said as the Low Moo drew near. The Low Moo's smile was ivory framed in copper. Her face possessed a soft childish look that still surprised Remo every time he thought back to how she had dealt with Horton Droney III.

"I have been looking for you, Remo. What happened to your hair?"

"It's not my hair I'm worried about, it's my fingernails," Remo said ruefully.

The Low Moo took Remo's hands in hers. "They are very long," she cooed. "Like talons, to claw and rend your enemies."

"I don't have any enemies at the moment."

"I know. Everyone likes you. Especially the peasant girls. Are you not tired of peasant girls by now? You have been on Moo a full week now."

"Yeah, actually I am."

The Low Moo's smile widened. It was dazzlingly white.

"That is good," she said, taking his forearm in her golden fingers.

"Uh-oh," Remo muttered.

"What is that you said?"

"It was English," Remo said quickly. "It means . . . you are very pretty today."

The Low Moo's smile broadened. She ran her fingers up to Remo's hard lean bicep, squeezing it hard, almost pinching it.

"Why do Moovian girls bite?" Remo asked suddenly. "Can you tell me that?"

"Because you are white. For generations, since the last white men came to our island and tried to make us embrace their one god, stories of the handsomeness of white men have been passed from mother to daughter. We have heard of your tallness, of your delectable white skin and potent organs."

"Organ. I only have one," said Remo. "I was just discussing the subject last night."

The Low Moo laughed.

"Do Moovian girls bite their own men?"

"Of course not. We kiss."

"Well, I'm still waiting for my first Moovian kiss."

"I will come to you tonight. But first I must ask my father an important favor."

"What's that?"

"Oh, I could not tell you. You might run away."

"Not me. There isn't anything I'm afraid of. And Chiun told me that you were probably a virgin anyway."

The Low Moo laughed. "There are no virgins on Moo. Not over the age of twelve."

"That's what I figured," Remo said dryly.

The Low Moo's face wrinkled suddenly. She glanced over Remo's shoulder. Remo turned.

"Why are those men not working?" she demanded petulantly.

"Them? Oh, I gave them a break," Remo lied.

"Their respite is not for another hour."

"What's the difference? They'll get back to work eventually. Besides, I don't see the point of all this beehive activity. You people have plenty of food for the taking. You should relax more."

"If my people did not have work, they would become lazy and lose their skills."

"I think they work too hard as it is."

"That is an attitude I would expect from a former slave. You do not understand rulership. How could my father and I rule if these peasants have no tasks set for them? Everyone would want to rule. Or none would. It would be terrible. Chaos. Like in the days after Old Moo disappeared under the waves." Saying that, the Low Moo stepped up to the squatting miners and, shaking her fists, began hectoring them in a high, bitter voice. She went on for several minutes, her beautiful face working in fury. She called them ungrateful for the purpose that work gave their indolent lives. She accused them of being lazy and disrespectful of tradition. Since the days of Old Moo, the empire had depended on the High Moo's coinage to maintain its power in the world. One day, thanks to their efforts, Moo would rise again as a great power. But not if the work stopped.

When she rejoined Remo, her features were soft and pliant again. It was as if a sudden tropical storm had come and gone.

"Okay, okay," Remo said. "You've made your point. I'll see that they don't slack off anymore."

"I will see you tonight," the Low Moo said gently. "I look forward to *pooning* you."

"Me too," said Remo. "Whatever you mean."

And the Low Moo ran off like a fawn, her tinkling laughter filtered through the leaves.

31

"This is it!" Shane Billiken shouted excitedly. "That's the island."

Dirk Edwards burst up from belowdeck. He was in his camouflage Jockey shorts. One hand gripped a nine-millimeter Browning that hung from a shoulder rig.

"You sure?" he growled.

"I dreamed on it last night."

"Yeah. And the last island you said was the right one turned out to be a guano preserve. So was the one before that. And you knew that was the right one because it was directly under the Little Dipper."

"Probably sunspot interference. I don't image well when there are sunspots. Look for a tall building. A temple."

"Let's look for the junk before we get carried away." Someone handed Dirk a set of binoculars. He trained them on the island.

"No sign of any junk," he reported.

"Probably on the other side," Shane said.

"I see unfriendlies, though. Natives."

"Let me see," Shane said, taking the glasses. He spied a number of natives at the shore. They wore few clothes. Their hair was black and their skin the color of cashews. They were busy dragging a sea turtle from the water.

"The girl looked like that!" Shane said. "The skin color is exactly right."

"Okay, we take them. Gus, line her up on that reef and then gun her. Everyone else, grab a piece and get ready to start shooting."

Shane Billiken found an M16 pushed into his hands.

"I don't know how to shoot one of these," he protested.

"You don't have to. That sucker spits out rounds faster than you can piss. Just wave it like a hose. It'll do the job."

The boat turned and dug in its stern. The bow lifted and salt spray washed Shane Billiken's face as the reef drew near. He hung on, trying to keep the rifle in his shuddering arm.

"Okay, burn them down!" Dirk Edwards hollered.

On the beach, the sound of the incoming boat made the natives freeze. Their black eyes—they reminded Shane Billiken of those of hapless seals before they were clubbed to death—stared out at them.

Dirk Edwards fired first. His weapon began popping. The others joined in. Coral shards flew off the reef. A native went down. Another, running madly, fell after a bullet stream sawed an arm off.

Shane Billiken forgot there was a weapon in his hands. He stared out over the bow. He had never seen people die before. It was mesmerizing. The gun sounds were puny. Just a sporadic popping. Firecracker sounds. The people on the reef didn't scream or yell. They ran and then they stumbled. There wasn't even that much visible blood. It was like watching television.

When it was over, the engines were throttled down and they drifted in toward shore.

Two men jumped onto the reef and took hold of thrown lines. The schooner was made secure, the anchor dropped.

Most of the natives were dead, Shane Billiken saw as he clambered onto the reef. One moaned, and Dirk Edwards beckoned him to the body.

"Finish him off," Edwards said.

"I don't know if I can," Shane muttered.

"It's easy."

"Isn't this your job? I hired you, after all."

"Look, we gotta head inland before the sounds get everyone on this rock organized. We're gonna need every man. So you're either part of the problem, sucker, or you're part of the solution."

And to a man, the mercenaries pointed their weapons at Shane Billiken.

Reluctantly Shane pointed his rifle at the native's twitching head, closed his eyes, and squeezed the trigger. The weapon gave a short snarl.

"Is it over?" he asked limply.

"Yeah," Dirk Edwards said politely. "You can look if you want."

Shane did. At the sight of the blood-streaked brains oozing out of the man's shattered face, he broke and ran for the waters. He got down on his stomach until he had emptied it into the beautiful blue water.

The mercenary team laughed uproariously.

"You'll get used to it. Now, come on. Let's find that village."

For three hours they penetrated the lush rain forest. They climbed a thickly overgrown hill. The terrain was rough. Shane's Adidas running shoes began to fall apart.

Finally they reached the crest of the hill. Below lay a mist-filled valley. Beyond the mists a tall shape loomed blue and indistinct.

"Let's make camp here," Dirk said. "The fog ought to burn off by noon. Maybe we can spot the village. Save us some humping."

They settled down to wait. As the morning progressed, the mists began to thin. A hill came into view. And another. And between them a tall landmark that was definitely not a hill.

"Shit!" said Dirk Edwards. "What the fuck is that?"

"It's the temple," Shane shouted. He was ignored.

"Looks like a building," said Gus.

"I know it's a fucking building. What I want to know is, what kind of building. Who's got the binoculars?"

Someone passed them to him. Dirk stood up and trained the lenses on the rapidly clearing object.

"I thought we were supposed to be looking for a primitive island," he said bitingly. "This thing is huge."

"We are," Shane Billiken said uncertainly. "I mean, it was supposed to be. Maybe it's some kind of mirage."

"Yeah? Well, this mirage says the 'Oahu Hilton' on it."

"What does that mean?" Shane wanted to know.

"It means, you flaky fuck, that we're in Hawaii and if we don't get out of here before those bodies are found, our asses are grass."

At that, everybody started running down the mountain at full tilt. In between puffing breaths, there was a discussion about whether to shoot Shane Billiken for getting them into this mess.

Shane Billiken was immensely relieved when the vote was decided, five to two in favor of not shooting him because one more shooting would only bring more trouble.

"Outstanding," said Dirk Edwards. "We'll wait till we're at sea."

32

Dolla-Dree, Low Moo of Moo, ran to her father's palace. Her bare feet skipped over the stones in her path. She felt light. Tonight she would enjoy the privilege that had not been accorded a Low Moo in hundreds of moons. The gift of a white man.

The oral tales of Moo were full of stories of the white men who once came to this remnant of Old Moo. None had come for so long that many believed the whites of the world had died out.

Dolla-Dree learned differently when she landed on the land of white men. But she had been on a mission. She could take no white man while she was a prisoner of the cruel magician who wore smoked glass over his eyes, yet was not blind.

Now she was home. Now she would ask her father.

Remo would be hers. Forever.

"Father! Father!" cried Dolla-Dree as she approached the palace.

The High Moo, Tu-Min-Ka, emerged from the palace, his face questioning.

"Is there trouble?" he demanded.

"No, no," said Dolla-Dree, dropping at his feet. She knelt before her father, bowing her long tresses. "I crave a boon. One that will make me one with the Low Moos of the past."

"Go on, daughter."

"I wish to buy the slave Remo. For I crave him greatly."

"He is no longer a slave. He has been freed. We do not have slaves on Moo."

"Only because there are not enough Moovians to have slaves as well as workers. We had slaves in the days of the white sailors."

"Which we freed at the proper time."

"And I vow to follow that tradition. I will buy Remo, and before I take him into myself, I will free him."

"Well-spoken. But he is already a free man."

"Oh, he will not be a slave long," the Low Moo implored. She grabbed her father's legs eagerly. Her face lifted. "I will treat him as we treated the white men of the long-ago days. He will be mine forever, one with my heart, identical with my soul, the flesh of my flesh."

"The Master of Sinanchu cares for this man," the High Moo reminded.

The Low Moo reared to her feet, her dark eyes snapping. "You deny me? Your daughter? The one who, alone in the world, loves you?"

The High Moo winced under the tongue-lashing. He relented.

"I will speak with the Master of Sinanchu," he said. "I will see what his feelings are toward Remo."

"I will await his decision," the Low Moo told him coolly. "Do not disappoint me, for I am all you have." She promptly disappeared into the palace, her haughty back radiating scorn.

His war club in hand, the High Moo called to his Red Feather Guard. They surrounded him as he set out in search of the Master of Sinanchu. The golden plume on his fillet crown dipped with each heavy step he took. It was a difficult thing his daughter had asked of him. The rite had not been performed since Rona-Ku was High Moo.

The monkeys chattered at him as he walked, and the High Moo shook his fist at them as if they were the cause of all his troubles.

They were nearing the rice fields when one of the guards walking before the High Moo seemed to stumble. He fell against a tree. He did not rise.

"See to him," the High Moo said shortly. "His head must have struck a stone."

The other guards surrounded the man. They shook him. He did not stir. They rolled him over on his back and everyone saw his glassy sightless stare. And they knew.

It was the High Moo who spotted the thorn sticking from the guard's foot. He pulled it free. A tiny drop of blood dripped from the tip.

"A stonefish spine," he growled. "It must have been set into the ground to trap me."

A rustling of the foliage ahead caught their attention. The remaining guards started after the skulker.

"No," cried the High Moo. "Do not leave me. There may be others lurking about. We will attend to that one later. I must see the Master of Sinanchu. You will carry my scared personage so that I do not fall prey to another vicious trap."

The Red Feather Guard hesitated. They looked down at their naked bronze feet.

"I have bestowed upon you the gift of being my guards," the High Moo growled. "Any who do not wish to enjoy the comforts that go with it may choose between the mines and the fields."

The guards looked at one another and two men took the High Moo by the legs while the third reached under his armpits. In this fashion they carried him from the path. They went with ginger steps, their questing eyes anxious.

When the Master of Sinanju saw the High Moo being carried in a supine position, his heart leapt at the thought that he had lost the only true emperor he had ever known.

"What has transpired?" he demanded of the guards as they set their ruler on his feet. "Is the High Moo ill?"

"I have escaped another base attempt upon my life," said the High Moo. "A stonefish spine placed in the road. One of my guards lies dead."

"He died knowing that he served you well," intoned Chiun. "He could ask for no greater destiny."

"I saw the one who did it," said a guard. All eyes turned to the man. "Through the trees. I recognized his face. It was Uk-Uk."

"Then Uk-Uk must die!" cried Chiun. "Point him out to me and I will rend him apart with infinite slowness." Like yellow talons, Chiun's hands flashed in the sunlight. He clawed the air, making flamboyant sweeping gestures. He hoped the High Moo would be impressed. But the High Moo's next words stunned the Master of Sinanju.

"No," he said unhappily. "Uk-Uk is my metalsmith."

"The old one?" Chiun demanded.

"Truly. I had thought him loyal. But he cannot die, for there is no other with the skill to fashion my coins."

"Then what would you have me do to him?" asked Chiun, who had never known an emperor to show mercy to a traitor. "I could pluck out one eye as an object lesson."

"No, for if he loses the other to disease or bird attack, he will be useless to me."

"I will leave the eyes, then. Select a limb for removal."

"I do not know," said the High Moo after a long pause. His broad coppery features were troubled. "But I have something more important to speak of now."

"Yes?" said Chiun, his eyes bright. What could be more important than the intrigues of the Shark Throne?

"My daughter, the Low Moo, has come to me. She craves your freed slave, Remo."

"Do you propose joining our houses in marriage?" Chiun asked slowly.

"If that is necessary to satisfy my daughter's need. But I would prefer to buy him."

Chiun's beard quivered. "Buy Remo? My Remo?"

"He was your slave in the outer world. Here, only we know that he has been liberated. Perhaps there is an honorable way you could unfree him. Then I would be prepared to discuss a price."

"Buy? Not marriage?" Chiun squeaked.

"I will do whatever is necessary, for my daughter's happiness is dear to me."

Chiun considered. "I will think on this matter. But I make no promise," he said hastily.

"Understood. Now I must return to my palace. For only there am I safe, it seems." The High Moo motioned for his guards to lift him off his feet.

Chiun watched as the High Moo was carried off. Then he went in search of Remo. He wore a slight smile of amusement on his parchment face, but it disappeared when he caught sight of Remo standing with his arms folded and looking bored while the miners worked half-heartedly.

"I have spoken with the High Moo," Chiun said solemnly. "His daughter desires you beyond all others."

"I got that impression when I talked to her."

"Indeed?"

"Yeah. She said she wanted to *poon* me."

"She said what?"

"*Poon.* Is it dirty?"

"It is obscene."

"Sounds interesting," Remo said. "I don't suppose you'd care to share a few details?"

"No. And you must have misunderstood her. Your command of the Moovian tongue is atrocious."

"Well, we'll find out tonight. She and I are having a tryst."

"Do not go to her, Remo. The High Moo has offered to buy you from me. I was going to tell you that I entertained the idea, but only as a jest. Now I tell you in full sincerity, do not meet with the Low Moo."

"I was starting to look forward to it. She's probably the only Moovian maiden I haven't made it with. Don't these people believe in marriage?"

"They marry. But it is not like other people marry. They are free to dally with whomever they wish. All children born on Moo are considered children of the mother and of the village. The concept of the father exists only in the royal house."

"That would explain the singular absence of irate husbands."

"There is other news. The metalsmith. Uk-Uk. He tried to kill the High Moo with a stonefish spine set on his path."

"Brrrr. Nasty," Remo said. "Does that mean he is an octopus worshiper?"

"Anyone can break a spine from a stonefish. And octopus worshipers are slaves to ritual. They always dress in imitation of Ru-Taki-Nuhu. Or leave a symbol of their evil, like the jug which contained a living octopus which was hurled at the High Moo. No, it means that the list of those who desire to topple the Shark Throne is longer than I would have believed. For the young assailant knew not of the metalsmith's designs."

"If you ask me, the way these people are worked, anybody could be out for his skin."

"We must expose the plotters tonight," Chiun said firmly. "All of them."

"Yeah? How, pray tell?"

"The metalsmith does not know he was seen. You will follow him if he leaves his hut tonight. I will guard the High Moo."

"What about the Low Moo? She's expecting me."

"Have nothing to do with her."

"That's gonna be hard. We're stuck on the same island."

"She is not your type, believe me."

"Since when do you know what attracts me?"

"On Moo, every swaying teat attracts you. I am surprised you have not been chasing the female monkeys."

"Har de har har har," Remo said. But his face flushed in embarrassment.

33

The physician in charge of patients at Folcroft Sanitarium was a rotund little man named Dr. Aldace Gerling. His white smock bulged at its lower buttons and Smith wondered as they walked down the two-tone green corridors of the sanitarium's psychiatric wing how a man could be a physician and yet allow his stomach to get so out of shape. If wasn't for his salt-and-pepper goatee, Smith would have suspected him, with his baby-fat features and soft voice, of being in the late stages of pregnancy.

"As I told you, Dr. Smith," Dr. Gerling was saying, "all rooms and patients have been accounted for."

"I know. But it's been nearly two weeks. I'm now convinced that Grumley never left the premises. There would have been police reports or incidents if he had."

"Then we will triple-check," Dr. Gerling said. His voice was a frown.

As they went from room to room, matching room numbers with a patient list Smith carried on a clipboard, Smith reflected that he had gotten nowhere with his other problem. Perhaps devoting more attention to this one would help clear his head. And there was still that nagging feeling he had that the two matters were connected somehow.

"And here is the unfortunate Mr. Purcell," Dr. Gerling said. They stopped at a heavily reinforced door.

"Oh, yes, Jeremiah Purcell," Smith said, peering in through the wire-mesh-reinforced porthole.

The walls of the room were gray and padded. A youngish man sat on the floor, wearing a straitjacket that confined his arms. He stared at a far corner of the ceiling as if it held the image of God.

"I have never seen such a case before," Dr. Gerling

remarked, pursing his wet lips. "The man's mind is totally blank. His state is beyond catatonia."

"He has not been a problem?"

"No more than a patch of catnip. He sleeps, he eats, he uses the toilet—although sometimes he forgets to put down the seat and falls in. Then he cries. Other than that, nothing. No words, no complaints. No nothing. His is a sad case."

Smith looked at the young man for several minutes. His hair was long and blond and the texture of cornsilk. His eyes were so blue they looked like neon points. But in back of them lay an uncomprehending opacity.

Jeremiah Purcell has been brought to Folcroft by Remo and Chiun. He was perhaps their greatest enemy living—a white man who possessed the powers of Sinanju and an additional faculty: the ability to project his thoughts as visible hallucinations. In their last encounter, the Dutchman—as Purcell was also known—had snapped mentally. His mind was an absolute blank slate.

No, Smith thought. Purcell would have nothing to do with this. This was not his style. There was no point to it. And every staff doctor had pronounced his mind a roiling confusion of thoughts.

Smith checked Purcell's name off and walked on.

"And this is Mr. Chiun's room," Dr. Gerling said when they rounded the corner to the guest wing.

Smith started. "Mr. Chiun?"

"Yes, the Alzheimer patient. The one who prattles on in the most astonishing ways. His stories about his village were most entertaining, if preposterous. As I recall, Dr. Smith, he once confided that he considered you to be his emperor. Is there a problem?"

"Mr. Chiun left us last month. Along with his guardian, Remo."

"Oh? Then who is in this room?" asked Dr. Gerling.

Smith pushed the door open. A man lay on a narrow bed. He slept. Smith shook his shoulder and the man roused slowly. He blinked uncomprehending eyes at them.

"This is not Mr. Chiun." Smith said.

Dr. Gerling looked at the patient's face. His own face loosened like a deflating balloon.

"But . . . but this man is Grumley," Dr. Gerling sputtered.

"Grumley! Are you certain?"

"Absolutely. I know Grumley. But what is he doing here?"

"Obviously he's hiding here. Why didn't you check this room more carefully?" Smith demanded.

Dr. Gerling drew himself up sternly. "You instructed me in quite explicit language, Dr. Smith, that the patient Chiun was not to be disturbed by the staff for any reason."

"Yes, yes, you are right. I did," Smith said distractedly.

"And you further neglected to inform me that Mr. Chiun had been discharged."

"It was quite sudden, actually," Smith admitted.

"Well, here is the solution to our little mystery. I shall escort Mr. Grumley back to his room."

"Yes, carry on. Thank you, doctor," said Dr. Harold W. Smith. He left the room hurriedly, clutching his clipboard.

Despite his acute embarrassment, Smith was relieved. He had indeed neglected to brief Dr. Gerling when Remo and Chiun had abruptly moved out of Folcroft. He had no idea where they had gone after that. They had promised to communicate with him once they were settled in a new location, but had not. It had been Smith's policy to relocate them at intervals. They had ended up residing at Folcroft by default.

Wherever they were, at least the disappearance of Gilbert Grumley had no connection with Smith's main problem. And that eliminated the possibility that Folcroft had been compromised.

Now it was time to close out that other matter.

34

Darkness fell upon the tiny island of Moo.

The cooking fires were doused with water. The riotous birds of day fell silent. Shining clouds hid the moon.

Yawning and stretching, the peasants of Moo retreated to their grass huts. The High Moo had already retired to his palace.

"I don't see the Low Moo," Remo whispered. They were on the roof parapet of the Royal Palace. The entire expanse of the island lay before them.

Chiun's face lifted to the freshening sea breeze, like a cat catching a scent.

"She is the least of our concerns this night," he said quietly. His hazel eyes, like polished agates, searched the village huts scattered like so many haphazard dice around the palace.

"You haven't seen her when she's angry."

"I will go below to guard the door to the High Moo's quarters," Chiun remarked after the last Moovian had slipped into his home.

"Check," Remo said. "I've got Uk-Uk's hut in my sights."

"If he leaves, or anyone else acts suspicious, take them alive."

"No problem."

"I go now. Remember—have nothing to do with the Low Moo this night."

"Yeah. Sure," Remo said vaguely.

Chiun paused. Then he slipped down the stone staircase. Remo was a willful pupil, he ruminated. But in the end, he could handle himself. It was not for Remo's safety that Chiun feared his tryst with the Low Moo. Remo had always had bad luck with women. He did not need a further shock to his opinion of the other sex.

* * *

Hours passed and Remo was growing bored. The clouds parted long past midnight, bathing the island in silver illumination. The moonlight was strong, but not strong enough to pick out colors. The breeze-worried jungle was a gray-and-white expanse. Out beyond the eastern shore, the Pacific danced with diamond-hard lights. The *Jonah Ark* bobbed like a grotesque cork.

Dolla-Dree, Low Moo of Moo, sauntered into the village far into the night. Remo watched as she stepped in and out of patches of moonlight. Her face was radiant with expectation. Her hips moved like the palms and Remo felt a momentary pang at the thought of Chiun's admonition to avoid her.

But business came first. Maybe he could explain it to the Low Moo before the night was over.

Then the Low Moo padded up to Remo's quarters and slipped in through the window.

Remo hesitated. He considered dropping to the ground to talk with her. But a stealthy shadow flitting from hut to hut drew his attention. He followed it with his eyes.

The shadow disappeared into a mangrove thicket. Probably a Moovian with an assignation, Remo decided. It was not Uk-Uk.

Then other figures crept out into the open. They went in different directions, apparently oblivious of one another. Some gathered together in the darkness and slipped off in groups. They were not always of opposite sexes. Oh, well, Remo thought. Anything that people did in civilization, they probably did on Moo.

The metalsmith, Uk-Uk, came out after most of the skulking had quieted down. Remo went over the parapet, hung by his fingers, and dropped to the dirt with no more sound than the clap of a baby's hands.

He trailed the metalsmith at a safe distance. The old man loped along toward the great cluster of mines cut into the sheer western wall of the Moovian plateau.

Along the way, Remo's acute hearing picked up voices.

"The High Moo must die tonight," a male voice whispered.

"I will tear his eyes out with my bare hands," a lilting young girl's voice promised vehemently.

Fixing the metalsmith's location in his mind, Remo slipped off the path. He eased in the direction of the voices. He dropped to one knee and parted the high turtle grass.

Three Moovians squatted under a banyan tree. They were discussing, in quiet, forceful tones, a variety of ways to kill the High Moo. Remo, concerned that the metal-smith would get away, memorized their faces and glided away unseen.

Other voices rose from the jungle as Remo crept along the path.

"The tyranny must end. We are as worthy as he is."

"The Low Moo is less royal than I am. Let her work in the mines."

"Why should we toil to fill the High Moo's coffers when all he fills is our stomachs?"

"Most of the stored rice goes to the insects anyway. We do not need to grow so much."

Remo counted twenty-seven plotters in groups of twos and threes. Worried, he pressed on. The ground dropped off sharply. Remo had to climb down.

Uk-Uk, the metalsmith, ducked into an active mine just as Remo caught up with him.

Remo drifted up to the entrance and put an ear to the solid bulwark of earth that framed its black maw. Vibrations of muttering voices carried through the dirt.

"No, not tonight." It was Uk-Uk's raspy voice. "Others plot tonight. Let them have their chance. If we have to kill them too, we will. But after the High Moo and his she-whelp are food for the sharks, only Uk-Uk will know the place where the coins are stored."

"What about the Master of Sinanchu and his slave?" someone asked.

"Let them return to their world. Moo is not for those with white skins."

"But the Master of Sinanchu has yellow skin."

"I have seen how he consorts with the white one. The Master of Sinanchu is like a banana. Yellow on the outside, but the meat within is white and soft."

The metalsmith's words were greeted with murmurs of assent.

"Let us retire to our homes and await future events," Uk-Uk said when quiet returned.

At that, Remo retreated. He had heard enough. It was

time to tell Chiun the bad news. Let him figure out how to break it to the High Moo.

The Master of Sinanju stood resolute. He stirred not. He blinked not. He was an unmoving rock standing between the High Moo and those who would topple him from his throne.

The corridor leading to the High Moo's quarters was darker than the stomach of an octopus. Darker even than the dreamless slumber of Ru-Taki-Nuhu, who dwells far from the life-giving rays of the sun. But Chiun saw it as clearly as if illuminated by pure moonlight. A spider scuttled into a crack and Chiun saw it plainly. And the spider, even with many eyes, saw him not.

Chiun had deployed the Red Feather Guard at every entrance. No one could enter the palace unchallenged. And if any did, he would face the Master of Sinanju.

Sinanju had lost few emperors in its long and glorious history. This Master of Sinanju was determined that the High Moo would not be one of them.

It lacked but an hour until dawn when angry, stealthy footsteps padded through the palace halls. Chiun's immobility melted. He stepped forward to confront the approaching figure.

The padding was familiar.

The silhouette coming down the hall, Chiun saw at last, was the swivel-hipped Low Moo. Her face was a tight mask.

"I would speak with my father," she said in an icy voice that pleased Chiun. It meant Remo had not met with her this night.

"He sleeps," Chiun said blandly, joining his hands within the open sleeves of his emerald-and-gold kimono.

"Then I will wake him. Or would you deny me the right to see my own father?"

Chiun stood unmoving. His thin lips parted and he bowed silently.

"I serve the House of Moo, of which you are an honored part." Chiun stepped aside silently.

The Low Moo pushed open the bamboo-and-rattan door. "Father, I would speak with you," she called loudly.

The door spanked shut behind her.

Chiun stood listening, his face intent, as the sounds of a low, intense argument began.

"He did not come to me," the Low Moo complained in a cat-spitting hiss. "And he is not in his room."

"I would have told you this," said the High Moo, "but you were nowhere to be found."

"I walked the beaches. I breathed prayers to the god of the waves who brings whites to our land. I thanked him abjectly, for you promised you would make this thing happen for me."

"You must be patient. The Master of Sinanchu has not yet given his blessing."

A bare foot spanked the stone floor. "I will not. I want him now. My hunger for him is great."

"He is not mine to give to you." The High Moo's voice was resigned.

"Then I will take him," the Low Moo hurled back.

"I warn you, do nothing to antagonize the Master of Sinanchu. Only he stands between our throne and these treasonous plotters."

"I will have him! I will feel the fire of his white *kuna* in my belly!"

"You are my daughter. You will obey me!"

"I am the Low Moo. I will not be denied the privileges that Low Moos of past time enjoyed."

The High Moo's answer was a strangled inarticulate rage. The Low Moo spat back a pungent curse. The exchange escalated and the Master of Sinanju heard a meaty slap, and there was the sound of a body falling.

There was silence in the room for a long time after.

When the Low Moo emerged from the room, her cheeks blazing with shame. One darkening eye had already begun to swell.

Chiun looked for tears, but there were none.

"My father slumbers," she said, closing the door after her. Her feet slapped the stone flooring angrily as she disappeared around a turn in the corridor.

The Master of Sinanju resumed his resolute stance before the High Moo's chambers. He was once more the impenetrable rock of safety for his emperor.

* * *

Remo Williams slipped up to the palace like a drifting shadow. He might have been a trick of the light caused by the moon ghosting in and out of low-flying cloud scud. He decided to climb in through his bedroom window in order to avoid the Red Feather Guards at every entrance.

"Remo, you have come." The voice was sullen. But it lifted toward the last.

"Dolla-Dree?" Remo asked. A shadowy figure sprawled on his sleeping mat.

"I have spoken to my father. He no longer stands against our union. I have waited long for you to come to me."

"Yeah? Gave us his blessing, did he?"

"Come," she said, rising on her hands. She lay there like a great tawny cat. Remo picked out the dark spots of her nipples. She wore only the lower portion of her costume. Her eyes were wide and unwinking, like black jewels. Her pupils were so distended that the smoky iris was all but invisible.

Remo joined her on the sleeping mat.

"I wanted to talk to Chiun first," he said uncertainly.

"It lacks but an hour until the sun's bright eye returns. Let us do what we will while he cannot see us."

She leaned into him, her smooth arms wrapping around his neck. She nipped at his right earlobe. Then playfully bit into the left. Remo felt his desire for her stir within him. It was more curiosity than need. Sinanju had burned out raw lust a long time ago. But the Low Moo was an attractive creature. The word popped into Remo's mind unbidden. She seemed in the half-light less a woman than a woman-child, and perhaps not quite that. There was something feral in her eyes. They were sullen and sexy at once. They made Remo feel a new emotion. Something subliminal. An anticipation, and a kind of tingling anxiousness too.

Remo sought her lips, but, teasing, she avoided them and sank perfect white teeth into his shoulder.

"Cut it out," Remo said lightly. The teeth tightened. Remo frowned.

"I need you, Remo. I need your strength," she said through her tightening teeth.

"How about you need me a little less hard?" Remo

asked gently but firmly, pushing her head away. He took her face in his hands.

"I get ahead of myself," she said. "Why do you not lie back?"

"You want to get on top?"

"I want you. All of you."

Remo let himself be pushed down. There was something in the air, something that was sexual but somehow outside of sex. He didn't know what it was. But he felt a little thrill course along his spine and the short hairs of his forearms lifted as if from static electricity.

Whatever the Low Moo had in mind, it was going to be very different, Remo decided. He closed his eyes as she mounted him. Let her surprise him.

The Master of Sinanju smelled blood.

His wrinkled face lifted suddenly. He sniffed in all directions. The scent emanated from the High Moo's quarters.

Chiun went through the door like a charging ram.

The High Moo lay on his bed, the golden plume of kingship drooping from his crown so that it brushed his broad nose.

A bone knife slanted up from the middle of his breastbone. He was not breathing.

Chiun fell upon the man. He didn't touch the knife. It had probably severed veins or arteries, and its blade might have sealed off the severed ends. To withdraw it would risk the free flow of royal blood.

Instead, the Master of Sinanju placed a fist over the High Moo's heart. It beat sluggishly. His mouth was open like a fish's.

Chiun pounded the fist with the flat of his other hand. Once. Again. Again. And again. The High Moo's bulk quaked and trembled. A whitish foam spilled from his lips and the coughing began. His eyes fluttered open stupidly.

"Move not," Chiun admonished. "I will tend to you."

Chiun examined the knife. It seemed to have gone in deeply. But when he touched the hilt, it wobbled. The blade had snapped going in. He lifted it free.

The blade had gone in at an angle. There was less damage than had been apparent. Chiun left the tip in.

"Sit up," Chiun said.

The High Moo pushed himself so that his torso and head were supported by the wall behind his sleeping mat.

"Who did this?" demanded Chiun.

"I know not," mumbled the High Moo. His eyes were glassy and blank. He seemed to be in shock, although the blood loss was insignificant.

The Master of Sinanju flew to the open window. He stuck his head out. A Red Feather Guard stopped pacing the open courtyard.

"You! Guard!" Chiun called. "Where have you been?"

"Here," the guard replied hastily.

Chiun motioned him close, and when he was within reach, the Master of Sinanju smashed the bone spear from his hand, and taking him by the throat, forced him to his knees. "Your emperor lies wounded by base assassins. I will ask you again. Who entered this window?"

"But, no one." Chiun squeezed harder. The guard's eyes bulged like frightened grapes. "I swear by the moon," he said.

Chiun's visage drew tighter. But the fear in the guard's voice told him that he spoke the truth as he knew it. No one had entered by the window. And only one person had entered by the door.

"See that no further harm comes to the High Moo," Chiun warned, "or it will be on your head." He released the guard and swept out of the room like a harried specter.

The Low Moo was not in her quarters. She was not in the eating room. Chiun began to ascend the stairs to the second floor, when he heard voices. Remo's. And one other.

He padded back to the first floor. The voices came from Remo's room.

Chiun burst in.

"Chiun!" Remo said in surprise. He lay on his back, the Low Moo atop him. She was pulling at her skirts, loosening them.

"Don't you believe in knocking first?" Remo asked sheepishly.

"I have learned who desires the High Moo's death," Chiun said.

"So have I," Remo said.

"Then why do I find you like this?"

Remo pushed the Low Moo away and sat up. "I was on my way to see you," he said. "Honest. But I happened to bump into her. One thing just led to another."

The Low Moo rearranged her skirts. She stared up at the Master of Sinanju, her eyes as big as a tomcat's.

"You consort with the enemy of him whom you are sworn to preserve," Chiun said coldly.

"What are you talking about?"

"You know who is trying to kill the High Moo?"

"Sure, I do," Remo said, getting to his feet. "Everybody."

"You are blind, Remo. The traitor lies at your feet."

"Her?" Remo said, aghast. "No way, Chiun. You got it all wrong. I was out in the jungle. There must be two dozen different plots being hatched. If you ask me, it's practically open season on the High Moo. I think he's been working everyone too hard. They're fed up."

"Spoken like a peasant," the Low Moo said sulkily.

Remo put his hands on his hips.

"Hey, what happened to wanting me?"

"I do want you," she hissed. "And I will have you!"

The Low Moo sprang to her feet. A bone knife flashed up from under her skirts. She came at Remo, the knife held low for a disemboweling slash.

"Hey!" Remo yelled, his eyes wide. Reflexively his hand caught her knife wrist. He twisted. The Low Moo squealed in pain. Remo kicked her ankles out from under her. She went down in a pile.

Chiun retrieved the viciously curved bone knife from the floor.

"Yes. It is the same design as the other."

"What's going on here?" Remo demanded hotly.

"She did not want you the way you think," Chiun said, examining the knife.

"Yeah? What other way is there?"

"She wanted to *poon* you."

"And she would have if you hadn't interrupted."

"She wanted to eat you," Chiun said. "*Poon* means 'to eat.' "

"No, *ai* means 'to eat,' " Remo said.

"*Ai* means 'to dine.' *Poon* means 'to consume.' "

Remo blinked. He looked into Chiun's unwavering eyes. His eyes flashed down to the Low Moo. She averted her gaze. Her pink tongue licked at her lips. She rubbed her bare belly as if from a stomachache.

"You mean . . ." Remo began to say.

Chiun nodded flintily.

Remo looked at the Low Moo again.

"It's not true, is it?" he asked quietly. "This wasn't what you meant by desiring my organ. To eat?"

"I deserved you. Other Low Moos enjoyed the Flesh Feast in the days of the whites who came to this island. Why should I not be like them? I earned my throne."

"Earned?" said Chiun sharply. Remo looked blank.

"Do you think that I was born Low Moo?" She laughed cruelly. "When Old Moo sank, the royal family escaped to the high plateau where the mountain palace stood. This palace. The peasants all drowned, but the royal family alone survived."

"You are *all* descendants of the House of Moo?" Chiun asked. "Every islander?"

The Low Moo nodded. "Ever since then it has been a struggle between those who sat upon the Shark Throne and those who did not. The strong ruled. The weak worked. My father slew the last High Moo only two years ago."

"In the Fifth Year of the Third Cycle," Chiun said, plucking the coin Remo had found from his sleeve. "The same year that the High Moo ascended the throne."

"There were four assassinations that year," the Low Moo went on. "Since then, my father has ruled through his might. There has been stability. Only the octopus worshipers vexed his kingdom. But now they are gone, and the troubles are worse."

"So you came to the throne with him?" Remo asked. "You weren't born a princess?" His voice was stunned. His features a little sick. The truth was starting to sink in.

The Low Moo shook her head. Her gaze was faraway. "I was the younger of two sisters. Tuka-Tee was Low Moo before me."

"What happened to her?" Remo wanted to know.

The Low Moo shrugged unconcernedly.

"I poisoned her. Crushed stonefish spines in her food."

Remo turned away. "I think I'm going to be sick."

"Not as sick as you would have been had I not come to your rescue," Chiun pointed out.

"She's a princess, for Christ's sake," Remo said to no one in particular. He towered over the Low Moo. "You're a princess!" he roared. The Low Moo cringed. "And you're a freaking cannibal."

"Do not be insulting," the Low Moo shot back. "Moovians do not eat one another. Only whites. And no one has eaten human flesh since the last white man came to these shores. They were made slaves for a time. When they were freed, there was a feast. The Low Moo always had her choice of the best meat. And only the Low Moo."

"Equal eating for the High Moo was out?" Remo said bitterly.

The Low Moo shrugged. "No white women ever came. The royal family does not eat members of the same sex. Do you think we are . . . perverts?"

"Perverts!" Remo shouted. "Listen, where I come from—"

"Enough," Chiun said. "Now you know the truth."

"Now I know," Remo said dully. He hadn't loved her, but somehow the truth hurt. He didn't understand why.

"What do we do with her?" Remo asked. "She's still the Low Moo."

"She stabbed her father."

"Yes," said the Low Moo. She sprang to her feet, her eyes flashing. Her bare breasts shook with the vehemence of her words. "The High Moo is dead. I possess the Shark Throne now. And all of its wealth. If you wish to claim any of the coins, you will do as I say."

"No," Chiun said, taking her by the wrist. The Low Moo struggled. The old Korean's fingers tightened like claws. "He lives, thanks to Sinanju."

And Chiun dragged the Low Moo, spitting and scratching, from the room. Remo went along uncertainly.

The Master of Sinanju threw the Low Moo at the feet of her father. She sprawled there, supine and frightened.

"I lay at your feet your assailant," Chiun said coldly. "Speak her fate and I will make it so." His hands went into his kimono sleeves. His spine straightened proudly.

"Wait a minute, Little Father," Remo began. A raised hand hushed him.

The High Moo's eyes were clearing.

"She is my daughter," he said dully. "There is no other I trust. Let her live. She is willful and cruel as a cat, but she only wanted to feel the white man's flesh between her teeth."

Remo shivered in spite of himself.

"There are others," Chiun went on. "Other plotters. Remo has uncovered their perfidy."

"Yeah, it's real bad," Remo offered. "Just about everyone on this anthill wants to kill you. Now I know why. It's their only chance for upward mobility. The Low Moo told us how it really is on your little tropical paradise."

"I need my peasants. Without them, there will be no one to mine the metal, make the coins, and grow the rice."

"Then choose one or two plotters," Chiun suggested. "I will make an example of them before the others. A few heads sitting on spears is a wonderful deterrent to plotters."

The High Moo shook his head slowly. "I need every peasant. We have already lost too many."

"Then what would you have me do?" Chiun demanded in an exasperated voice.

"Let them go."

"Go! I am royal assassin to the House of Moo. How can I protect you if I cannot deal justice to pretenders to the throne? Where is the deterrent? What is your power?"

"My power lies here," said the High Moo, pointing to his right arm. He lifted his war club feebly. "And in the wealth of my treasure, which every Moovian covets but no one may possess but me."

"In other words," Remo said, "you have nothing."

"Well-spoken," said Chiun, distaste thickening his voice.

"I would sleep," said the High Moo. "Leave me. We will speak of these matters after the sun has restored the color to my empire."

"Some empire," said Remo, turning to go from the room.

The Master of Sinanju beheld the supine figure of the Low Moo, and the great snoring bulk of the High Moo. They no longer appeared royal to his wise eyes. He saw only a fat man with a feather drooping over his thick features and a spiteful and treacherous girl.

He left them without a word.

35

They asked Shane Billiken if he could swim and he said yes.

They asked Shane Billiken if he could swim with his hands tied behind him and his feet weighted with vats of cheese.

"Of course not," he snapped.

"Then it's settled," Dirk Edwards said. "You go over the side."

It took three of them to hold Shane Billiken down on the deck while a fourth tied his wrists behind his back with rope. Getting the goat cheese tied to his feet proved more difficult. For one thing, they found they would have to drill holes through the vats for the ropes to go through. For another, Shane kept kicking the wooden vats to pieces with his frantic feet.

"Let's think this through," Dirk Edwards said at last.

"Great idea," said Shane Billiken. "Let's not rush into anything."

"I meant how we're going to do it, not if," Dirk Edwards said. "You got us into this fool operation."

"I hired you. I gave you all my money."

"Your mistake. Besides, we aren't in this for the money. We're soldiers. We have a soldier's pride. How the fuck do you think this operation will look written up in the pages of *Soldier of Fortune*?"

"Not so hot if it comes out that you murdered your employer," Shane pointed out.

"Exactly. Not to mention all the screwing around these islands we've done. Gus, find something we can use as a plank."

"Plank?" Shane said blankly.

"Yeah, it's traditional during mutinies to make the captain walk the plank. And I'm a traditional kind of guy."

"I don't think you guys are considering the karmic repercussions of this."

"You're right. We're not."

"Look, I can pay you more money. Just don't kill me."

"We got all your money. You just said so."

"Then I'll cut you in on the treasure. Did I tell you guys about the treasure? Half for me, half for you guys to split up."

"We don't need you to find any treasure."

"Sure you do. Only I know what the girl looks like. And the two with her."

"A white guy and a gook in a party dress. How many of them can there be in the South Pacific?"

"You never know. Synchronicity is one of the great misunderstood forces of the cosmos."

"So are sharks. Hey, somebody see if there's any red meat left. Throw it in the water. It'll be more fun if we toss him into a mess of man-eaters."

"No, not that. Anything but that."

"No, not that," Dirk Edwards mimicked. "Anything but that. You sound like a pansy. I hate pansies. I gotta kill you for that reason alone."

"And for the cheese," someone joined in.

"Yeah. For the damned cheese. I shoulder never have signed on without checking you out more carefully."

"There's no more meat," a voice called up from below.

"Damn. I guess it's back to the cheese."

Shane Billiken resumed kicking wildly.

"No, no, no!" he screamed.

"Hey, shut up! Shut him up." It was Gus. His voice was excited.

Dirk Edwards dropped into a crouch and clamped a dirty hand over Billiken's wide mouth. "What is it?" he hissed.

"I see an island."

"Steer clear of it. The Hawaiian authorities probably have the whole South Pacific on the lookout for us."

"Maybe. But not this island."

"Say again?"

"There's a junk lying at anchor on this side."

Dirk Edwards replaced his hand with a boot and stood up. Shane Billiken tried to shake the boot out of his mouth, but that only made the boot press down harder. He stopped struggling.

"Yeah, yeah," Dirk said, his voice rising.

Shane Billiken felt the boot go away and two hands yank him to his feet.

"That the junk?" Edwards demanded, pointing.

Shane Billiken said, "Yes!" He would have said yes if he had been asked if Peking was the capital of Alaska.

"Change in plans," Dirk said. "We ain't going to kill you. But you gotta do everything we say from now on."

"Done," said Shane Billiken. "Thank you."

"We ain't doing this for you. We can't kill you without noise and I ain't blowing our chance to salvage something from this miserable operation."

"Whatever works," said Shane Billiken gratefully.

"Okay. Pull down the sails. Cut the engines. Douse the lights. And everybody listen up. You too, Billiken. You play your hand right and we'll cut you in for a piece of the treasure."

"Half?"

Stone faces stared at him.

"A quarter?"

"Aww, Dirk, why don't we just strangle him and get it over with?" Gus drawled.

"We need every hand. Provided we get cooperation."

"Ten percent!" Shane called out. "Ten percent works for me."

"You get five—if you pull your weight."

And Shane Billiken found his hands being untied and an M16 placed into his trembling fingers. This was his last chance and he knew it. He promised to pull his weight from now on. He used his most convincing voice. Anything to avoid the sharks. Shane knew everything there was to know about sharks. He had seen every *Jaws* film. Talk about unevolved.

36

Michael P. Brunt's voice was jaunty over the long-distance line.

"Brunt the Grunt," he said. "You point and I do."

"This is Brown," Harold Smith said. "Have you completed your assignment?"

"Mission accomplished."

"You have recovered the tea service?" Smith asked blankly.

"What if I said yes?" Brunt asked. Smith could hear a raspy scratching noise. It sounded like Brunt was scratching his beard stubble.

"Please stop talking in circles. What did you find?"

"Nothing. No tea service. No furniture, unless you count a TV and a bunch of boxes. If you want my opinion, the guy took it on the lam, as we detectives like to say."

"Boxes? What kind of boxes?"

"What do you care?"

"What was in them?"

"Got me. They were padlocked. For all I know, they were booby-trapped too."

"Could you describe them?"

"Oh, about four or five feet long. Kind of like footlockers. Some of them had brass handles and fittings. They came in an assortment of colors. Gaudy, too. Designer luggage they definitely weren't."

"And you did not open them?"

"My job was to go in and recover the tea service without disturbing the domestic environment, correct?"

"Yes," Smith admitted glumly.

"Those babies were secured with monster brass padlocks. Not the combination kind, which I could have cracked, but the kind you open with a key. A big brass key. Get it?"

"Clearly," Smith sighed. "You dared not open them."

"Not without the big brass key, which I did not find, or a hammer and cold chisel, which I must have left in my other suit. Did I do right?"

"Yes, of course," Brunt suggested, "for more bucks, I could take another whack at it. Maybe you want your tea service so much you don't mind if I make a mess."

"I do mind. The occupant must never know his dwelling was penetrated."

"Burglarized, you mean. Only CIA types say 'penetrated.' "

"Yes. Burglarized."

"So now what?"

Smith considered. The scratching came over the line again.

"If I need you, I will call you again," he said at last.

"Sounds like a kiss-off to me."

"You have your check."

"Cashed and spent already. I could use more. My secretary keeps asking for a raise."

"Good-bye, Mr. Brunt," said Smith, hanging up. He swiveled in his cracked leather chair, his gray eyes regarding Long Island Sound through the office picture window.

"Boxes," he muttered. What could these boxes contain? Armaments, perhaps. Brunt had described them as footlockers. Assault weapons were often shipped in similar boxes. Or weapons components. Stinger missiles, for example. Or in the case of a more complex device, such as a portable rocket launcher, the components were often transported in several boxes of the type Brunt described.

Was the house being used as a weapons-storage site? Was Smith the target of terrorists? If so, why hadn't they made their move? If not, who was their target?

This was too critical now for a broken-down private investigator. Smith would have to get into the house himself, despite the risk. He must learn the contents of those boxes.

The time for waiting was over. Smith went to his file cabinet and from a folder deep in back extracted an Army-issue .45 automatic and two clips. He inserted a clip and sent a round into the chamber to check the action. Then he placed them in his briefcase, where they nestled in a false compartment under the telephone hookup.

Dr. Harold W. Smith left his office, a gray man with a cold white face and a purposeful stride that made the guards in the lobby dispense with their usual tipped-hat acknowledgments. They had seen that look on Smith's face before. It usually foreshadowed someone getting fired.

37

Shane Billiken felt positively transformational. He really did.

Under cover of darkness, they had heaved to outside the lagoon. Dirk "Ed the Eradicator" Edwards and his men donned their jungle fatigues and greased their faces with green and black camouflage paint. They slid survival knives into ankle sheaths and taped magazine clips together to make reloading easier. Then they went over the side in rubber rafts, which they scuttled in shallow water. From there, they waded.

Shane Billiken carried an M16 assault rifle over his head and clutched a marlin spike between his teeth. His shirt pockets were stuffed with spare clips and extra rounds and Gouda cheese. He hadn't any camouflage clothes, so he settled for rubbing his white ducks with borrowed jungle paint, not forgetting to anoint the triangle of hairy chest exposed by his buttonless shirt. At the last moment, he kept his mood amulet because, happily, the bull had turned green. It blended in perfectly.

He felt truly in touch with his animal side. There was just one nagging doubt to be resolved.

"Does it get easier?" Shane wanted to know as they waded onto the crushed-shell beach. "The killing stuff. I mean."

Dirk shot him a wolfish grin. "Sure it does. Hardly anybody ever throws up the second time."

"That's good," said Shane. "I hate throwing up. It's so, you know, primal."

"Nothing's more primal than killing," Dirk snorted. "Right, boys?"

They scaled the island's steep western slope. The face was riddled with square openings shored up with bamboo beams.

"Are these tunnels?" Gus demanded. "I was in Nam. I don't dig tunnel action. Gives me the creeps."

Dirk Edwards waved them into a crouch. He eased forward to one of the dark openings. He sniffed. No animal smells. He pulled a flashlight from his belt and shone the light in.

"Looks to me like a mine," he whispered.

"Maybe the treasure's in there," Shane said eagerly.

"Yeah," Dirk said slowly. He detected faint stirrings inside the mine. "Maybe it is. What say we check it out?"

"Suits me," Shane said, slipping the safety off his rifle.

"Glad to hear it. You go first."

"Me?" Shane was shoved forward by several of the others. His eyes were sick. Dirk grinned at him. Shane decided the tunnel was less threatening than Dirk's grin. He crept in.

A murmur of laughter rippled up from the others. They waited, listening. The sound of Shane Billiken's stumblings echoed from the mine.

"The fool don't have sense enough to take off his sunglasses," Dirk guffawed.

His laughter died suddenly when sounds of firing came from the tunnel. Shane burst out, his face a twisted warp of panic.

Dirk pulled him down. "What was it?" he spat. "What'd you find?"

"Eyes. I saw eyes. Human eyes. I shot at them. I think they're all dead."

"Natives," a man hissed. "They'll be all over us."

"Don't panic," Dirk barked. "Tunnel probably muffled the sound so it didn't carry.""

Shane Billiken started to gag. Everybody saw it coming. They piled on him, stuffing headbands and belts into his mouth to stifle the vomiting sounds. When Shane's convulsions stopped, they let him go. He spent fifteen minutes quietly spitting chunky yellowish fluid out of his mouth. He rinsed his mouth out with dirt.

"I thought you said it never happened that way twice," Shane gasped. His breath smelled like sour cheese.

"Some people have to get used to blood," Dirk replied. ""Okay, we press on. Stay away from the tunnels. There's a big building on the high ground. I'm betting that's the treasure house."

"No," Shane said. "I dreamed on it again."

"You gonna start that bilge all over?"

"No, the building is the sacred temple. I saw it in the dream. The treasure house will be near it, though."

"Yeah, and did you dream its location?" Dirk asked sarcastically.

"No, but I brought along an attuned way of finding it."

"What's that?"

"This," Shane said, pulling a Y-shaped branch from under his silk shirt. "It's a dowsing rod," he explained when confronted with a circle of blank camouflage-painted looks.

"Ain't those used for finding ground water?" someone asked.

"This is a willow branch. It will find anything I want. Including treasure. Watch."

Shane Billiken put down his rifle and stood up. He held the dowsing rod by its forked ends, with the tail of the Y pointing outward. The branch quivered in his hands. His hands quivered too. It was impossible to tell which was affecting the other.

"I can feel the magnetic pull already!" he declared. "Come on!" Shane went up the hill. The others hung back uncertainly.

"Wood ain't magnetic," Gus pointed out.

"No," Dirk growled, "but we ain't got any more clue where that treasure's at than he does. We got nothing to lose. Saddle up."

They trailed after Shane Billiken in a ragged line, dropping into defensive crouches every time Billiken tripped over a rock or ground root, their eyes sharp and their weapons pointed out in all directions.

After the third time, Dirk Edwards snatched the Ray-Bans off Shane's face and threw them away.

"Hey!" Shane protested. "Those are my trademark."

"They'll mark your gravestone if you fuck up one more time." Shane received an ungentle shove. "Now, get going!"

Shane pressed on. He seemed to do better now that he could see. He tripped only once more, and that was because his Adidas sneakers were coming off his feet like bad tires.

"Damn!" he said as he pulled himself to his feet. The others had dropped into a defensive circle, their hearts in their mouths and blood in their eyes.

"Lemme shoot him, Dirk," Gus moaned. "Please."

They were on level ground, near a hidden path they had discovered.

"What's wrong now?" Dirk called out. "Besides your usual clumsiness?"

"I fell and broke the rod."

"What a tragedy."

"You don't understand. I was close. I could feel the odyllic vibrations." Shane reached down to recover the willow pieces, which had fallen under a lightning-scorched tree. He leaned into the tree to steady himself and it cracked like a burnt twig. He fell across a wide flat and was surprised to feel his right foot sink down into something clammy and wet.

"Oh, God," he moaned. "I'm wounded. My foot's all wet."

"Maybe he pissed himself," someone said dryly.

Dirk Edwards came to his side. He examined Shane's foot. It disappeared into the top of a wide stump. He pulled it free.

"Is there much blood?" Shane moaned, looking away.

"None," said Dirk. He wasn't even looking at Shane's foot anymore. He was looking into the stump, where silver glints rippled under disturbed water. He turned to his men. "I want you all to get a grip on yourselves, understand? No shouting. No hooting. No bullshit. I don't know how, but this idiot found the treasure for us."

"I did?" Shane asked blankly.

He climbed to his feet and joined the group clustering around the stump to drink in the sight of stack upon stack of round silvery coins. The moonlight made them shimmer.

"I did!" Shane exulted. Everyone piled on him. They wrestled him to the ground, a dozen hands clamping on his mouth and throat.

When they finally let go, Shane Billiken's eyes were feverish. "I did. I did. I did," he whispered over and over again. "Didn't I? I made a positive affirmation and it worked. Finally."

'Everybody grab as much as they can carry," Dirk ordered. "We'll take this stuff back to the boat in rotating groups of threes. The first group stays with the ship to guard that end. The main force will remain here with the treasure. If we hustle our butts, we can have all this stuff on the boat before dawn."

"Then we sail home, right?" Shane said.

"No. There's natives on this island. I've been at sea without a woman for more than a week. I feel like having me some island girls. When we're done loading, we'll see what we can rustle up in the way of enforced R-and-R. Everybody with me on that?"

Everybody was. Except Shane Billiken. He volunteered to stay with the treasure. His offer was accepted.

The Master of Sinanju sat in the courtyard of the High Moo's palace. He faced the east, his eyes closed. The rising sun warmed his parchment countenance. Sea breezes toyed with the wisps of hair that decorated his wise face. He was transcending with the sun, an old Sinanju custom.

When he had finished meditating, he laid his hands upon his knees and arose like a straightening sunflower.

Remo sauntered up from the jungle. He carried something black and shiny in one hand.

"I have decided," Chiun said gravely. "We will leave Moo today. My heart is heavy, but my mind is clear."

"Don't say your good-byes just yet," Remo said evenly. "We have problems."

"I absolve us of any problems associated with the House of Moo. It has sunk into evil ways."

"Not them. I was out for a walk and I found these."

Remo held up a pair of Ray-Ban Wayfarer sunglasses.

"Elvis is on this island," he said.

"Nonsense," Chiun snapped. "Elvis is dead. Or living in Minnesota. Reports vary."

"Not Elvis Presley. Our old pal Shane Billiken."

"Oh, him," Chiun said, waving dismissively. "A mere annoyance."

"Maybe, but there's a ship outside the lagoon and it's crawling with jungle fatigues. And they're armed to the gills."

"Our ship is safe?" Chiun demanded.

"So far. But the news gets worse. I happened to walk by the ol' treasure stump. It's been emptied."

"My coins!" Chiun squeaked.

Remo nodded grimly. "Everybody's coins. And I tracked bootprints leading down to the lagoon. The coins must be on that boat."

"They will rue this day," Chiun cried, shaking a tiny fist.

"Why should they be any different than us?" Remo asked rhetorically.

Together the Master of Sinanju and his pupil descended from the lofty summit of Moo. Chiun was a driving storm cloud in an azure kimono. His chin jutted forward. He scorned the treacherous path to the shore and instead took the direct approach. Branches and mangrove thickets were crushed from his path.

"Where are the peasants?" Chiun asked at one point. "I do not see them at their toil."

"While you were transcending with the sun, I had a little talk with them about labor-management relations."

"Be good enough to speak English, not American."

"They're on a sit-down strike on the back part of the island. They won't stand up until the High Moo makes certain concessions. I've been appointed strike leader."

"You are poisoning their minds with foolish notions, Remo," Chiun scolded. "These people need their High Moo."

"The High Moo needs them, you mean. Uh-uh. After today, things are going to be different. Hold it," Remo said suddenly.

Remo and Chiun froze. Down below, white men were running in and out of the mines, trailing lengths of wire. Others hunkered down in the mangroves, confident they were invisible in their fatigues.

"I count five on land," Remo said.

"Yes, five. Let us cut their number."

"Hold on," Remo said. ""They're up to something in the mines."

"Not for very long," Chiun vowed.

Dirk Edwards waited until the last man was out of the mines.

"Okay, everybody get down," he said as he lifted his clenched fist to signal the men with the detonators to be ready.

"Remember," he said, "when they blow, it will bring the natives out where we can pick them off. Just shoot the males. We can handle the women easy. Maybe we'll get lucky and dislodge same of whatever they're mining, too."

And then he brought his fist down and twisted the handle of his own detonator.

The ground lifted under Remo and Chiun's feet. They reacted instantly, leaping into the treetops with the graceful alacrity of gazelles. The palms shook like dust mops in angry hands. They began toppling. The ground beneath collapsed like the sand at the top of an hourglass pouring down.

"The whole slope is crumbling!" Remo shouted.

"Higher ground," Chiun called. He leapt into the next tree, Remo following. They swung from tree to tree as the whole slope seemed to cave to behind them. Remo paused long enough to look back. The sheer western face of Moo, which was riddled with mines and tunnels, was falling like an avalanche. Instead of cascading snows, it was a nightmare of soil and foliage and palms sliding into the sea. The roar of moving earth was like a freight train.

Dirk Edwards saw that he had miscalculated. He called retreat.

"Every fucker for himself!"

They broke for the beach. They splashed into the surf ahead of a tidal wave of soil and stones. Some abandoned their weapons as they swam for the ship.

Belowdeck on the *New Age Hope*, Shane Billiken was happily counting coins.

"Seventy-seven . . . seventy-eight . . . seventy—"

The concussion sent the kerosene lamps gyrating in their gimbals. Shane plunged up the companionway. The two men on watch, Gus and Miles, were at the rail pointing toward Moo, their mouths hanging open in stupefaction.

It looked as if the entire island was coming down. Birds

flew into the air. Shane saw a scampering monkey buried alive. A faint dust cloud lifted and kept on rising, and Shane realized it was the insects of Moo, fleeing the collapse of land.

"Where are they? Can you see them?" Miles shouted hoarsely.

"No. Wait! There—in the water. They're swimming for it."

Shane saw Dirk Edwards stroking like mad, the others not far behind. One slow swimmer was caught by the sliding wall of soil. He went under a bubbling mixture of newly created mud.

Shane's mind crystallized instantly. The treasure was below. The others were in the water. And he was alone on deck with only two men.

He looked around and spotted an assault rifle leaning beside the mainmast. He tiptoed back and took it in his sweaty hands. His thumb squeezed off the safety and he crept forward.

He shot Gus first. He shot him point-blank in the back of the head, scattering his face across the water. Miles whirled and Shane riddled his chest. Miles staggered back. His mouth gulped like a beached fish's.

While Miles teetered against the rail. Shane sent a foot into his caved-in chest. He went overboard. Shane then hoisted Gus's carcass over the side.

Within what seemed like only seconds, the water was full of churning sharks. They attacked like hungry dogs, turning the water pinkish-white.

Shane called down encouragement to the sharks. "Hey, do what you love!" He started to raise anchor and then took the wheel. He kicked both engines to life. The schooner dug in and raced away.

Shane Billiken was very pleased with himself. He didn't feel like vomiting in the least. In fact, he felt hungry. He decided that once he had cleared the island, he would go below for a good fistful of Limburger, and maybe finish counting his coins.

38

The roaring, rumbling, snapping, and splintering sounds began to subside at last.

Remo and Chiun dropped from the shivering trees to the ground on the summit of Moo. They ran to the Royal Palace. Moovians were milling about the palace, their voices high and plaintive.

"So much for my strike," Remo muttered. He gazed back to the lagoon. "Looks like Elvis is taking a powder."

The ship was heading for open water. But down in the lagoon, whose deep blue water was turning slowly milk chocolate, tiny figures floundered. They were swimming away from a spot of water that churned white and pink.

"Sharks," Chiun said. "Those men must return to land."

"We better clean them out before they get organized. They'll be after the junk next."

"Yes." Chiun turned to the milling Moovians. "Never fear," he cried. "We will deal ruthlessly with these interlopers. Inform the High Moo that the Master of Sinanju will not let this atrocity go unpunished."

"I thought you'd gotten over your High Moo worship," Remo said bitterly as they raced down the loosened and tangled western slope.

"We have not taken our leave yet."

There was no white beach there anymore. Just a soaking apron of mud. The moisture was creeping upward. The soil, made heavy by seawater, fell in occasional mudslides.

Dirk Edwards and his men crawled onto this mud, carrying their weapons. They were met by two resolute figures. Remo and Chiun.

Dirk took one look and growled out a low order.

"Waste them."

The order was easier given than carried out. Dirk raised his AK-47 and got off a short snarling burst at the white man. He peered past the thinning gunsmoke and the white man was running toward him, dead-on. He pulled the tape-doubled clip out and inserted the other end. He tried single shots, but the white man zig-zagged between the shots somehow. Dirk plucked out a hand grenade, pulled the pin with his teeth, and let fly.

The white guy stopped, looked up at the descending object. Dirk's wolfish grin wreathed his muddy features. It died when the white man casually caught the grenade like a pop fly ball and tossed it back in Dirk's shocked face.

Dirk had no place to run. He burrowed into the mud like a clam. He stuck his fingers in his ears to ward off concussion damage. The explosion was muffled. When it subsided, Dirk stuck his head out. Smearing the mud from his eyes, he looked around.

His men were deploying frantically. They fired every which way, like amateurs. What the hell was wrong with them?

Then he saw. The old guy. The gook. He was systematically taking them out with what looked like kung-fu moves, but were not. The old man vented no heart-freezing cries. His punches and kicks were not swift and flamboyant. They were more graceful. There was an economy of movement that Dirk Edwards have never seen before. It was too pure for kung-fu, he told himself. And the thought surprised him. He had great respect for kung-fu.

The white guy was moving in and out of the tangles of uprooted palms. Dirk had trouble spotting him even though his bare white chest should have been a dead giveaway. He was like a ghost.

One of his men slunk past a clump of bushes and suddenly the white guy was behind him. He came out of nowhere, chopped once at the back of the neck, and Dirk didn't have to hear the ugly crunching noise to know he had lost another man. The weird angle of his neck as he fell told him that.

The white guy moved on.

Dirk scrambled out of the mud. He went from body to body, collecting plastic explosive charges. He still had a detonator strapped to his belt. He felt his pockets. Yeah, a few blasting caps too. He circled away from the fighting—it was more like a massacre than a fight—until he came to open beach. He clambered up the hilly island. There were other mines here too. He found one as close to the damaged western slope as he dared go and crawled in.

In a matter of moments he had planted a charge. He fixed the rest in other strategic places, trailing wire back to the shelter of a coral outcropping. He hooked the wires to the detonator.

"So long, suckers!" he shouted, and twisted the plunger.

Gouts of fiery soil jumped into the air. The ground shuddered. Dirk grinned. He waited for the shuddering to subside. Strangely, it kept on going. Like an echo chamber.

Puzzled, Dirk peered over the outcropping.

What he saw made his blood run cold. The island was coming down like a sandpile. Not just the part he had blasted. All of it. Water came pouring out of the mines. High above, on the summit, the stone building was sinking as if into quicksand.

A wail rose from the summit. Screams. Terrible screams of terror. But Dirk Edwards didn't hear the screams. His own were too loud.

A wave of loose earth was coming at him and he plunged for the blue water.

Chiun realized it first.

"Moo is falling into the sea."

"Can't be," Remo said hotly. He clutched a mercenary in his hands. He waved his long fingernails before the man's face and suddenly it looked like the pink side of a watermelon rind.

"These nails are good for something, at least," Remo said, dropping the body.

"Lo!" Chiun pointed upward.

"Christ," Remo said anxiously. "What do we do?"

"The junk. Come."

Remo hesitated. The ground under his feet was separating like cornmeal. "We can't abandon everyone," he shouted.

"And we will not. We will bring the junk closer to land. It is their only hope. And ours."

"I'm with you," Remo said quickly.

Together they plunged into the brown water. They

struck out for the junk, taking care to swim wide of the feeding frenzy of hammerheads.

Remo spotted another swimmer angling across their bearing. He was also making for the junk.

"He's mine," Remo called, pointing him out.

"I will ready the ship," Chiun said.

Remo slipped under the surface. He found himself once again in a fantasy world of multihued coral. Old Moo. He homed in on Dirk Edwards' kicking feet. Remo darted for them like a dolphin.

Remo came up from below. He pulled Dirk Edwards down by the ankles. Then he grabbed his throat, holding him underwater. Remo gave Dirk just enough time to see the wrath on his face before he shattered his shoulder joints.

Dirk Edward's face registered surprise when he found that his arms would not move. They hung limp. Stupid arms. He needed them to swim with. He kicked, but suddenly there was pain in his hips.

He looked down and saw that he no longer had hips. His pelvis felt mushy, no longer solid. And his legs hung straight down like cooked noodles.

Then he was sinking, down, down into a beautiful world of coral reefs. He looked to see where he would land, and there was a gap in the reef below. He slipping down through it and all became black.

At first Dirk couldn't tell if he was dead or in some kind of dark hollow place. He decided he was dead, and further decided it didn't feel so bad after all. Then his eyes became accustomed to the dim light and he saw that he was surrounded by shelf upon shelf of dead people, all in big jars like bugs in specimen bottles.

The shelves shook, causing the jugs to wobble and topple. They broke, unleashing their contents in a dark red cloud like blood. Dead eyes stared at him accusingly and Dirk suddenly wondered if they were really dead. Some of them seemed to be pointed at him.

Dirk screamed then. His lungs emptied and the breathing reflex that could not be denied demanded that he inhale. He swallowed the water into his mouth and stomach and lungs. Odd, it tasted like wine.

He was dead when he floated down to solid ground, settling on a tiled floor like a discarded marionette.

Remo clambered up the *Jonah Ark*'s hull and over the rail. Chiun had the foresail down. The wind filled it.

"Take the tiller," the Master of Sinanju snapped.

Remo leaned into the tiller, and the junk came about slowly. He cursed its slow response time. The bow lined up on the shrinking island of Moo.

It was an incredible sight. Like a sand castle drying in the sun, Moo simply crumbled. The Royal Palace was sinking as the supporting ground disintegrated.

All around Moo, the water was turning to brownish-black mud.

"Can't we move faster?" Remo cried.

"The wind is not with us," Chiun returned. He stood on the bow, his feet apart, his back stiff.

"How can it just sink like that?" Remo moaned.

"It is not. Use your eyes, not your heart to see, Remo."

Moo was not sinking. It was spreading out. It lost height. It lost shape. With sick eyes Remo saw tiny figures being pulled under the shifting porous volcanic soil. It was like dry quicksand. Others climbed palms and rode them down to the water. The boles snapped apart with thunderous splinterings. Remo lost sight of every tiny figure he picked out.

The junk wallowed closer. Remo's eyes searched the water for survivors. He saw none. He pushed at the tiller, sending the boat around.

"Might be some survivors on the other side," he called.

Chiun said nothing in reply. Remo couldn't see his face. He wondered what thoughts were going through the Master of Sinanju's mind as he watched an important link to Sinanju's past crumble.

On the far end of the island, the soil was spreading even further into the water. The summit of Moo was barely ten feet above sea level now. And still it shifted and spread. It was all going to go.

"There!" Chiun cried. "I see the High Moo."

Remo peered past the rakish sails. He spotted the High Moo splashing helplessly in the water. His arms waved at them. He called for them to rescue him.

"Hurry, Remo," Chiun called back. He went to the rail.

"I can't get out and push this thing," Remo snapped back.

Then other figures appeared in the water. They surrounded the High Moo. At first Remo feared they were sharks. But they were Moovians. They grabbed at the High Moo, pulling at his face and hair and arms. They were beating on him, dragging him down with them.

They pulled him below the brown water, which was turning chlorophyll green from crushed vegetation.

Bubbles marked the spot where the High Moo disappeared. One head surfaced after a while. A girl's. Remo thought he recognized her although her wet hair was plastered to her face. It was the Low Moo.

"Hold on," he called in Moovian.

"*Nah,*" the Low Moo called back. "I am the last. All the others have perished. There are no more. Go away. Moo is no more. I have no subjects, no throne. There is no place for one such as I in your world. I no longer wish to live. Go, Remo, but never forget us."

"No chance," Remo said, diving into the water.

He set out for the Low Moo, but she saw his intentions and jacknifed under the water. Remo slipped down after her. He followed the trail of air bubbles that spilled from her open mouth. She wasn't even trying to hold her breath. She went as limp as a starfish and Remo knew before he reached her that she was gone.

He pulled her to the surface and tried desperately to squeeze the water from her lungs. He touched his lips to hers, and puffed steady breaths into them. "Come on, come on," he urged.

Her lips remained cold, her eyes closed. Reluctantly Remo let her go. The Low Moo floated away, her face brown and composed and nearly innocent.

Remo fought back the burning sensation in his eyes as he climbed aboard the junk. He couldn't understand why he should care that the cruel Low Mo had perished. He took the tiller, sending the junk around for another circuit of the island.

There were few bodies. They floated facedown, many of them.

The hammerhead sharks closed in.

"Shouldn't we stop them?" Remo asked. Chiun kept his back to him.

"No," Chiun said distantly. "It is the way of the sea."

"That was the Low Moo I tried to rescue back there, you know."

"So?"

"I know it sounds strange, but I wish I could have saved her."

"Why?" Chiun asked in a cold voice. "If we took her back to America, she would only try to eat you again."

"Hey," Remo said angrily. He stormed up to Chiun and spun him around. "That was uncalled-for."

But then he saw the tears rilling down Chiun's lined cheeks and he swallowed.

"Sorry," he muttered sheepishly.

"History had repeated itself," Chiun said slowly. "Greed destroyed Old Moo, and greed has claimed what had survived almost five thousand years."

"Greed, nothing. It was those killers and their explosives."

"No, my son. Mere explosives would not have done all this. Old Moo sank because the High Moos of those days also forced their people to mine every foot of land in search of coin metal. Eventually they undermined the very earth, and the seas claimed Old Moo. Now the greedy sea has drunk the last of Moo, and the last poor Moovian."

As they watched, the final patch of dry ground grew dark with moisture and soon it was indistinguishable from the ugly brown of the sea.

Steam rose in mighty tendrils from the place where Moo had been.

"Behold, Remo. Do you see those mighty arms reaching up to the very sky?"

"Yeah. Steam from the hot jungle growth. So what?"

"They only appear to be steam. For those are the very tentacles of Ru-Taki-Nuhu itself, holding up the sky."

"Bull," said Remo. But he stared into the swirling steam uncertainly. Did he see suckers?

39

It was four days later. The mouth-watering smell of hot egg-lemon soup woke Remo Williams. He jumped out of his bunk and made his way to the junk's galley, where he found the Master of Sinanju hovering over the galley stove.

"Do I smell my favorite soup?" he asked brightly.

"You do," replied Chiun in a happy voice. He turned, a steaming wooden bowl in his hands.

At the sight of Remo's face, Chiun let out a screech.

"Aiiee!" he cried.

"Yeah, I know," Remo said, holding up his hands. His nails were long and curved. "Aren't they gross?"

"Your nails are perfect. It is your hair. And beard."

"Huh?"

"They are a sickly yellow." Chiun looked into the bowl. His eyes narrowed. His lips thinned. "Lemon yellow."

He marched to an open porthole and emptied the bowl's contents overboard.

"My breakfast!" Remo cried.

"No more egg-lemon soup for you," Chiun muttered angrily as he dumped the remaining potful after the bowl. "It has had an unforeseen effect upon your ridiculous white consitution."

"Unforeseen?" Remo folded his arms. He tapped a foot impatiently. "Chiun, I think you have some explaining to do." He was looking at his fingernails.

40

Dr. Harold W. Smith noticed the shiny blue Buick in the next-door driveway when he pulled into his own. His lips thinned. They were home, his mysterious neighbors. That changed everything.

As he put his house key in the front door, the portable phone in his briefcase buzzed. Perhaps it was Remo calling, Smith thought, his heart racing. He fumbled the door open.

Smith plunged into his living room. Mrs. Smith was sitting in an overstuffed chair, facing an identical high-backed chair.

"Oh, Harold, I'm so glad you're home," Mrs. Smith gushed excitedly. "I'd like you to meet—"

"One moment, please," Smith said curtly. "I have some phone calls to make." And he hurried into the den, leaving his wife to mutter apologies to her guest.

"He's not like that, really. It's just that he's been so overworked."

"I recognized him as a man of responsibility," the other voice said gravely. "And have I told you that you brew excellent tea?"

Smith opened the briefcase at his desk. He lifted the receiver.

"Yes?" he said crisply.

"Smitty? Remo here."

"Remo!" Smith bit out. "Where have you been? Never mind. That's not important now. We have a crisis."

"I'll be right over."

"No, I'm not at Folcroft. I'm home."

"I know. I saw you drive up."

"You did? You're in the neighborhood? Wonderful. Listen carefully: unknown agents have bought the house next door to mine. There's something very wrong there. I don't have time to explain the details, but I want you to look into this. Find out who they are and what they're up to. I believe that at the very least, they're storing munitions over there. The apparent leader is a man who calls himself James Churchward."

"I'm already on top of it, Smitty."

Smith gulped. He was so relieved that his normally ashen face flushed with perspiration. "You are?"

"Look out your window," Remo suggested.

Smith hesitated. Carrying the briefcase awkwardly, he moved over to the window. It faced the house next door. Smith peered through the chintz curtains.

Framed in the opposite window, Smith saw a blond man with a full golden beard. He was holding a telephone receiver to his face. His lips moved. The words they mouthed were reproduced in Smith's unbelieving ear.

"Hi, neighbor," Remo's voice chirped. "Come on over."

"Stay right there," Smith hissed. He slipped out the back door and crept to the rear of the other house. He knocked gingerly. The door opened.

"Don't mind the place," Remo said casually. "Chiun and I are still working on it."

Smith walked in on leaden feet. His face drained of color.

Remo led him to the living room, which was bare except for a projection TV and two reed sitting mats. In the middle of the room stood a huge cardboard container.

"Grab a piece of floor, Smitty. I'll be just a minute. This arrived today. It was the first thing I bought after I closed on the house. I never thought I'd have an urgent use for it."

Smith's eyes focused slowly.

"Your hair," he croaked. "That beard."

Remo touched his blond head. "One of Chiun's little schemes gone wrong," he said as he attacked the cardboard box with curved talonlike fingers.

"Your nails."

"Exhibit B," Remo said. The box lay in strips, exposing a tractor lawn mower. Remo pushed it over on its side, revealing sharp rotary steel blades. He began filing his nails on the sharpest blade. It sounded like two steel files rasping one another. Remo talked as he worked.

"I have to admit Chiun fooled me this time. I thought

the soup was a special treat. You know, a celebration because we'd finally bought a house."

"This is your house," Smith said hoarsely.

"Yup. We answered an ad. Hey, imagine our surprise when we found out it was next door to yours." A fingernail dropped to the floor. Remo started to work on the next one.

"Imagine . . ." Smith's eyes were sick. He looked away, and through an open door he saw stacks of brass-bound lacquered boxes in the next room. They were festooned with old-fashioned padlocks. Chiun's steamer trunks. They fit Brunt's description perfectly. Smith didn't know whether to laugh or cry. So he swallowed uncomfortably.

"Naturally," Remo was saying, "I objected at first. But Chiun convinced me. He said the emperor's assassin should dwell no more than twenty cubits from his emperor. I didn't measure, but I guess we've got twenty cubits between us. Besides, we'd been living at Folcroft for over a year now, so I figured security wouldn't suffer."

"No. But I have. Do you have any idea what I've been going through for the last two weeks?"

"No," Remo said as he went to work on his other hand, "but I can guarantee you it's nothing compared to what Chiun and I have experienced. So do me the favor of not telling me your story and I'll return it. Okay?"

"Who is James Churchward?" Smith wanted to know. His hands hung limply.

"That's me. Sorta. It's one of the aliases you gave me. I used it when I bought this place. Don't tell me you forgot?"

"Oh, my God," said Smith. "No wonder I recognized the name. No wonder the computers couldn't access those files. I was fighting my own rebuff programs." He sank to the floor and took his head in his hands. He pulled at his gray hair. "I never thought to check your alias file. I never dreamed you were connected to this."

"Join the human race," Remo said when the last dead fingernail clipping clicked to the floor. "Now you know you're not perfect."

"Where is Chiun?" Smith asked hollowly.

"Next door. Paying a courtesy call on Mrs. Smith."

Smith's head shot up. "My wife?"

"Yeah, she recognized us from that time we met at

Folcroft. She invited us over to tea, but I had my manicure to do. To tell you the truth, I think the only reason Chiun accepted was that he knows I'm still pissed at him over the egg-lemon trick."

"Egg-lemon?" Smith's voice was drained of emotion.

"Yeah, he's been feeding me egg-lemon soup for two weeks now. It's mostly lemon, but it's got eggshell bits in it. I've been drinking it by the gallon, little dreaming that the eggshells were making my nails grow faster and harder. You know how Chiun's always on my case to grow mine like his. But the joke turned out to be on him. The stuff turned my hair yellow. It freaked Chiun out. He says a true Master of Sinanju should not go around looking like a fuzzy lemon. And all the time I was on Moo, I thought the soft bone knives were the problem. These nails are ridiculous. They couldn't have been cut with anything less than tempered steel."

"Moo?"

Remo's hands shot up. "Forget I mentioned it. I'm just happy to be home. My roots are coming up brown again, so I figure I'll be completely normal in a week or two. Oh, well, live and learn. It could have been worse."

"How so?"

"It could have been egg-*lime* soup." Remo grinned, brushing at his hair.

When Smith didn't join in his laughter, Remo remarked, "You're aging just like vinegar, Smitty."

"I feel as if I've aged a year since I saw you last."

"Better let me help you to your feet," Remo said solicitously.

Dr. Harold W. Smith allowed himself to be helped to his feet. He winced at the pain in his arthritic knee.

The Master of Sinanju came in through the front door, and at the sight of Smith, he bowed formally.

"Greetings of the day, O tolerant Harold. I have been conversing with the Empress Maude. She is a sterling woman, truly worthy of one such as you."

"You don't have to lay it on too thick," Remo said. "He's not as upset as you expected."

"I am laying nothing on, thick or thin," Chiun protested. "I am merely offering up my thanks now that we will be neighbors with Emperor Smith. I trust while Remo and I were taking our much-overdue and thankfully received vacation, no villains troubled your kingdom?"

"You are supposed to check in every day, if you are not in a prearranged location," Smith pointed out sternly.

"Exactly what I told that innkeeper," Chiun said quickly. "And you should have been there to witness the tongue-lashing I gave him. Do you know that scoundrel did not have a single working telephone?"

"I'm going home now," Smith said, shaking his head. "I do not feel well."

"A wise decision," Chiun said. "You look pale—but at least you are not a sickly yellow." Chiun shot Remo a distasteful glance. Remo stuck his tongue out at him.

After Smith had gone, Remo showed his spread fingers. "Notice anything?"

"Yes," Chiun said. "You have maimed yourself. Tonight I will lie awake, deprived of sleep, wondering what will be next. A ring in your nose? Tattoos?"

"Actually, my next goal in life is duck in orange sauce. I never thought I'd say this, but after all that soup, I'm really looking forward to duck."

"You may look forward to it, but we have unfinished business."

"Billiken?"

"He has the treasure of Moo. Including Sinanju's rightful share. He must not be allowed to go unpunished or word will get out that Sinanju has lost its mighty vigilance. Then the vultures will circle my village and the treasure of Sinanju will be prey to any fool who covets it. For it is our reputation that does most of our work for us. Otherwise we could not enjoy this splendid home, but instead be forced to dwell forever in the village of Sinanju, safeguarding our property. Such a day will never dawn while I am reigning Master. If it happens on your watch, it will be on your head, but as long as I live—"

"Stow the lecture," Remo said. "I'll be with you as soon as I get rid of these toenails and shave."

"I cannot bear to look," Chiun said, turning his back as Remo tried to figure out a safe way to trim his toenails with a lawn mower.

41

The British Museum in London wouldn't accept Shane Billiken's call.

He got through to the Smithsonian, but when the curator realized who he was, he hung up.

The Museum of Fine Arts in Boston was no better. They transferred Shane Billiken to their public-relations staff, and Shane hung up on them.

"What's wrong with people?" Shane demanded, slamming down the receiver. He was in the living room of his Malibu home. Stacks of Moovian coins surrounded him. Shane had counted them seven times, each time coming up with a different total. The exact number didn't matter. He was rich. If only someone would believe his story.

Frustrated, Shane riffled through the mail that had come while he was away. There was a postcard from Glinda. She was shacked up with a rock singer in Rio. He threw the card away. The bank statement said he was overdrawn by nearly six hundred dollars. And the mortgage on the house was due in a few days. Although surrounded by the entire wealth of the vanished Moovian empire, Shane Billiken was flat, dead, sucking-wind broke.

"No problem," he said suddenly snapping his fingers. He grabbed the Yellow Pages and looked up the listing for coin dealers. There was one in Beverly Hills. They'd know how to treat him. He picked out a dozen coins and piled into his Ferrari.

"But you don't understand," Shane was explaining heatedly to the proprietor not twenty minutes later. "These are rare ancient coins. From Mu. Don't tell me you never heard of Mu. It was a great continent that existed before the dawn of time. It sank. But not all of it. A little bit of high ground stuck up. Except that it sank too. Recently. Last week, as a matter of fact. And before it went, I rescued these coins. There aren't any more left. I got them all."

"Sank?" asked the coin dealer.

"Yes!"

"Twice?"

"Yes! That's it. You've seized the concept perfectly. You must be highly evolved to catch on so quickly. Congratulations. Don't ever change."

"But you're willing to sell them to me, instead of to the Smithsonian?"

"The Smithsonian people are nimnoids, and I've got a minor short-term cash-flow thing going on right now. I've got more of these coins. Tons. Otherwise I wouldn't be making you this truly excellent deal. So how much?"

"I see," said the coin dealer. "Tell me something. I thought I recognized you when you walked in. Haven't I seen you on TV?"

"That's right!" Shane Billiken said eagerly.

"On the Donahue show. You're Shane Billiken."

Shane Billiken's hairy chest puffed up. His mood amulet turned from orange to blue.

"That's right."

"The New Age guru?"

"Exactly!" Shane Billiken said. He fairly shouted it.

"The one who's always talking about Atlantis and Nirvana and other mythical places?"

Shane's chest deflated. His face fell. He seemed to shrink.

"That was different. Mu is real. Or it was."

"But it sank."

"Well, yes."

"So there's no proof?"

Shane pounded the glass counter. "The coins! The coins are your proof! Some of them are thousands of years old. Probably."

"They look pretty new to me. Besides, why should I believe you now when I didn't believe in your Atlantean high priestess, what was her name again?"

"Princess Shastra," Shane said in an injured tone. "She was my Soul Mate."

"Is that so?" said the coin dealer. "But when I was in

high school, she was my classmate. Only then she called herself Glinda Thirp and her tits were real."

Shane Billiken's face slowly turned gray.

"What will you give me for the metal content?" he asked in a small voice.

"Oh, about six cents, depending on weight."

"You robber. These are pure silver. Maybe platinum."

The coin dealer shook his head soberly.

"Tin," he said firmly.

"Tin? It can't be."

" 'Fraid so."

"Tin," Shane Billiken said dully. "Tin." Slowly, carefully he swept the coins back into a paper bag. His eyes were wounded. His lips moved soundlessly. His mood medallion slowly turned from blue to black.

He walked out of the coin shop, his tread as heavy as a deep-sea diver's walking in lead boots.

The coin dealer watched him go. He wondered what Shane Billiken meant as he went out the door. He kept muttering one thing over and over:

"Tin. I don't believe it. I shipped tin again."

When Shane Billiken returned home, the unpaid mortgage loomed suddenly larger than a mountain. It was all gone. He had no hope left. He couldn't summon up a positive affirmation to save his life.

He noticed the stack of newspapers that had come while he was away, Woodenly he went through them one by one, page by page.

His eyes bugged behind his sunglasses when he came to the entertainment section of the previous day's paper.

The woods were full of Roy Orbison impersonators. There was a Roy Sorbison, a Roy Orb-Son, a Sun-Ray Orison, a Ray-Ban Bisonor and many others. Their similar puffy features, masked by identical sunglasses, stared out at him mockingly. Every ad had "Sold Out" printed over it in funeral-black letters. With a sick clutching in the pit of his stomach, Shane Billiken lifted his thumb and saw that there was even one thief who called himself Roy Orbit Sun. And he was playing in the Hollywood Bowl.

"No! No! No!" Shane Billiken moaned, not noticing that he was making a negative affirmation. He tore through the stack of papers, looking for the item he had for years dreamed of reading, but which he now dreaded. He found it on page one of a week-old paper:

POP BALLADEER ROY ORBISON, DEAD AT 52

The great Orbison had passed away of a massive heart attack a week ago Tuesday, while Shane was at sea.

As he collapsed in his beanbag chair, the terrible irony of it descended on Shane Billiken like an Egyptian curse. His window of opportunity was lost. He couldn't compete with all those other Roy Orbison clones. It was booming industry now.

Desperately Shane closed his eyes. There was one last hope, one last shot to take. He would employ a technique he described in *The Elbow of Enlightenment* as "Uncreating the Reality."

"It never happened, it never happened," he chanted, mantra-like. "Roy's alive, he really is. I never left home. I never left home. Everything is fine. Everything is cool. Everything is fine. Everything is cool."

Shane's tense expression softened. He felt better already. Meditation had always worked for him. Soon, he would open his eyes and all would be well. Was there anything else he should wish for, he wondered, now that the Wheel of Destiny was under his control. Oh, yes.

"Glinda's back, too," he murmured. "And she's naked. All is well, all is good. There's no place like home. There's no place like home," he added, thinking why not? It had worked for Judy Garland.

But when he opened his eyes, the repeating images of Roy Orbison impersonators stared back at him like a blind army, and Roy the Boy was still dead. He searched the house for Glinda, but she was nowhere to be found, either.

Shane Billiken, high priest of positivity, felt very, very negative.

And so Shane Billiken piled the coins of Moo into the reed boat which he had repaired with Krazy Glue and shoved it into the surf behind his home. He placed his favorite guitar in the bow next to a bottle of gasoline siphoned from his Ferrari. He pushed off.

When the boat was afloat, he clambered aboard. The sun was setting, its twin reflection showed on his Ray-Bans. It was a cool, sweet night. The stars were right.

Shane had done his horoscope. It had assured him that it would be a good night to die. Either that, or he had cancer. It was hard to say. His tears dripped all over the chart, making the ink run.

Shane waited until he was far out to sea before he shook the gasoline all throughout the boat. He poured the remainder over his head. Then he applied flame from his Zippo lighter to the stern. It caught slowly because the boat was already wet.

Then, taking up his guitar, he began to sing what had become the theme song of his life in a pain-choked voice.

"It's ooooovvvvveeeeeerrrrr," he wailed.

He faced the setting sun, his back to the wavering yellow flames. Shane Billiken was going out like a Viking, a song on his lips. He wondered if he had been a Viking in a past life. Or maybe he would become a Viking in the next. Was it possible to be reincarnated into the past? Shane hadn't studied that, but he hoped all knowledge would soon be revealed to him. He had earned it.

He wondered what was taking the flames so long to reach him. And why did his feet feel so wet? He looked down.

The boat was sinking. Strange long fingernails were piercing the bottom. They withdrew.

"Damn!" he said. The flames hissed as seawater quenched them. In seconds he was floating in a gasoline slick, clutching his Ovation guitar like a life preserver.

A head popped up beside him.

"Remember us?" Remo asked.

"You have my treasure," Chiun said. He surfaced on the other side. His eyes were angry and narrow.

"Hey, you can't do this. This is my funeral. I'm going to die. And you can't stop it. My horoscope foretold this."

"Yes," Chiun said gravely. "You will die, but for your base temerity, you will not die the death you prefer, but the one I choose for you. For you have been the instrument of great tragedy."

"You got me wrong. It wasn't me that wrecked that island. It was those mercenaries. Talk to them. I'm just a leaf in the karmic wind."

"No," Chiun said. "You will talk to them for me. I wish you to deliver a message."

"Yeah? And what's that?"

"No one trifles with the possessions of the House of Sinanju."

And suddenly the old Oriental's hand was in Shane's face, and he never heard his Ray-Bans crack and never felt the bone chip fly back from the bridge of his nose all the way through his brain and out the back of his skull. He just sank to the bottom, where he became one with the food chain.

The Master of Sinanju emerged from the surf, his arms full of coins.

"Going back for more?" Remo asked, wringing seawater out of his pant legs.

"No. This is the amount we earned. The remainder do not matter."

"Be a shame to leave the rest out there with Billiken."

"Pah!" Chiun spat. "They are worthless."

"What do you mean, worthless? They're pure silver. Aren't they?"

Chiun shook his wise head. "Impure tin. It is not the metal that makes Moovian coins so valuable. It is that they are Moovian."

"Then why bother with your share? And why kill Billiken over it?"

"Because, worthless or not, these are the property of Sinanju. Just because others do not treasure it does not mean that we do not. Besides," Chiun added, "These have sentimental value. And as far as any know, they are the only Moovian coins left. The fewer there are, the more valuable they will be. Who knows, one day America might sink and take with it all its precious metal. Even tin might become valuable then."

"Don't hold your breath," Remo said, plunging back into the surf.

"Where are you going?"

"To salvage a couple more coins," Remo called back. "I'm famished. Maybe I can convince some unsuspecting restaurant owner to take them in trade for an order of duck with orange sauce."